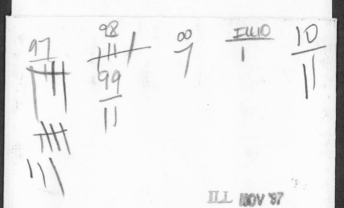

out west

out west

fred g. leebron

doubleday new york
london
toronto
sydney
auckland

PUBLISHED BY DOUBLEDAY
a division of Bantam Doubleday Dell Publishing Group, Inc.
1540 Broadway, New York, New York 10036

DOUBLEDAY and the portrayal of an anchor
with a dolphin are trademarks of Doubleday
a division of Bantam Doubleday Dell Publishing Group, Inc.

Library of Congress Cataloging-in-Publication Data
Leebron, Fred.
Out West / Fred Leebron. — 1st ed.
p.   cm.
1. Man-woman relationships—California—San Francisco—Fiction.
2. Murderers—California—San Francisco—Fiction.   I. Title.
PS3562.E3666O98   1996
813'.54—dc20   96-11607
CIP

ISBN 0-385-48420-8

1   3   5   7   9   10   8   6   4   2

Book design by Claire Naylon Vaccaro

Thanks to Roger Skillings, Bruce Tracy, Lynne Raughley, Peter Ho Davies, Jennifer Rudolph Walsh, Geoff Becker, Steve Rinehart, Deb West, Yoji Yamaguchi, John Skoyles, and especially Kathryn Rhett.

For support during the writing of this book, special thanks to Pat de Groot, Alan Watahara, the Tenderloin Neighborhood Development Corporation, the Fine Arts Work Center in Provincetown, and James Michener and the Copernicus Society.

A portion of *Out West* appeared in different form in *Ploughshares* as "Lovelock," and was reprinted in *Voices of the Xiled.* Thanks to Don Lee and *Ploughshares* for permission to reprint, and to Mel and Denise Cohen for the financial support of the Cohen Prize.

. . . it is a test,
this riding out the dying of the West.

—ROBERT HASS

for kathryn and cade

out west

lovelock

The billboards into Lovelock, Nevada, promised dinner and drink coupons, a roll of quarters, hot showers, cable television, king-sized beds, breakfast coupons, twenty-four hour free coffee, air conditioning, and a swimming pool all for only $39.99, and Benjamin West, after three nights dozing in rest stops by the side of the interstate, could not help but be swayed. Lovelock came up on the lefthand side in the middle of the Nevada flats, a one-street town with a skyline of gas stations, hotel-motel-casinos, fast-food restaurants, auto dealers, insurance brokers, a combined elementary-junior high-high school, a chamber of commerce. West took the Chevy down main street, keeping his eye out for a name from one of the highway advertisements. The Lickety Split, the Bellwether, It's Your Night, On the House, Holiday Inn, Motel 6—their signs lighting up in the dusk like struck pinball targets. West pulled into

the lot of Lucky Andy's Roadside Hotel-Motel-Casino, the one
with the $5 in quarters and $20 worth of coupons. He had $111
left.

In the refrigerated lobby a slot machine stood to either side of
the registration desk. West peeled off two $20 bills and lay them
before a woman with tall blond hair and platinum painted fingernails. "Will that do?" he said.

"Sure will." She smiled at him. "Do you want an upper rack or
a lower rack?"

He looked at her in numb confusion.

"First floor or second floor," she said.

"Second."

She gave him a key, a roll of quarters, and a wad of coupons,
her fingertips grazing his knuckles. He glanced at her quickly,
but she was already occupied with something else.

He walked stiff-legged back out to the car, as if he'd been
riding a horse for the last four days. Over the course of the past
twenty-seven hundred miles he'd given up stopping regularly,
and drove until he couldn't take the pain and the cramping and
the stiffness anymore. When he slept at the rest stops, he folded
himself into the front seat, worried that one of the unsavory types
who populated these urine-soaked places all night would try to
steal the car out from under him. He was a tired motherfucker,
and he found himself adopting the personality he suspected of
every state he passed through. In Iowa he had been bland and
unassuming, slumped low in the car as he drove, an old man. But
by North Platte, Nebraska, where the roar of motorcycles cut into
his sleep, he'd begun to swagger and curse, and bought a six-pack
for a last two-hour dash down the interstate before sleep overcame
him again. When he dipped into the tip of Colorado, he felt

unaccountably swank, wealthy, and he tucked in his shirt and nodded gravely at gas station attendants, touched two fingers to his forehead even though there was no hat there. Now Nevada, whorehouses and casinos alongside McDonald's and Motel 6.

West sauntered over to the car, reveling in the not small accomplishment of traversing the bulk of the country without a driver's license. From the trunk he pulled out a set of clean clothes, and hobbled up the fire-escape-style stairway to his second-floor room.

In the airless mush of humidity and disinfectant he undressed and got in the shower. After four days without a shower, he was so ripe with odor that it seemed to line him like a second skin, the smell of Iowa corn and pigsties, Nebraska wheat and truck exhaust, Wyoming slag, Utah salt. When he'd driven across the Great Salt Lake, he'd pulled over, gotten out, and taken a few steps toward the hills shimmering like quartz in the heat. He felt as if he were walking on the moon, the thick bed of shifting, sucking salt suspending rules of gravity and air. He could barely breathe. He got back in the car and gingerly got through Utah, the road lined with scallops of tires burst open and shredded by heat and traffic.

Now in the shower he held his mouth up to the gush of water and rinsed his teeth first, the four-day grit of fast-food hamburgers and funny sandwiches snatched from the glass coolers of gas station convenience stores, the thick sugary film of two dozen caffeine soft drinks, the occasional chocolate bar for energy and digestion, the odd six-pack of beer drunk on the sly over the last bit of midnight road before fatigue closed in and shut him down at desolate rest stops in Iowa City, Ogallala, Rock Springs. He enjoyed the taste of the water, a chemical pureness of chlorine and fluoride and Nevada minerals, as if it were some post-nuclear solution that could cleanse him of the smell of the country and the car and the interstate.

He changed into the fresh clothes and descended the metal staircase, each step pinging under his tired weight, to the parking lot, packed with RVs, station wagons, minivans, economy cars. He passed the outside of the casino again, not at all curious. West had been eighteen when Atlantic City had opened up its massive hotels to gambling, and at first he'd been hooked, driving out every weekend during his senior year in high school with slick-talking friends who convinced him that he only had to *know* he could win, and then he *would* win. After losing five hundred dollars over six consecutive weekends, he recognized the myth of it. Now he fingered the roll of quarters in his pocket, counting up how many drinks it would buy.

He ate dinner at the restaurant, a curtain-draped wood-paneled spectacle done up as a Spanish galleon, then crossed through the lobby to the casino, feeling woozy from the oversized T-bone and pitcher of Bud. He sat at the horseshoe-shaped bar and ordered a bourbon on the rocks. An inlaid video poker game stared up at him. EASY MONEY! EASY MONEY! He moved down a seat. At the slot machines fifty- and sixty-year-old ladies in blue jeans and neckerchiefs loaded coins in five at a time, accompanied by the whoops of yet older men in cowboy hats and Levi's.

He sipped at his drink. Two seventy-five. He had to go slow. His clean clothes made him sleepy. Twenty-seven hundred miles and he was not even in San Francisco yet. He just wanted to be there. When he'd finally gotten a hold of Bob Fields, he'd felt reassured. "You just take as much time as you need," Bob had said. "The job's waiting for you, it isn't going anywhere. Seven days, eight days. I'd say nine maximum. Can you make it in nine?" West had counted his money. "Would it be a problem if I got there a little ahead of schedule?" "No problem at all," Bob said. "We're on a day-to-day contract with the security company."

The job paid room, board, and benefits, plus five hundred dollars a month—a pretty good deal. It would give him a chance to put some distance between himself and prison, to figure out what the next step was. He missed the kids at the Institute, but they wouldn't hire him back now. He still had nightmares about Nathan, who had to wear a hockey helmet even when he slept. And the ululations of Melissa, funky-limbed, strapped in her wheelchair, chortling to herself like a bird gurgling water. In his ten years he had not worked with more than twenty children. You got them for a year at a time, possibly longer, until they were shipped to the next research facility or their parents removed them to home for a spell. He never wanted to have kids.

He held up his empty glass and waited to catch the bartender's eye. He was not so drunk as he thought he should be. Perhaps Lucky Andy's watered their drinks. What had intoxicated West most about the Atlantic City casinos was that, when he was gambling, they gave him drinks *free.* But that had not helped him in the quixotic struggle to convince himself that he would win. Now he saw that he had lost five hundred dollars not because the theory was wrong, but because he had failed, ultimately, in *knowing.* He looked at the video poker game and reached into his pocket for the quarters.

"Hey, buddy."

The damn thing apparently talked. He glared at it.

"Hey, buddy. Over here." Someone was knocking on his shoulder as if it were a door. "On your right."

West swirled the bar stool around. His interlocutor, his rescuer, was a man of thirty-odd years and six and a half feet, a white cowboy hat cocked on his head like a second grin, a strong jaw, five o'clock face. An open-lipped toothy smile, waiting for the go-ahead to continue talking. West was delighted to discover that he was drunk, after all, and at the back of his mind he was frightened by it, too, he could feel it coming on like a train through a tunnel, and there would be nothing he could do but get up after it had run him over. He wondered if he would have to throw up.

"What," he said uneasily.

The smile drew shut in a line of gratitude, at having been recognized by the chair. The chair nodded for him to go on.

"I've got my hands full, buddy, if you know what I mean," the smile said. "Two ladies." The hat wagged in a direction West could not follow. "I was wondering if you might help me out." He clapped West on the shoulder. "How about it?"

West looked at him. It was some kind of scam, belied by the easy smile, the white teeth, the glad face.

"What the hell," West said. He slouched off the barstool. "Where are they?"

The smile steered him around the curve of the bar. "Name's Jack," he said.

"Scott," West lied, his favorite of fake names.

"Well, Scott, by the end of the night you'll be thanking me. I just know it."

They pulled up at the far end of the bar, underneath a cold shaft of air conditioning, where two women in their twenties sat stirring their drinks. One of the women looked up. She had long dirty-blond hair waved around a thin face. A smirk spread, which she did not attempt to hide. West had to admit that she was beautiful. "You found somebody," she said.

"This is Scott," Jack said.

"I'm Lisa." The woman frowned at West and gave a sideways nod of her head. "This is my sister Ana. Don't fuck with her."

Ana looked up at West frankly, with incautious eyes. Her short brown hair was parted incidentally in the middle, and faint freckles rose with a blush in her face. "Be nice," she said to Lisa. She took West's hand and shook it. Her wrist seemed as thin as his thumb. "I'm pleased to meet you," she said.

"He's a jerk," Lisa said. She jabbed West in the shoulder with her index finger. "I'll repeat myself. Don't fuck with her."

"I'm out of here," West said. He turned to go. Somebody caught his arm and he assumed it was Jack, but when he looked down it was Ana.

Jack laughed. "Okay, babe. I did my end." He offered the crook of his elbow to Lisa, and she took it and rose off the stool. She was wearing a tank top and very tight jeans, and she undulated as she arranged herself next to Jack.

"You two be good." She smiled fakely at the both of them, while Jack began to lead her away. "Honestly," she said. "I don't care what you do."

West watched them go, two tapered backs. Ana still held on to him, and he could not bring himself to move. He shut his eyes and then opened them, expecting to find himself staring down at the video poker game. She let go and patted the empty seat beside her.

"Join me," she said.

Obediently he sat on the stool.

She touched his hair lightly. "I like your hair," she said. "It's clean." He tensed, liking her touch, wanting her to go further. She selected a lock and stretched it unpainfully between two fingers. "Don't you worry about Lisa. She's my younger sister but I frustrate her terribly." She said it in an even way, without irony.

"The way she was"—West felt for each word—"I thought she was older."

"It's because I'm a little slow," Ana said. She let go of the hair and turned his head to face her. "Mildly retarded. Would you mind kissing someone like me?"

"No," West said, a weird joke, but he'd play along. "I wouldn't."

She pulled his head to her and kissed him, long and tight-lipped, as if she had learned by watching television, her face moving instead of her mouth. It was still a nice kiss. He drew back.

"Did you like it?" she said. Her finger traced his face.

"Sure." West glanced around the casino to see if anyone had noticed that her head as she kissed had slowly ticked back and forth like a metronome, that the sweet pout of her lips was infantile. He rubbed the back of his neck. He liked her bangs and how small her nose was. He felt as if the back of his head had been shot off and all the air was rushing in. He reached for the back of his head. He wondered if this were the train of his drunk finally coming, to knock him out.

"Can I buy you a drink?" she said. "I have ten dollars." She took out a plastic purse from a little red pocketbook and showed him the money. She handed him a personal identification card that said TENNESSEE in a hologram across her face. She pointed at the birthdate. "I'm twenty-five," she said. "See." Effortlessly she flagged down the bartender. "What are you drinking?"

West shook his head and swallowed to see how close the drink was to overpowering him. It was not close enough. "Bourbon," he said hoarsely.

"Bourbon," she said. The bartender nodded and went off to make the drink. "Bourbon," she said again, drawing out the *r,* tasting the n on the roof of her mouth. West could see her that clearly. "What's it like?"

He'd never thought much about it. "It's like," he began. He swallowed. "It's like water mixed with the skin of red apples. Like the very sweet bitterness of apple skin."

"It doesn't sound very good," she said.

"It isn't," he agreed. But it was sure as hell going to stop him, which was lucky.

The bartender returned with the drink, straight up. West nodded at Ana and forced a sip. He hated warm bourbon. He made himself take a gulp. Bile rose halfway up his throat. "Thank you," he said.

"Do you have a room here," Ana said. She touched his hair again and he froze. "Jack has a room. Lisa and I share a room. I think I'd like to see your room." Her hand fell lightly to the back of his neck, and she squeezed it tenderly between her thumb and index finger. He shivered. He looked at her. The air conditioning fluttered her bangs. She took in his look with what appeared to be mild interest. "Are you ready?"

She was behind the curve but she was not that far behind. But she was far enough behind as to be behind the curve. She was capable of complex thought the way a twelve-year-old was capable of complex thought—serendipitously. It was a long word and he took a dip with it into the bourbon. He wished he did not have a room. He wished he were back at his old seat at the other end of the horseshoe bar. He wished—almost—that he were back in prison.

"How exactly," he said. "How exactly did we get into this?" He leaned his head into his hands, her fingers falling down his back, and shut his eyes, saw explosions of light, and opened them again.

"I think you're nice," she said.

"Oh, I'm nice." He sighed. "I'm very nice." He drained his drink. He could feel his train of drunkenness coming through and it was not going to knock him down, it was going to take him with it. He reared off the stool. "Let's go."

She stood, reached for his hand, caught it. They walked out of the casino, hand in hand, she holding on tight enough so that he knew not to break loose, but loose enough to seem as if she understood he would not think of leaving her. The bright light of the lobby hit him suddenly, and he reeled. She guided him to the door and opened it.

They were outside, in the night. He hoped the air would help, but it was flat, dry, desert air. She led him toward the parking lot, the cars caged in their heat and grease.

"Where's your car?" she said.

"Don't know." He could see it quite easily, the black vinyl hood, the wide brown body. The Pennsylvania license plate peeking out between the Winnebago and the pickup.

"Ours is over there."

He looked at her arm as she pointed, the way it extended out of her short-sleeved dress in a stunning, naked pureness, the subtle looseness of flesh around the upper arm, the taut forearm with a hint of muscle, the impossibly narrow wrist, the fingers long and slender. He wanted to eat them. Their car was a four-door dull silver Toyota that looked almost blue in the sparsely lighted parking lot.

"We're going to visit our aunt and uncle in San Diego," she said. "Where are you going?"

"Los Angeles," West said.

"Maybe I could see you on our way back. That would be in two weeks." She pressed his hand.

"Absolutely." He touched her arm, followed it up toward the shoulder, just to see if he could. He certainly could. His fingertips felt for the sleeve opening and he was in and feeling the very light titillating growth of hair at her underarm, then past and lightly pressing the swell of her breast, touching it at the very base of the bra before the nylon consumed it, measuring its potential size. Already he was hard. He wanted to bring around her hand that so persistently was locked in his and make her touch it. He was aghast to discover that that was just what he was doing.

"Not in the parking lot," she said.

They led each other through the rows of cars and vans and pickups and campers to the metal staircase.

"The second rack," she said.

Up the stairs, the loud pinging like coins dropping down a well, and along the thinly carpeted balcony to his room. He fought with the key for a moment, wanting it to take long enough to allow her to escape. Instead, she moved out of his light to give him a better chance to open the door. She strode in without invitation, and he followed, turning on the light and at first hesitating but then shutting the door firmly and flicking on the air conditioning.

"It's just like ours," she said. "I knew it would be."

He started for the television, to get some more noise in the room, but she intercepted him. She caught him and hugged him tightly, her cheek against his, as if they were saying good-bye. He looked forlornly beyond her to the television, which he now realized he had considered his last hope. Against his chest her breasts seemed to be throbbing, demanding his attention.

The buttons down the back of her dress came easily to him, and he unhooked each of the four disks while her hands slipped down to his buttocks. Her dress fell from her shoulders to her forearms. The straw-basket shade of the overhead lamp released thin sheaves of illumination, the creamy part of her neck, the soft cups of her bra. Without waiting for her to step from her dress, he unhooked the bra. She was undressed in such a way that it looked as if perhaps she was trying to dress. He hesitated, and she came out of her pumps and her dress and her bra all at once.

He fell onto the bed with her and bucked against her, squirming to kick out of his sneakers and jeans and trying to get her underwear down her legs. She sighed. He could not tell whether it was a sigh of resignation or enjoyment, and again he stopped. It struck him, taking her in—the incautious eyes, the incidental part in her bangs, the calm breasts with the inerect nipples—it struck him that it was a sigh of indifference. The bourbon rose in his throat and he shut it down, willed it back to a place he had yet to discover. He was atop her.

"What's that?" she said.

She was fingering a pimple on his right buttock.

"It's a pimple," he said. "I've got a pimple there." He forced his tongue inside her mouth.

"Oh," she said around it. "A pimple." She giggled, another word whose sound she seemed to like.

He slid his hand along the inside of her thigh, and at the same time moved her under him so soon her free hand would be where he wanted it to be. He felt the hair between her legs and then probed inside. She was a little wet, not quite wet enough. He was terribly hard. She touched him, then gripped him. He massaged her wetness.

"I have to ask you something," she said, slightly out of breath, holding onto him. "Should you be doing this?"

"Yes." From his perspective, it was just too late, the train had

come through and he was on it and he just had to ride it. He just
had to follow this through. He pulled against her grip, trying to
get loose.

"It's a strange hotel," she said, her face turned to the side so
that she appeared to be examining the loud air conditioner and
the green curtains that quivered against it.

"You're not kidding." He was finally where he wanted to be.
He started.

"You sure you should be doing this?" she asked again.

"Yes." Now retreat was impossible. He had no choice.

"How does it feel?"

He didn't answer her, he kept at it. She clung to him.

"Do you like it?" she asked.

"Yes." He did.

She squirmed, as if to push him out. "I think we should stop."

"Soon." He pinned his weight to her, and held himself inside.
She lay still. He gripped her buttocks and made her move.

"Are we going to stop?"

"Yes."

She touched his face. "When are we going to stop?"

"Soon." If she would just be quiet, he was almost ready.

"I don't like it."

"I know." He stopped. Through the sheaves of light he could
see her eyes, wide open and indifferent. She had certainly had
experience in masturbation, but it had not prepared her to understand. He was sure she would be all right. He pulled out.

"Los Angeles," she said.

He came against the bedspread, unable and unwilling to rein it
in. It seemed to him that he came for a long time, but he could
not be sure. He tried to hide it from her. She was already pulling
on her underwear.

"Can I use your bathroom?"

He clutched a swath of bedspread around him, began to dry himself off while he still came. "Of course," he managed.

She moved to the bathroom, picking up pieces of clothing as she went. She shut the door behind her, then laughed, and opened it. He turned his back to the sound of her, felt the light of the bathroom on his shoulders. She hummed and made water at the same time, like a song with instrumentals. He finished with the bedspread and began to get into his clothes. She got off the toilet and flushed and washed her hands in the sink. She was fully dressed and he was trying to shimmy into his jeans.

"We leave at seven tomorrow for San Diego," she said, touching his back with her clean hand. "Will you come see us off?"

"Sure." He finally had his jeans on. Where was his shirt? Frantically he scanned the room.

"I have to go."

He nodded his agreement. He spied the shirt under the corner of the bed and bent to pick it up. Behind him she started for the door.

"Won't you kiss me good night?" she said.

Relieved, he stood. They kissed each other on the cheek. She opened the door and was through and shut it quickly behind her. He listened. She did not walk immediately away. She called in, softly, "Don't forget tomorrow morning—7 A.M." He nodded at the door, even though he couldn't see her, even though she couldn't see him. Finally, he heard her leave.

He went to the sink in the bathroom and splashed water on his face. In the yellow light his hands looked green. He felt a little green. He located the toilet, lifted the seat, got down on his knees, and stuck his finger down his throat. He gagged around his finger. At last, it came, so much liquid as if he'd not eaten anything in a long time. He let it come, he tried to encourage it to come, he tried to be patient. Sweat popped out on his back. His throat was raw. He reached for the sink, and drank tap water from the cup of his palm. He put his mouth to the tap, rinsed. He considered taking another shower, but concluded he could not spare the time.

He gathered up his dirty clothes, and shut off all the lights. He stood at the door. It was past midnight. He opened the door, slipped through, and closed it softly. Lightly he made his way down the metal stairs to the parking lot, the steps almost silent, making only the faintest jangle.

He navigated the rows of vehicles to his car. Only after he had turned right out of the lot and was on Main Street did he switch on his headlights. The road was lined with twenty-four-hour convenience stores, and he was thirsty. Straight ahead and beyond the town, in the blackness of the flats, occasional lights of solitary traffic scudded across the overpass. He did not think he could afford to stop. In his mouth was the taste of tap water and vomit. The still sunbaked car smelled of it and of his new sweat and of the old sweat that he'd been unable to air out. Once he got on the interstate, he would allow himself to roll down the windows. He would stick his head out the window as he drove, taking in the air like a dog.

Now he was up on the interstate, over Lovelock and past it. He could not quite risk rolling down the windows yet. He was terribly paranoid. He deserved paranoia. Almost suffocating with the smell of himself, he drove through the flats.

The dial on the washing machine in the basement of the Golden Gate Residence was jammed, stuck on

BRIGHT COLORS, and Amber Keenan had been twisting and hammering at it for a while, she had already poured in her detergent and load of clothes—underwear, bras, T-shirts, blouses, sheets, towels, everything white. Of the other three machines, one lacked a lid, the second needed an agitator, and the third was without a control dial. She gave up and pushed in the loaded quarters.

She walked out from the damp heat of the laundry room to the vending machines, where she lit a cigarette. She inhaled deeply, feeling for the borders of her lungs. She had quit smoking after Dean, just a few months ago. It had been easy. Every cigarette reminded her of him, his thick, arrogant lips, the way he dismissively tapped the ashes out, manipulating with disinterest the cigarette between his middle finger and index finger. She exhaled. She was not allowed to smoke in the basement.

She brushed the hair out of her face and went back in to check the machine; at this rate she'd be up until one-thirty. She leaned against one of the broken washing machines and took another drag, watched the tip of the cigarette burn, and toyed with the idea of setting the laundry room on fire. Above her the ceiling was an open maze of crisscrossing wood beams and electrical wiring. A dried-out mat of carpeting covered the floor of the vending machine area. Several splintered wooden chairs could serve as kindling. It was a complicated job, but with a high likelihood of success. She flicked the ash into the chamber of the broken washer, and wandered out past the vending machines.

The basement corridors were lit by intermittent light bulbs noosed from the open ceiling. The door to the children's room was locked. Once before, she had seen a television inside. Up on the lobby floor were two lounges, each with a television. She wouldn't have minded a television and a couple of beers. Drinking and sleeping were prohibited in the public spaces, and smoking was confined to one of the lobby lounges. She had tried to smoke there yesterday. She had felt as if she were sitting in an ashtray, even the fake crushed velour of the cheap sofa and chairs had a soft crumbly texture. She levered her knee against the children's room door and pushed.

"No esta abierto," said a man softly behind her.

She turned. It was the security guard, his hands clasped behind his back. He smiled and nodded at her, immediately apparent that he'd followed her downstairs, waiting, pausing, selecting this moment, the two of them alone in the basement. In an odd way, she was touched.

"Can't you open it?" she said. She jiggled the doorknob.

"Mas tarde."

She remembered her cigarette, looked at it, and waited for him to say something about her smoking. He shrugged. She reached into her breast pocket and pulled out the pack, held it out to him.

"Gracias." He took one.

She offered her lighter. He came forward, awkwardly. She lit his cigarette, his face bending shyly toward the flame, a boy's face, a bristle of moustache, faint acne. His round head glistened with pomade. The strands of her cut-offs teased the backs of her thighs. She laughed.

"What's your name?"

He inhaled carefully on his cigarette, as if it were hot. He backed away, keeping his eyes on her. She thought he might fall, or at least cough out his smoke like a teenager.

"I'm Amber," she tried again. "What's your name?"

"I should." He pointed to the ceiling with his cigarette.

"Don't let me keep you."

He started backing away again, then turned and hurried for the stairs.

"Hey!" she said. He turned. She pointed to his cigarette. He looked at it. "You better not smoke on the job."

He smiled and bowed his head to her, then took a deep, extended drag on his cigarette. He held it in, smirked at her, and in one motion expertly pinched out his cigarette and exhaled, the smoke engulfing her face. She could hear him laughing, as he raced up the steps away from her.

She wiped her mouth and walked back to the laundry room. The whites still sloshed in the wash cycle. She ought to go upstairs to him, plant her backside on his desk and prod her breasts at him. She would have to wait until she was not thinking about him, and then it would come to her, unanticipated but ultimately expected, the perfect way to fuck with him.

She stabbed out her cigarette and hit the button for the elevator. When it arrived, she got on and rode it to the second floor, its cables clanking. In her room she locked the door and sat on the bed. She was having difficulty breathing. She could not seem to remember how it was done, it no longer felt instinctive, but as mechanical and tenuous as the elevator. Was breathing supposed to be shallow or deep? Where was the median between slow and fast? She just wanted to calm herself. Every guy had the potential to be Dean, but that did not mean she had to feel vengeful with every guy. With Dean, she had overwhelmed herself. She had seen his key in her apartment, picked it up, studied it, and suddenly she knew. She knew. She knew when he was in his apartment and when he was out, which café he sat in with his loud stupid laugh, which black jacket he wore to which café— leather to Warner's, cotton to the Highball, denim to Yosemite.

She knew the way his head tilted back when he laughed, and how his laughter came up from his chest, that hollow cavity, and echoed in the café as if the sound of it could not rest until it hit walls and came back at you. She knew his walk when he languidly rose to retrieve a second cup of coffee, a stalking walk, long strides as if he were used to covering great distances, though his greatest distance on his feet was the twenty yards between his apartment door and the bus stop. He used to say he was the only white person he knew who rode the buses in Los Angeles. His fingers, skeletal and thin, felt almost like taut cables against her shoulders. The stories he told her, that he told all his women. Dean's lore. "When I was seventeen, I found a wedding ring in the lining of a coat I bought at a thrift store on Venice Beach. It fit me." "My father is the CEO at a toothpaste conglomerate, but I never accept any of his money. He disgusts me." "I'll tell you this about me, I almost died. Twice. A friend was struck by lightning on the limb above me as we both sat in a tree waiting out a thunderstorm. He fell to the ground. His face was smoked. The other time? The other time it was so bad I can't remember it." Stories so narcissistic they had a pathetic charm to them. But she knew this about him—she knew he accepted money from his mother, that he had recurring venereal warts, that he ripped the knees of his jeans before he would wear them in public. His studio with the kitchenette and the bathroom the size of a phone booth smelled of feet and stale ashtrays; and he didn't have to work, he lived off money from his father funneled through his mother. For all the time Amber had lived with him, working her forty-hour weeks, they kept a little stuffed lamb and stuffed bear in their bed. They performed puppet shows for each other. The lamb learned to fuck the bear. In the evenings they'd smoke cigarettes and cook curry dishes over the blue flame of the gas stovetop, sip wine and do the puppet show. Wake to a night that still had possibilities, put on the right clothes, and go to Warner's or Noc-Noc to listen to music so loud it didn't matter it was canned. He liked to wear a black satin demi-cape that flapped like wings when he stalked down the street and made his Dean entrance into a club or café, his loud voice booming somehow modulated greetings to people who for the most part didn't like him. She loved him, she understood the lamb and the bear. They used handcuffs, rope, nothing. She learned, cultivated, rings of sensation to his penetration. They watched each other shit, pee, the door to the bathroom thrown open like an invitation. He would stand over her, naked, watching, his dick swaying until it rose and was in her face and she sucked him while she sat on the toilet, she learned to do two functions at once, and it gave her pleasure. It was natural.

He never held a steady job, the three years she lived with him. Sometimes he taught composition or literature at a private college run by Jesuits. He had never allowed her to come watch him teach, but she could imagine it, the booming voice, the stalking walk, how he wanted to make them cower and for the most part they did. The Jesuits kept letting him go after each quarter and then, a quarter later, rehiring him. He had an evangelical quality that they could not resist. Some students were terribly loyal to him, because he demanded loyalty, and in demanding it he was bound, occasionally, to achieve it. They followed him from course to course—composition to introduction to literature to nineteenth-century poetry. He did not sleep with any of them, although she knew that the loyalists were women, attracted to him ripping apart their writing, stripping it to expose their instinctive intelligence.

But he did not sleep with them. He would have told her.

Instead, he slept with another teacher; Amber did not even want to know her name, sometimes she had gone with Dean to young teacher parties and felt humiliated to say that she worked as an assistant librarian at a law firm. But Dean had told her who it was. He'd come home late, stalk-walked into the studio, sat down at the stupid little table where they shared all their meals. "I fucked Andrea in the faculty bathroom today," he said, lighting a cigarette—it was always the first thing he did when he came in, light a cigarette—looking at her critically, because he was Dean and he was allowed to say and do whatever the fuck he wanted, he was *supposed* to.

"Dean," Amber had said, feeling for a seat at the table.

"It was not a mistake." He offered her a cigarette across the little table. "I think I'd like to start seeing her."

"I don't believe this." Amber looked around the room, willing every object to confirm that she was here and that this was happening. The bear and the lamb lay across the pillows, turned in such a way that they could not see her.

"I'm not saying that we're over," Dean said. "I don't know about that. I can't say. I just have to follow this thing with Andrea, and then I'll know. I don't want you to be East Coast about this. You're just going to have to go with it." He twiddled his cigarette between his middle finger and index finger. She wanted to reach across the table and snap the fingers in her hands.

"You're an asshole," she said.

Dean laughed, that hollow laugh that he liked so much. "Hey, babe, you should know."

She had tried to hit him, but failed to crack his prominent cheekbone with her knuckles. She packed a suitcase, called a cab, and retreated to a Motel 6 out on Santa Monica. Within a week she moved into her own shoebox of a studio and, knowing his teaching schedule and pattern of clubs and cafés, she was able to retrieve the rest of her things without having to deal with him or anybody else. Pieces of the new woman were already occupying the studio—a plate she hadn't seen before, slippers, a towel. She tried to think of it all as relatively painless. She never told him where she had moved, and she kept her phone number unlisted so that she would not have the false and masochistic hope that he would call.

She had dreams about him, dreams where she was successfully tearing at his face, gouging at the mouth that emitted the painful laugh, and dreams where he easily batted her away, mocked her, let loose his laugh on her. She sat in her studio at night, idly watched the black-and-white television she had forced herself to purchase (reduced to a television! Dean would have never allowed it), and began to understand that she had to bring this thing with him to some closure, on her terms, before she could move on.

When the plan came upon her, she tried to rationalize it away. It was too easy, too extreme. It could not possibly work. Or, it could work but who was she to decide that he deserved it. She tried to nurture the plan, to develop it so thoroughly that by simply having fully imagined it, it would be enough for her, it would suffice. Everywhere, every day, men hurt women and women hurt men. Who was she to take such an offense at being cheated on and dumped? She had done it to somebody as well. But the way he did it to her, as if it were his birthright. She worked on her plan from the inside out, developed it and redeveloped it to an organic whole without any potential for dissolution or failure. At night, her dreams convinced her. He kept waving her off, his laugh pounding at her, whittling her away. She was no longer able to rip at his face, while he laughed at her, ignored her, and worked his wart dick into a willing

Andrea. She woke five, six times a night, with hate, envy, fear. Weeks passed. She felt him fading away, escaping unpunished. At night his laugh shook her studio. She turned up the volume of the television. The downstairs neighbors knocked on her floor with broomsticks or tennis rackets, she kept turning the television down and then, without realizing it, turning it up again, until the neighbors knocked again like something kicking inside her. At work the librarian told her, unsolicited, that the only way out of anything was through the middle. She pondered what that meant. She had no idea, but by this time she had lived with her little plot so long it was no longer extreme, it was natural. Like baking bread. Like cooking dinner.

She kept the key to his apartment in a celadon-green ashtray that they had swiped together from a chic club. She knew his schedule, knew that the afternoon class on Wednesday led to a stop at a café with the other young teachers, then home for a late dinner, a fuck and a nap, out again to a club. On such a Wednesday he had come home to announce his realized interest in Andrea. Had he closed the lid on the toilet and sat, and Andrea then sat on top of him, or had he leaned her over the toilet, her hands resting on the water closet, while he entered from behind? Amber had been too demure to ask, "Dean, just which way did you fuck her?"

On the first Wednesday in May, six weeks after she had moved out from Dean's, and four weeks before she would move to San Francisco, she called in sick to the office. Her voice sounded strange and distant, as if she were talking to a large audience, and heat rose in her face.

"Are you crying?" the librarian said, lowering her voice to a whisper. "Is it an abortion, honey?"

"Just the flu," Amber said. "I'll be in tomorrow."

She had drawn attention to herself, calling in sick. But she could not use cabs, and what she planned required more time than her lunch hour. What choice did she have? She hummed inanely to herself, did the few dishes in the sink, made her bed, showered, shaved her legs, reread her acceptance letter from VISTA, and waited. At noon she went out. The weather was absurd, at least ninety-five degrees. She walked quickly away from the apartment building, as if she had stolen something. She walked five blocks, turning corners, getting as far away from her place as possible, as necessary. At Kirkland she drew out from her pocket a scarf, silky and deep blue. She unfurled it and tied it around her head, put on a pair of cheap mirrored sunglasses she had bought for the occasion. Last she pulled on a pair of black stretch gloves, stylish and affected enough so as not to attract suspicion. She felt like a tawdry Gloria Vanderbilt as she drifted through the midday heat another seven blocks, to the bus stop, passing the sad little sun-drenched bungalows of West Los Angeles. At the bus stop she waited twenty-seven minutes, and when the Thirty-nine came, it wheezed to a halt, beeped, and knelt for her as if she were an old woman. She got on gingerly, gave up her money to the machine, and took a seat by the middle door.

It was almost two by the time she got off eight blocks from Dean's apartment, the scarf and her head damp with perspiration, her eyes swimming in a mist of haze. She crossed to one block parallel to the bus route, and walked a street of stolid adobe houses and occasional stunted palm trees. At Dean's cross street she stood out on the corner, hooding her eyes against the sun so bright it seemed to penetrate easily both the scarf and the sunglasses, and waited until the next bus passed. Then she started up the block to his building.

It was a four-story apartment complex with twenty units. Because of the insulated, mutually entwined life she and Dean had lived, she could not recall what any of the other tenants looked like or did, she could only dimly recall seeing U-Hauls and Ryder rent-a-trucks parked in the usual seasons on the street in front of the building, bringing in or taking away the unfamiliar faces and bodies.

She strode briskly up the paved walkway to the door, and let herself in. Her step was light on the wooden staircase, but it did not matter. She had the clear and almost happy sensation that no one was around, in the middle of the weekday, in the middle of such heat. The landlord prohibited air conditioning due to faulty wiring.

At Dean's door she was tempted to knock, but the noise seemed unnecessary, and if for some reason he were in, then it was fate, and she could accept fate. Or at least she would try to hit him again. She let herself in, quickly shutting the door behind her.

He—or they—had changed things around, but the one thing that had not changed was his obsession with the windows. They were all shut, despite the heat. He distrusted air. The bed sat like an altar in the middle of the room, up on its four legs. The little table now had a cloth over it, black of course, with matching black mugs still half-filled with coffee. Inside her gloves her hands were sweating. The shallow closet had some of Andrea's clothes; she favored metallic knits and leather and stirrup pants. On the floor of the closet, underneath a pair of ankle boots, was the stuffed lamb. It lay on its side, one eye staring up at her. She wanted to pick it up, to hold it to her. She shut the closet door.

She looked through the drawers of his rickety desk. He and Andrea had compartmentalized—his students' papers in the top drawer, her students' papers in the middle drawer, departmental correspondence in the bottom drawer. They had fallen behind in their grading.

She checked the windows again. As tightly shut as she could have hoped. She had to get on with it, but where was the bear? She wanted to check on the bear. Almost frantically she searched the apartment, the little kitchenette, the bathroom. She would not be able to bring herself to finish if she couldn't find the bear. Finally, she saw it. It had fallen behind the bookcase, and lay face down on the floor, its round butt and stubby tail pitched in the air. She wanted to see its face. She remembered it had the most simple expression—so flat you could not tell whether it was mournful or serene. She reached for it, caught herself. Sweat was streaming from her. When she wiped her face her glove came away damp from the pressure inside and damp from the perspiration of her face. Quickly she crossed the room, around the center-piece of the bed, to the kitchenette. She opened the door of the gas oven and made sure no improvements had been made in her absence. She turned it on to see if it would light. She waited ten seconds, fifteen seconds. It did not light, you still had to light it yourself. She shut the door, leaving the oven on. She waited another thirty seconds, then checked again. Still no flame, no pilot light. The sound of the gas was like a last, endless exhalation. She again shut the oven. It was three-thirty. In four hours Dean and Andrea would return, fresh from class and the café. They would come in, shut the door, perhaps she would slip off her shoes. But the very first thing he would do, would be to light a cigarette.

Perhaps Andrea, more observant than Dean, would remark on the smell of the gas when they came in, but Amber thought not. She had come to terms with this uncertainty. She could live with it either way. It would at the very least scare the shit out of him. She had found closure.

As she walked back down the street parallel to the bus route, she finally shed her gloves. She could have wrung them out. Five blocks from Dean's building, she dropped them in a garbage can. Her hands were free. Three blocks later, she crossed back up to the bus route. The world viewed through her sunglasses seemed like an aquarium, green and watery. The bus came. Again, it knelt for her. She climbed on nimbly, and blithely fed the machine precise change. She swayed, almost swaggered, to the back of the bus. She took a seat by the window, slid it open, and let the damp afternoon wind come in. She smiled in it, a face hidden by sunglasses and scarf, a woman of indeterminate age and sanity, on her way home from the business of the day.

Through the Nevada desert West searched the landscape for signs that he had not driven the same way once already, that he'd only imagined it. That he'd only imagined taking this route before convincing himself to return to Lovelock, where he had found the two sisters hurriedly loading their car even though it was the middle of the night. They had both put on shorts, their legs stretching out of them like swords. He'd said he was sorry for what he'd done, and Ana had kissed him and thanked him for coming to see her off. Lisa had slammed the trunk shut and demanded what the hell else he needed. Ana had said she was fine and that she'd wanted to do what they had done. And then she had held out her hand to him and asked her sister if they were going to call the police.

Now the moon lit the bed of rock and sand into shades of blue, and the night sky met the land with walls of depthless black. He couldn't tell any more what else had happened, what else was said. He knew what he regretted, he felt the crustiness in the crotch of his jeans, he had not dreamed it. How he'd gripped her and made her move under him. He recalled kneeling in the face of the toilet, after she'd left his hotel room. He took a long swallow of soda and waited. He could feel it coming. He pulled over onto the shoulder of the road and quickly got out of the car. He descended a soft slope into the flats, the ground hard under his feet, loose crumbles of land like marbles against the thin soles of his sneakers. Rocks jutted out across the desert, their points glinting. He could still feel it coming. It bent him at the waist and the seat of his jeans was suddenly damp with his sweat. He vomited.

Was it what he had done, or what he had drunk? His eyes filled with tears from the effort and pain of puking. "Don't you know what you've done," Lisa had said. "Sorry doesn't do a whole hell of a lot for her." Around him he could feel the dry earth soaking him up. He was careful not to fall. When he finished, he walked a good distance away, and peed.

Afterward he climbed the soft slope to the road and stepped out onto the middle of the pavement. He could still feel the heat of the sun rising from it. Above and around him the night was turning, fading, draining into day. Blue crept into the sky. He would still reach San Francisco by the end of this one, provided Lisa didn't notify anyone. She did not seem the type. She had dismissed him instead. He could live with that. He did not mind being dismissed. In the distance he heard something coming, and he turned and saw about a mile back down the interstate a truck making its way toward him, the lights atop its cab standing out like a hairline. The truck honked two times, as if it could see him. He crossed back to the side of the road and got into his Chevy. What was left of the soda had spilled over onto the floormat, sweet fumes and a dark stain. He opened a second can and took a sip. He swished it around in his mouth, and spit it out the window. He tried another sip. It tasted better. Up ahead the truck was still coming, lumbering across the flats toward him. He started the Chevy.

It moved weightily over the road, through the flats, as if it knew it had been this way before and resented having to repeat it. He laughed and gulped at the soda. The truck came up from the other direction and shot past him in a clatter of wind and metal and tire flaps. He finished his drink and tried to lick the film of it from his teeth. Clouds approached in the gradual blueing of dawn. A paper bag caromed across the flats. From a great distance he spied another oncoming truck. It was just him and the truck and the paper bag. He wondered why he had even returned in the first place. To leave nothing undone, nothing to chance. To save a remnant of his conscience. To extend a trip that was bound to end in the hollow disappointment of a crummy job. To stall the onset of the rest of his life. But California, he was going to California! That was *someplace,* by God. He tried the radio. Nothing, not even static. The sky around him filled with the flat whiteness of heat and haze. He had somehow missed the actual sunrise, and now the sun had slipped out of view, already above the car somewhere. He could feel it through the vinyl roof, but it wasn't even six yet. Yes, it was. It was exactly six. California in thirty miles, Reno swelling beside the interstate. He ought to slow down. He didn't want to get to San Francisco just yet, in case what awaited him proved unpleasant or worse. He ought to be stretching this out, the passing rockscape, the dry, cracked barrenness, the hot wind coming into the car. This feat of motion. He turned the steering wheel slightly, drifted into the right lane, then back to the left and over toward the double yellow line. He could still do whatever he wanted. It was almost mid-June, the steady relentless ripening approach of summer, particles of heat shimmering in waves off the asphalt. Soon he would be in California, with a job, an apartment, resigning himself to routine, a city, the deadening haul of daily work. He jiggled the steering wheel again, it was still with him, it made the car respond. He adjusted his rearview mirror to see if anyone was coming. There was no one. When he turned his attention back to the road in front of him, the second truck was upon him. He jerked awake, jerking the car with him to the right, then correcting himself. The truck was already fifty feet past, curving toward the east. It had not even been close.

Within ten miles of the state border the car caught a tail wind that made it go faster than he thought it should, the wide trunk buffeting in the swirl of air. His hands on the steering wheel were greasy with sweat. He braked just to see if he could. The car slowed, but not as much as he had hoped, the distant mountains growing large and darkly vertiginous. They gave the flats color and a skyline. Just as he thought that perhaps the border had passed him by, the road opened into the Sierras and he was irreversibly ascending on a three-lane switchback, up too quickly into thinner air until a sign said California. The car skated down the Truckee off-ramp and he pulled into the parking lot of a delicatessen, turned off the motor, got out, stretched his legs, looked up at the sky, and kicked at the loose gravel, to see if he had changed his mind about all this.

He went into the delicatessen. A rippled Formica counter was lined with filled stools of hairy, bearded men in trucker's caps and bib overalls. Lean, deeply tanned women in their thirties and forties crammed into the few booths. Smoking was not allowed.

He bought an iced sun tea and drank it standing up in the unisex rest room. He urinated, splashed water on his face, and ran his fingers through his hair like a comb.

He sat in the Chevy, gazing out at the road. In the hotel room at Lucky Andy's thin sheaves of light had illuminated aspects of Ana, the creamy part of her neck, her incautious eyes. He'd tasted her nipples, a salty sweetness. He started the car and drove from the lot. An altitude headache gnawed at his hangover. The highway glinted with four-by-fours and camper trailers. Of this much he was certain: That from the driver seat of her departing car Lisa had leaned over and opened the door for Ana, and Ana had backed away from him and stepped into the car. That her foot had caught and she had fallen against the seat, her legs sticking out. That she had curled them up to her chest, those bare legs, and her sister had reached around her and pulled the door shut. She had stared at him through the window, Lisa had, as if she'd had one last thing to say to him but she couldn't remember what it was. It could have been *I'm sorry for you,* it could have been *I hate you,* it could have been *I knew.* Instead she had just shaken her head, and turned toward the interstate.

Around him as he descended through the Sierras, the mountains were steep and green and pointed. He would have liked to see some snow, but he supposed that was impossible in this season, that you couldn't get up high enough in just a Chevy. He would miss it, when he sold it, but he'd be relieved as well. You could get in trouble with a car.

On her way to the literacy center, Amber walked quickly, careful not to bump into anybody, careful not to make extended eye contact while at the same time letting everybody know that she knew they were there. The sidewalk was sticky with urine and alcohol. A large iron and cement trash receptacle lay overturned on the sidewalk, uprooted from its foundation. Bright clumps of mottled green and orange produce spilled into the street. She chucked her coffee cup into the hole where the receptacle had once stood, stepped around a prostrate man on the pavement, and passed the early line at a soup and shelter joint. At the corner she braced herself for the next block.

"Fuck you, you tightass babe," someone shouted behind her.

She crossed Turk against the light, keeping her eyes forward, lowering her shoulder as if she were fighting a wind. A couple of guys hunched over in front of a chain link fence, setting out pieces of an antiquated stereo alongside car radios and an eggbeater. A woman with a red scarf knotted at her throat sat against the third parking meter. Amber nodded to her, she had seen her every day along this route. The woman nodded back.

"How you doing," Amber said.

The woman raised her eyebrows and looked out into the street. Across the way a man was hitting at a woman with seemingly ineffectual woodpeckerlike punches. The woman shrank but did not make an attempt to move out from the blows. Amber told herself it was not her business.

At Eddy the light was green, but she stopped and carefully looked both ways. A block down, a week ago, on her way home from work, she had come upon a heavyset man lying on his side in the street, knife slashes in his back and throat, blood soaking his T-shirt. Sirens screamed from both directions, even though Eddy was one-way. Children giggled and came out from doorways. It was a plain black face, expressionless, eyes partly open, loose lips giving way to a bubble of saliva. "Don't ask me," an old guy said, sliding away along a wall. "Get lost."

Now she crossed Eddy and started up the rise toward Ellis. Once or twice she'd seen the girls this early, their too-short shorts creased with night wear, their skin in the cold morning like skim milk. She passed a couple of Korean coffee joints, packed with drowsy tense people hunched over their cups, waiting for the day to start. At Ellis she turned right. The Tenderloin Literacy Center occupied a caged storefront pocked with pigeon turds and shiny slicks of dried liquor. She wrenched the dirty handle and let herself in.

"Hey, Amber," Rose said without looking up, the six-dollar-an-hour receptionist. Amber made about that much, but somehow her job had prestige. She taught, she was funded by the government, and she made so little for her college education and teaching load that nobody bothered clocking her time.

"Sister Frances wants to see you," Rose said.

"Me?"

"She's upstairs in her office."

No one had ever wanted to see her before. "Do you know what it's about?" Amber said nonchalantly.

"Nope." Rose shut a manila folder and finally looked up at her. She wore her hair curled at the shoulders like a southern belle; each of her fingernails was at least an inch long. "Just go on up," Rose said. "She isn't going to hurt you."

Amber blushed and hurried into the other room. It had thread-bare green carpeting and a high ceiling, and was divided up by flimsy partitions. The largest section had thirty school chairs with attached arm-length desks. A computer literacy center was partitioned within a five-foot square, three monitors side by side on a table constructed of a slab of wood on trestles, Amber's desk across from it in a tiny cubicle. She fished out a notebook and pen from the only working drawer and headed up the wooden staircase to Sister Frances' office.

She sat at her computer with her back to the doorway. Amber knocked, and Sister Frances swiveled around, a pleasant, sweet-faced woman who sported the boyish haircut that all the Sisters seemed to favor. Her desk, a huge oak contraption with eroded corners and a cracked base, looked like it had fallen off a truck. Sister Frances gestured across it to a shaky Goodwill-donated chair. "Come in, dear. Have a seat."

Amber gingerly took a seat.

"So how are you?" Sister Frances said.

"Fine. Everything is going great."

"Good. Good. I just wanted to talk with you about your VISTA goals."

Amber nodded. She hadn't forgotten about her VISTA goals.

"We ought to formulate a plan of action," Sister Frances said.

"I was just thinking," Amber said. "I was just thinking that maybe that wasn't appropriate for the community." She couldn't imagine transforming the people she saw on the street into an orderly corps of tutors and learners.

Sister Frances smiled and sucked in on her dentures. She nodded slowly and put both hands on the desk, as if she gained her power from it. "You could start with the churches, going around to all the churches. You could try the drug and alcohol treatment centers, see if we could have a partnership in rehabbing their adults, putting them to work teaching in the center. You could put up flyers and hold a few receptions for people in the community. How does that all sound?"

"I guess it sounds fine," Amber said.

"It's what the last VISTA worker did. You know, dear, it's simply not possible for you to take on all the teaching yourself. We need you to train teachers. That's the way you were intended to be used."

Amber stood up. "I'll take care of it."

"Very fine. I knew you would."

Amber made her way back down the stairs. She had fifteen minutes until class, and then she had class for seven and a half of the next eight hours. At her VISTA interview they'd asked her what she knew about organizing and she'd admitted not much, and they'd said that was fine, it was all theory anyway and the only way to be successful at it was not to have any preconceptions, just to do it. She inhaled deeply on her cigarette and blew smoke up into the rest of the room.

Through the plywood she heard the classroom filling behind her. She liked the individual sessions better, where she recorded life stories in essential phrases, and helped the learners read them back to her. She liked learning the stories, and in the five minutes allotted between each session, she would shut her eyes and imagine how she would distill her own story. She looked over the partitions to the open space of the classroom. There were about twenty today, of which she recognized maybe half. It was nine o'clock. Intermediate meant that they read at the third-grade level. She could not recall a damn thing she had read in third grade, her teacher's vague perfume, the globe in the corner, the view of the parking lot from the classroom window. The blackboard that covered the entire wall, the colored chalk that the teacher broke out for special occasions—the pumpkin she drew for Halloween, the turkey for Thanksgiving, the Santa Claus for Christmas—the grainy color on the black slate.

In third grade there was a black girl that everybody had decided to hate, and her father had to come every day at recess to play with her. They bounced a basketball back and forth on the asphalt court, they ate lunch together in the cafeteria, his butt bulging out from the small chair. Amber could not remember why they had all decided to hate her, and she had neither gone along with it nor gone against it. She herself always ate lunch quickly, as if she were afraid someone would steal her food from her. After the third grade, the father pulled the black girl from the school. Amber remembered the shouts of triumph in the fall of fourth grade, the giggling and clapping in the cloakroom. Her mother had once asked her, during the year of third grade, if she had anything to do with the ostracization. Amber shook her head no. "You better not," her mother said. "I don't want you being part of anything vicious." She pulled Amber to her and hugged her. It was late in the afternoon, almost evening, and she smelled of the tomatoes and garlic that she was cooking down into spaghetti sauce. Amber's father would be coming home from the office soon, he worked downtown as a lawyer, in Baltimore. He would have one drink of onion and sweetness—a Gibson—and then they would eat, her brother across the table chewing with his mouth open. She watched his food appear and reappear as if it were a secret.

Third grade, fourth grade, fifth grade. All grades and years that she hated. By fifth grade she refused to take the school bus, and her mother had to drive her, and then she refused to stay at school, she would run off at the first chance, only to be discovered by her mother or one of her mother's friends on the three-mile walk between school and home. Her mother had to come to school every day, to sit in the lobby while Amber was in class, so Amber could wave to her between classes. In the sixth grade, during a checkup, it was all explained. She had a thyroid disorder. She had thought she had just known that life was going to be miserable, and that's why she'd been a miserable child—but they'd found a medical explanation for it. She took pills for two years and was cured. Tell that to Dean. She was cured!

She stood before the twenty adults, smiling, fanning herself with the primer. They looked at her, expectantly, tiredly, angrily, indifferently—the usual range for the morning class, padded with people from the street who wanted a peaceful place to sit for a while. An older, heavy man wore his bathrobe and slippers. A bald woman with earrings through her lips and nose smirked at Amber and looked away. From Rose's desk in the other room came the rising voice of an argument in progress. Amber scanned the class, looking for a face she could fall back on. In the middle row, on the left side, was a woman with her head wrapped in a blue bandanna. A purplish welt rose under one eye. She frowned at Amber.

"All right," Amber said. "If you all could turn to page thirty-six, we can begin."

As Amber leafed through the pages, she stole another look at the bruised woman. She was the one Amber had seen being beaten on the street on her way to work. The woman glanced up sharply, catching Amber's stare. Behind her, Amber noticed, sat the man who'd been beating her, his head leaning forward so that his chin almost touched her shoulder.

"We have a lot to cover today," Amber said, stalling, as she walked around the chairs to stand at the side of the class, directly next to the man and woman. The class swiveled to look at her. Behind her was a bookcase of primers and manuals. "I'll be referring to some of these manuals during class." She picked up a manual for the alphabet, and turned to the first letter. She held it up to the class. "You all know the letter A. You know how *a* can separate itself from the rest of the word, be its own syllable. About. Abroad." She paused and took a breath. "Abuse. Today we could talk about abuse. Yes. Why don't we do that." She hovered closer to the man behind the bruised woman. "We could begin with you. What do you know about the word *abuse?*"

"You ought to get back up there where we can all get a look at you," the man said.

"Just teach the plan," someone else said. "I thought we were on consonants today."

"The library's open at ten." The man behind the woman stood. He pulled her up by her shoulder. "But I can tolerate the wait. Come on, we'll hang on the street."

Amber got between him and the door.

"Don't fuck with me," he said.

"Just sit down," she said. "I'll go back up to the front if you just sit down."

"You got that right," he said. "But we're still going." He pulled the woman along with him.

Amber reached for his arm. "Look—"

He wheeled back and punched her in the stomach. His fist seemed to break a wall in her skin. She hit the floor and sat there, coughing, her feet splayed out in front of her as if they belonged to someone else. She gasped, trying to catch her breath.

"Later," he said.

She could not look up. She saw and then sensed them moving around her, beyond her to the outer room. She collected herself and stood. Her diaphragm felt all punched in. Some of the learners were half rising in their chairs. She waved them off.

"It's all right," she said. "It was my fault."

In the front row a woman with a pale forehead and a runny nose, a woman she recognized instantly as a class regular, turned and nodded in assent. Amber knew she should not have touched him. She should not have interfered. Her second week of classes and already this. She sucked in her breath, a sharp pain. She made her way to the front of the class. On the stairs above the partitions Sister Frances appeared, a learner in tow.

"You okay, dear? Did you hurt yourself."

"No, I'm fine." Amber shook her head. She squinted to see if she could recognize the learner, an older woman, missing teeth, with patchy brown skin. "Marie. If you can come on back, we'll start again."

Marie descended the stairs past Sister Frances, disappeared for a moment among the partitions, and came back out in the classroom. Sister Frances waited on the stairway.

Amber stood facing the learners, catching her breath. A tang of bile sat in her throat. She swallowed it down. The taste remained, inert, insoluble. She wished she had a hot coffee. She wished she had a real job. She wished she had a future. She'd been educated. What the hell had happened?

"Page thirty-six," she said.

No one moved. They had arrived at the page ahead of her and were waiting for her to catch up. From the stairway Sister Frances folded her arms across her chest and watched. Quickly, Amber counted the students left. Fifteen. She retreated to the blackboard and wrote "S-h" and "T-h" on the slate. "You remember the difference?" she said.

"Show," a woman in the front row said.

"Thaw," a man called from the third row.

"Exactly," Amber said. She wrote the two words on the blackboard. Shit, she thought. This. This is shit.

the tenderloin

the tenderloin

The Golden Gate Residence was an eight-story ivory-colored building, about ten windows wide, SINCE 1912 written in brown paint under its large empty store-front windows. Across the street were a Popeye's Chicken, a Church of Scientology Reading Room, and a twenty-four-hour adult film and bookstore. The air tasted sugared and leaden. Benjamin West rang the buzzer at the glass double doors. For a moment, nothing happened, and he put his face to the door. He could see a wide blurry lobby, at the end of which, tucked under a staircase, was a receptionist's desk with iron grillwork rising around it. He'd have to work in a cage. The door buzzed back and he opened it and let himself in.

He headed straight for the cage, past two tall columns, under a high ceiling and broad walls of heavy white wainscoting and moldings. The front desk was a frontier-style teller's window, with a burnished wood counter and thick iron bars.

He smiled at the small Latino woman behind it.

"I'm Benjamin West. I'm looking for Bob Fields."

She nodded noncommittally and picked up a phone. "Bob," she said. "There's a Benjamin West here to see you." She pursed her lips. "All right." She hung up. "Just a minute," she told West. She hooked a faded sign to the bars that said BACK IN FIVE and let herself out from the cage through a door to the side. She touched West's arm. "Follow me."

Together they walked past the desk and began to ascend a wide marble staircase with a wrought-iron railing.

"So you're going to be working here," she said as they climbed the steps. "I hope you'll like it. This is the mezzanine."

They had reached a wide step on the staircase, with a knee-high door off to the left. West stared at the door.

"It's a joke," the woman said. "But we do call it the mezzanine."

They continued up the stairs. At the second floor she pointed to an apartment that took up the entire street frontage. "That's the Homeless Vietnam Veterans' office. They have a lounge, a couple of program people. You probably won't have much to do with the staff, seeing how you work nights." She guided West along by the elbow. "Down here is Bob's office."

They passed through an antechamber with an unmanned desk and framed advertisements for various operas covering the walls.

"He's a big opera fan," the woman said. "He knows Beverly Sills and Domingo."

Out the other end of the antechamber was a slightly dimmer office shaded by a curtained-off window and papered from floor to ceiling with opera memorabilia. Sheet music stood in piles on a filing cabinet. A bald man with earring studs in both ears and a cigarette between his fingers rose from behind a cluttered desk.

"Benjamin West?" he said. "Delighted to meet you. I'm Bob Fields."

The hand, extended, quivered almost imperceptibly. They shook hands. The room was outfitted with a walker, two canes, and a tank of oxygen. Fields looked to be in his late fifties or early sixties.

"Nice to meet you," West said.

"Thank you, Cecilia," Bob said.

She tapped West's wrist. "I'll see you."

West sat and leaned forward on the chair, waiting.

"Cigarette?" Fields offered a pack. They were menthol lights.

"No, thanks." West took out his own pack. He was not much of a smoker but he always carried a pack. Benson & Hedges Ultra Lights Deluxe, his ex-girl friend's brand. He was moderately embarrassed by them. Fields stared at him from behind delicate horn-rimmed glasses, his thin shoulders slumped in a white linen sport coat, light green button-down shirt. His curled heavily-ringed fingers. All the opera souvenirs. The guy had money.

"How was your trip?"

"Fine." West reached over to tap the ash off his cigarette, but there was no ash yet.

"I'm from back east." Fields inhaled off his cigarette. "New York. Then I was in the service. Did some odd jobs in Chicago. Became an alcoholic. Spent time," he raised his eyebrows, "in prison. Then moved out here and reformed myself."

"You knew?" West said.

"Your credentials were just too impressive for this kind of

work." He coughed something from his throat and spat it into a handkerchief tugged from his breast pocket. "Excuse me." He took a drink of water from a glass on his desk. "There are some papers for you to sign. Then we'll spend a couple of minutes being frank with each other, what I need from you, what you need from me, what the building needs from both of us. After that I'll have Cecilia take you around. Any questions so far?"

"My car's illegally parked outside. Should I move it?"

"Benjamin." Fields laughed and shook his head. "We both know your driving days are over. A few tickets before you sell the thing won't hurt." He leafed through the papers on his desk and produced a set of stapled pages. "Here's your contract. Read it, sign it, then we can get started." He maneuvered the cigarette to the corner of his mouth and clamped down on it. He picked up the phone and looked at West. "If you want to start tonight you've got to let me know now, so I can cancel security."

West glanced quickly at the contract. Turn on and off lights. Keep the cafeteria locked. Monitor the front door. Man the phone. Screen all visitors. He looked up at Fields, who was smiling benignly at him. It might be depressing, but at least it wasn't going to be difficult. "Sure," he said. "I can start tonight."

West was not allowed to strike a tenant, not even in self-defense. He was not allowed to carry a weapon, drink on the job, have controlled substances on his person or in his room, make long-distance phone calls without paying for them. There were significant amounts of lead in the water and in the paint at the Golden Gate, but exposure to it wasn't going to kill him. His status was probationary for three months. His first paycheck would arrive in eight days, after which he would be paid every second Friday. No overtime without prior approval of his supervisor. No health benefits for the first month of employment. When West explained to Fields that he had only thirteen dollars left, Fields reached into his pocket and offered him a twenty. "That should last until you sell the car," he said. "You'll probably want to do that tomorrow."

West thanked him, shook hands again, and quit the hospital odor of the manager's office. On the staircase he stopped. There were now people in the lobby, mostly elderly, occupying the faded sofas and chairs. They would long be in bed by the time eleven o'clock and the start of his shift rolled around. "The younger tenants will concern you most," Fields had said. "If it gets confrontational, just stay in the cage and call the cops. But your job is to defuse any situation, not to ignite it."

"I'm the only employee who lives on-site?"

"I'll give you my home number. And, Benjamin," Fields shook his finger at him, "try not to get involved with any of the tenants. That's always where we get into trouble with our desk clerks."

A slow line was forming down past the reception desk into what had to be the cafeteria, hairless men in suspenders and baggy-assed trousers; wigged women in frocks and elasticized stockings, cheap perfume and denture rinse and alcohol-swabbed ears. Fields had said some of them had been living in the residence for thirty or forty years. West still liked the frontier feel of the cage. He wondered where exactly his room was. Fields had said that Cecilia would take him to it—like the butler in a horror movie.

"Excuse me." Someone pushed at his shoulder. "You're blocking the stairway."

He stepped aside and turned at the same time, almost tripping himself. A woman shouldered past, laughing quietly but distinctly at him.

"Don't hurt yourself," she said.

He caught the railing and watched her cross the lobby. She wore tight jeans and a T-shirt that said, THE FAMILY TREE STOPS HERE. When she reached back to flip her hair away from the neck, her shoulders under the shirt seemed fragile, her elbows narrow, almost pointed, and she walked with a gentle sway that if he looked long and close enough he could follow. She got in the line into the cafeteria and turned his way, glared at him and looked away. Her face was white, untanned, her hair parted in the middle, her breasts through the T-shirt round and pronounced.

He approached the desk and told Cecilia, in a too-loud voice, that he was ready to be shown around. She posted the BACK IN FIVE sign, and came out from the cage. She pointed past the line into the cafeteria. "That's the cafeteria," she said. "You can see it on your own. The food is okay."

They cut through the line to the elevator.

"If you're ever in a hurry, don't take the elevator." Cecilia pressed the button a few times. "As it happens, we're not in a hurry."

The line behind them disappeared into a long yellow room with a salty, milky smell like overcooked beef in a thickened stew. He tried to catch a glimpse of the woman in the T-shirt, but she was far down the line. They waited for the elevator.

"So what do you think?" Cecilia said.

"It seems like a nice place."

She guffawed and clapped him on the back. "Sure. If you don't mind the needles in the shower stalls and the occasional suicide. Bob is a nice guy, too nice. But, Benjamin," she squeezed his elbow familiarly, "we're dealing with some real assholes here. You watch yourself, okay? You'll go weeks at a time when nothing will happen, and then, bam. Suddenly you got a mouthful of blood and it's you they're firing."

West rubbed the back of his head. "Is that what happened to the last desk clerk?"

"That asshole? He wouldn't take a punch if his life depended on it."

The elevator came and they got on. Cecilia squinted as the door shut, the carpeting soggy and the color of dirt, and the walls bare and scarred as if layers of paint and papering had been ripped from them. The ceiling had loose white panels under a single tube of fluorescent lighting.

"Some people need to be toilet-trained all over again," she said. "At least you've got your own bathroom."

They rode for a moment in silence, West still thinking of the woman in the T-shirt, he could not help it. "There are two kinds of men in this world," the judge who sentenced him said, even though the girl in question had been seventeen and had testified on his behalf. "I don't have to tell you which kind you are."

"What's on your mind?" Cecilia said suspiciously.

"Nothing." The elevator clanked upward; they had not even reached the third floor. The smell of the carpet hit him again and he breathed through his mouth. "How long you been working here?"

"Three years. I live in one of the other buildings."

"Other buildings?" West said.

"Yeah, I live in one of the nicer ones." She looked at West and shook her head. "Bob neglected to tell you that we all work for a management company, didn't he? It doesn't make any difference.

The bottom is the bottom, no matter how big whatever it is that's above it. We're the bottom. How many other people you know are still making six an hour in the nineties?"

The elevator stopped and the doors opened onto the eighth floor.

"Showing around somebody new always gets to me." Cecilia stepped out into the corridor. "I should just shut up."

He followed her up a narrow staircase to a fire door and she pulled it open and they climbed through onto the roof.

"I always bring new hires up here," she said over the wind.

Across the parapet, he could see the fog coming off the hills down into the valley of the city, stacks of apartment and office buildings, their windows like peepholes through the dusk, blocks of tin-roofed warehouses and single-story homes. All around him were air and light, a thin, almost negligible pollution. He felt he could breathe.

"The water heater's up here, if you're curious." She looked a last time, not bothering to point it out. "It's a maintenance problem anyway. Come on, I'll show you where you're living."

Down the flights of stairs, they passed discarded sandwiches, half-eaten and laid out open-faced as if for birds to eat. Over a waist-high wall was an interior air shaft. He peered over cautiously.

"That's not where they jump," Cecilia said. "They like to hit the street."

On the third-floor landing she opened the door by the elevator, and they stepped into a hallway that ended abruptly at a locked door. Inside were two rooms, beige carpeting, white walls, a built-in kitchen of a stovetop and sink. A narrow wooden bed frame topped by a lumpy, stained mattress, a wood-colored plastic card table, two folding chairs, an old black phone that had no mechanism for dialing. He opened a cupboard and found a set of plastic plates and cups, and a small metal kettle.

"It's not bad," he said.

"It's not good," Cecilia admitted. "But you could fit a sofa and a television in here no problem. You have any money saved?"

"I've got an old car to sell."

"Is it smog-checked?"

West shrugged; he had no idea what she was talking about.

"Then good luck selling it."

He went into a small booth with a toilet crammed in next to a shower stall and sink. At the drain in the shower lay a belly-up skeleton of a cockroach the color of rust.

"Pretty disgusting," Cecilia said. She bent, picked it up for him, and deposited it in a miniature plastic trash bucket.

He tested the single-bulb overhead lights. They made the walls look yellow and the brown furniture green. At least it was hard to see if the carpet was clean or not.

Cecilia patted her curly black hair and smiled at him. "You ready to see the basement?"

"All right," he said. He'd stick it out for a few months, and then he'd quit. What he would do for money he had no idea, but he had no doubt that this was not it.

In the basement Cecilia showed him various rooms that were to be locked and unlocked at certain times, and the vending machine area which he was to patrol twice a night. "Sometimes people get fucked up, they don't have any money, they're hungry. That's when they break the machines. Don't let them, if you can help it. But like I said, don't get yourself hurt trying to save a couple of candy bars."

Here were exposed overhead wiring, noosed light bulbs, a dank laundry room, pathways that disappeared around sharp corners. He'd make it a point not to check on the basement much.

"You've seen enough?" Cecilia said.

West nodded.

She checked her watch. "You relieve me in about four hours. I guess I'll show you how to work the desk then." She started toward the stairs, then stopped and turned. "Don't get too depressed about this, Benjamin. It's not worth it. And it's not as hard as it looks. I used to work nights." She flashed a grin. "Until I got promoted."

He waited until he was sure he would not catch up with her. Then he ascended the stairs to the lobby. Cecilia was already in the cage, busy with the phone. He hurried out to the street, where his car sat flashing its lights as if complaining at his absence. A ticket flapped on the windshield. He read it, then reinserted it under the wiper. From the trunk he dragged out the metal box that held his clothes. He bent there, balancing the weight of the box on the car. It was not quite dark, the sun still hinting from a blind corner of the city.

He rang the bell and Cecilia buzzed him in. He carried the trunk in front of him, then hoisted it to one shoulder as he pressed the elevator button, Cecilia's eyes on him. Some elderly people departing the cafeteria stopped to stare at him. The elevator came and he got on and turned around, looked straight at Cecilia as the doors were shutting. She had an expression on her face that was so empathic he could hardly bear it. "The new night desk clerk," he heard her tell one of the tenants, and she shook her head and made a clicking sound with her tongue.

Amber came up the short flight of stairs onto the roof and saw him leaning into the chest-high retaining wall, staring out like a dog over a high fence.

She glanced up the hill toward where the ocean was supposed to be, and dug her hands into the front pocket of her sweatshirt. He was not much older than she, if at all. Benjamin West. From the east. The moon sat in the purple hills, partially shrouded in fog. Lights came on. The air fell degrees in seconds. She hugged herself. Cecilia had brought her up here a few days ago, and now she had a routine, same time, a certain spot. Watching the bleeding of sunset into evening, the sidewalks running with over-dressed civil servants from ornate buildings, in search of buses, cabs, parking garages.

She turned and looked back at his narrow shoulders, the collar of his jean jacket pulled up against the cold. He wore gym shorts, and it made her want to laugh at him and hold him at the same time.

"Hey," she called to him. He looked over, startled, embarrassed, slightly territorial. "You have a car?"

He touched his hand to his shorts pocket, said something. His voice didn't carry. Cecilia had told her that he'd had his eye on her, but now he was shy.

"I'm Amber," she said, walking toward him. "You're Benjamin West. I'm a VISTA worker. I live here. It's kind of part of my job."

"Oh," he managed.

"So, I heard you have a car. Do you want to go for a drive? I wouldn't mind getting out of the neighborhood for a little while."

He ran his fingers through his hair, looked down at Market Street. She looked with him, tried to see it through his eyes, a veil of gradual darkness layering itself over departures and emptiness.

"I'd like that," he said.

She pointed at his shorts. "Did you want to change?"

"It's all right."

She led him back down the partial flight of stairs to the elevator. She hit the button and they waited.

"Which floor do you live on?" he asked.

"Second. They give you a nice place?"

"No."

The elevator came, and they got on. She wanted to urge him to change into pants, but she understood what he was going through. It was California. You ought to be able to wear shorts.

Outside, West said, "Where do you want to go?" He held the door of a brown and black car open for her.

"The beach."

He smiled a shy smile. "You want anything?"

Several parking tickets flapped on the windshield. He meant alcohol, maybe some pot, a suggestion to dissolve inhibition.

"It's probably not a good idea," she said. "But I wouldn't mind if you wouldn't."

They drove past the library, toward the various government buildings. In a broad expanse of concrete walkways and potted trees, flocks of tourists perched on benches and gathered around a dry fountain, their long silver buses leaning top-heavy at a shallow curbside. The dome of city hall kaleidoscopically caught the dusk. West pulled over at a deli.

"I'll get us some beer," he said.

In his gym shorts and jean jacket, he hurried around the front of the car and into the store. She was wearing a baggy gray sweatshirt and white leg warmers and black leggings, the cotton blend sealing her calves as if her body were unexplored territory. She touched her smoothed knee. She wasn't quite thirty, living in San Francisco, working a comparatively meaningful job. There was something to say in favor of all of that.

West came back out with a six-pack under his arm. Fields had most likely slipped him a twenty and now he was spending it on her. Fields was always slipping everybody a twenty. He'd inherited two million dollars from a woman in Brooklyn whose groceries he used to carry, and now he lived in a large house in Pacific Heights with a manservant and a phalanx of medical equipment. People in the cafeteria said it was like going to Disneyland.

"You said the beach," West said.

"I'm not even sure which direction it is," Amber admitted.

He pulled away from the curb, and at the light took a left. She opened him a beer, then one for herself.

"This feels right," he said.

They followed Turk. On Van Ness were movie theaters, restaurants, a bookstore, tennis courts in a diagonal valley and beyond that flatlands gleaming with streetlights and the lit windows of houses. Then came rows of identical slapped-together apartment blocks, with raddled roofs, beige siding, chain link fences, graffittied sidewalks. Past a windowless police station painted metallic blue, they ascended a hill. She looked back at a patchwork of public housing, a thin line of commerce, and the mud-colored Tenderloin. The sun still hadn't set and she had half-finished her beer. West's was already empty. She opened another bottle and exchanged it for the empty one. Their hands touched briefly in the transaction.

"You don't go out much?" he said. She shook her head. "What's a VISTA worker do anyway?"

"It's hard to explain," she said. "A lot of things."

She sipped her beer and looked out at blank homes and apartments, tile roofs, tar roofs, cars parked on the meterless street, a small university that seemed more like a high school but a sign said UNIVERSITY and she was not going to argue with it, then a line of grocery stores, laundries, Chinese and Korean restaurants, then more houses and apartments.

"It's nice to be out of the neighborhood and in a car." She smiled at him. "Not that I'm using you or anything."

He laughed. "I have to sell the car tomorrow."

"Tomorrow?"

"I can't afford it."

At the end was the ocean, speckled with dusk. She pushed her door open against a wind, and got out, the air furiously cold. The sun still hadn't fully set. On the gray and purple beach a man tossed a Frisbee up thirty, forty feet in the air, pirouetted, pranced, and then pirouetted again just as he caught it. He wore nothing but a bikini swimsuit.

Amber descended a short flight of stairs to the beach, bent down, and felt the sand with her hand, cold and granular. She glanced up at West, standing a few feet away, torn between watching the guy with the Frisbee and watching her. She felt childlike looking up at his face. She stood.

"Is it what you expected?" she said.

He shivered and bit his lip. "I try not to have any expectations. But, yeah, I like it."

"You're cold," she said. She pulled him to her just as he made a reach for her. She could feel a narrow roll of flesh above his waist. They walked along the beach, holding each other, the last frayed edges of sun lighting the tips of clouds. The wind tried to cut between them, and he held her tightly around the waist. She let her hand slip to the outside of his bare leg, his skin colder than her hand. He drank at his beer.

"Are we going to walk far," he said.

"I don't know." She rubbed his outer thigh, tried to warm a patch of skin shot through with a thin thrush of hair. They followed the water south against a wind that came from all sides. Around an illegal fire a circle of teenagers screamed and laughed at each other. One of them pointed at her and waved her in with a hand. She pulled West that way.

"I don't think so," he said, steering her against the water.

"It might be fun," she said.

"No."

Far out at sea, the sun dropped below the waterline, the sky streaking with purples and oranges. She swallowed the last of her beer. It was hard to keep track of time or distance, too loud and cold to talk. The beach seemed lusher, warmer, as it grew dark. He was fighting to keep his teeth from chattering.

"We can go back," she said.

"I don't mind."

They turned and started north. Around the fire the teen-agers were breaking bottles. She hadn't thought they were all boys, but they were. They rose and staggered in her general direction, their heads lunging like spikes. She pushed herself into West.

"It's all right," he said into her ear.

The outline of a large restaurant on a hill lay far in front of them, its windows lit. Beyond it were the dark shoulders of mountains. The teenagers ran flailing and shrieking into the water.

The man with the Frisbee stood on the seawall, toweling himself. He nodded at the bobbing heads in the ocean. "Pack of animals."

"They're not that bad," Amber said.

"I come out here every nice day." The man sniffed as he picked sand from between his toes. "I've had to use Mace about five times."

"Maybe if you weren't such an exhibitionist," Amber said.

He pointed something that looked like a cigarette lighter. "Do I have to?"

"Hey," West said. "Just both of you give it a rest."

In the car she lit a cigarette, her hand shaking, opened the last beer, and gave it to him. He took a sip and handed it back. She drank slowly, the mouth of the bottle warm with his saliva and the beer cold.

"Thanks for taking me to the beach," she said.

"I wanted to see it, too."

Warm air from the heater was rushing at her legs. She moved across the broad seat closer to him. He swung his arm around her shoulder and drove one-handed. She felt the outline of his bare knee, ran her finger toward his thigh. His knee tensed and his leg opened for her. She rested her hand atop his thigh. A park followed them alongside the car. She pulled the ashtray from under the radio, and tapped off her cigarette.

"Didn't you think that guy was an asshole?" she said, her hand on his knee.

"Everyone's an asshole," West said. "I'm an asshole."

She fought a compulsion to tell him something personal about herself. "No," she said. She wanted to give him the beer to finish, but he didn't have a free hand. She held the bottle to his lips, tilted, and he swallowed.

"You drink a lot," she said. "I don't mind. You probably didn't get that much to drink in prison."

He choked on the beer, and it ran out his nose onto the bottle. She took the beer back and leaned herself against him.

"I didn't think it was such a big deal," she said. "It's not like you hurt anybody." There was a disagreeable silence. "It was pot, wasn't it?"

"Yeah."

"Anything else?"

"No."

She held the beer back up to him, and helped him finish it.

"Does everybody know?" he said.

She shrugged. "Probably."

"I guess it doesn't matter."

"Where we live," she said, "it shouldn't."

Cecilia laughed a little too heartily as she buzzed them in. They headed directly for the stairs. On the second floor West stopped. "I'll be down in a minute."

"Can't I see your room?" Amber said.

"Sure."

She followed him up to the third floor, through a door by the elevator, into a dark, tiny hallway. He let her in. It was not much, but still more than she had. He stood awkwardly by as she walked through the outer room into the half-room, a mattress covered with a yellow bottom sheet torn at one corner and an old gray army blanket. The radiator next to the bed had been left on. On the other side was an oversized wardrobe that filled the wall. She sat on the bed.

He came and reached over the bed to the wardrobe. Pairs of jeans and work pants hung folded on metal hangers, along with button-down cotton and flannel shirts. From a shelf above the hangers protruded three or four folded sweaters. He took down a dark blue sweater and a pair of jeans and held them in front of him over his shorts. She just sat on the bed looking at him, looking around the room, looking out into the other room.

"Maybe you want to go into the other room while I change," he said.

She touched the army blanket. "The bed's really the only piece of furniture."

He got out of his shorts, holding the new clothes over himself. He tried to step into the jeans.

"Hey," she said softly. She reached over and took away the sweater. He hadn't been wearing any underwear. She pulled him down to her as he tried to pull her up, and they fell, he on top of her, onto the bed. He kissed her, their mouths opening. Her leggings and underwear snagged against her leg warmers. He was naked from the waist down. She lifted her caught legs and he bent down and came up within the circle made by her legs, his face again touching hers. He was trying to get in and she was trying to help him. Then he was in and they were kissing and her hands were under his shirt and he was moving well and her feet were hooked around his back, around his jean jacket, with the collar still pulled up, even though they had been inside for a while.

Outside the air was icy and she stretched in it, trying to make herself feel clean. She got into his car and they drove out McAllister.

"What do you feel like?" West said.

"Food." Amber stayed to her side of the seat, looking through the window at the city. "Any kind." She took out a cigarette, lit it, inhaled once, and crushed it in the ashtray.

The floor of the diner they chose was black rubber with a million little nipples, the walls a gleaming white, the menu covers fluorescent orange. A hostess showed them to a booth near the kitchen, even though there were several better tables. West pinched at his lower lip and his eyes blinked rapidly. They squeezed into opposite sides of the booth. He smoothed his hair back with both hands and smiled at her. She smiled back and concentrated on the menu. From the kitchen came the clatter of slapped around dishes.

They both ordered the tuna melt; he grinned as if that meant something. She asked for a coffee. He ordered a beer, and shrugged apologetically. The drinks came quickly and he folded his arms on the table. She couldn't think of a thing to say. She gave him a smile and glanced at her coffee. It had a brown scalded look to it. She lifted the cup, knowing the coffee would burn her tongue and trying to position herself so that it wouldn't. Her life had boiled down to this, to trying to outsmart a cup of coffee. She took a loud, slow sip, sucking in air through her teeth.

"What's going on?" West said.

She shrugged. "I guess I don't feel like talking."

From the ceiling was strung a gigantic inflated cola bottle. The booths were done in blue vinyl, the tables an off white with tiny black specks. A solitary couple ate hamburgers by a large picture window while looking out on a row of parked cars. A streetcar passed and the nippled rubber floor rumbled beneath Amber's feet. At the front door, behind a plastic reception stand, the hostess applied bright red lipstick to her pale face.

The waitress brought out the tuna melts. A bed of French fries soaked up and added to their grease. West began to eat, a shred of fish sticking on the corner of his mouth. His beer was already finished. He looked down at his plate as he chewed, his shoulders big under the bulk of the jean jacket and sweater. It was a nice sweater, cabled. She liked his clothes. They were simple, work-manlike. He wore them well.

"How is it?" she said. She did not know why she suddenly did not like him.

He nodded, too polite to talk with his mouth full. She picked up a half sandwich and took a bite, chewed it with effort.

"Isn't it all right?" he said.

"It's fine." The tuna through the mayonnaise was brown. Me-thodically, she began to finish her sandwich. West ordered an-other beer before she could stop him.

When the waitress came to see if they wanted dessert, Amber brought out ten dollars as an answer. She read the waitress's watch as she made out the bill. Only eight-thirty. Her limbs ached, and she was sore. It had been a long time. Since Dean.

"Let me get this," West said.

She looked at him and was surprised to see he really wanted to.

"That's all right," she said.

He insisted on giving her change on the ten. "I had the beers," he explained. "You just had coffee."

"You're very fair," she said. She intended irony, but she hated going out with people who split the checks down the middle even though they didn't eat fifty-fifty. Dean had always done it when they were out with other couples, and on the walk home afterward he'd gloat about it.

Across the street from the diner was a large, brightly lit Chi-nese restaurant with a lot of people inside. She stopped on the sidewalk, staring at it. First dates were so much about chance, about where you ate and whether it was good and the atmosphere festive, about what movie you saw and how it left you. She could remember guys she thought she should have liked, but didn't, and guys she should have never liked, but did. It was like every-thing else. The way you could walk through a doorway and have the light and the air catch you in such a manner that you'd think about something or somebody that you hadn't thought about in years. The small, turning moments. His modesty as he took off his clothes. But would that last against the diner? She doubted it.

"Did you like it?" he said.

"Not really."

"No." As he drove, he looked intently through the windshield. "Neither did I."

At the Golden Gate he could not immediately find a parking space. The car idled outside the door.

"Should I just drop you off?"

She supposed she should offer to go with him. "That would be nice," she said. She leaned over and kissed him indifferently on the lips. "Thanks for everything." She opened the door and got out. "Good luck on your first night."

"I'm off at seven-thirty. Could I come up and see you then?"

She was beginning to pull away from the car so she could shut the door. "I don't think that's a good idea."

"What—"

She shut the door before he could say anything else. She crossed between two parked cars to the entrance and hit the buzzer, then stood there, hugging herself in her sweatshirt, breathing clouds of air against the door. Finally Cecilia rang her in. Not until she was pulling the door behind her did she see West had stayed, the car hovering, watching to make sure she made it safely.

He was in a dream—two women, yellow sheets, greenish rooms, a desertscape—when the pounding woke him. He'd left the lights on. There was no spyhole, and he blindly opened the door.

"What the fuck, Benjamin?" A short Latino woman pushed her way into the room. "This isn't such a hot start."

"Shit." He looked at himself, still in clothes and sneakers. At least he was dressed and ready to go.

"I tried calling you, man." Cecilia pointed at the black phone without the dial. "You wouldn't answer. First night, you're out getting your dick wet. Unbelievable."

"Is it your business?" He held up his hand and started from the room. "Lock the door, would you?"

"It's automatic." She was at his heels.

"Are you always this obnoxious?"

She patted him on the back while he headed for the stairs. "Only with people I like."

His mouth was dry and he had a hangover behind his eyes rising to his forehead. Son of a bitch.

At the darkened lobby she let him in behind the lighted reception counter, the cage a smell of mold and paper, the back wall lined with an archaic rack of mail slots, the front grillwork interspersed by wide gaps between bars.

"If they start reaching in," Cecilia said. "Just keep backing away." She pointed to the phone. "And don't think about the switchboard for now. You don't need to let any calls through on your shift anyway, so don't try to figure it out. You wake one of the tenants in the middle of the night, you're stuck with him. That's your night, man. So forget about it. If they say it's an emergency, don't believe them. There's plenty of time in the morning for emergencies, and most of the people in here don't know anybody anyway."

She looked around quickly, while he tried to rouse himself.

"Anything else?" she said. "Oh, yeah. Don't forget to check the basement at least twice. If someone's shooting up or something, just write it in the log." She gestured at a black spiral notebook on a small desk under the stairs. "If anyone catches you sleeping on the job, you get two warnings. Then you're terminated. You don't have to sweep or anything. Housekeeping arrives at six. Don't let anybody in who isn't an employee or tenant. Of course," she winked at him, "anybody can go out. Questions?"

He shook his head. "How you getting home?"

She squeezed past him out of the cage and turned back to shut him in. "Hey, don't you worry about me. I'm from New York."

As he watched her through the bars, she crossed hurriedly to the door, opened it, then turned back. "You behave yourself," she said. "Your girl friend's kind of an insomniac, so you might be seeing her. No sex in the lobby, right?"

"Right," he said drily.

"Read the house rules. They're posted behind the counter." The door shut behind her. "Good luck," she shouted, muffled by the glass.

He stood drowsily at the counter. The desk under the stairs had a shaded lamp and a little wooden chair. On the reception counter was an old-fashioned oblong reading lamp, and a few feet above him was suspended a single one-hundred-watt light bulb. The bars in front of him were inch-thick rectangular poles with circular notches three inches from the top and three inches from the bottom; the base of the poles descended into a darkly stained wood frame. It was, indisputably, a kind of cell. He liked it.

He pocketed the key from the slot in the cage door and took a seat on an antiquated sofa in the middle of the dark lobby. The lighted reception area glowed cheerily. He felt himself dozing off. He got up and pushed himself over to a chair. Fragments of dust rose as he sat. He got up again. Beyond the front door, the sidewalk and road were empty and lacquered under the glow of a near streetlamp and a distant stoplight, the Popeye's dark behind caged windows. Through the cold door he could hear glass breaking somewhere out of sight, and a scream of tires or people.

He wondered when Amber would be coming down. The mail slots behind the reception desk were marked by room number only, and he could not find any directory near the phone. He did not want to call her, but he wouldn't mind knowing where she lived, what her last name was. Cecilia would know, but he could just imagine having to ask her. "She already trying to give you the slip?" she would laugh. "I'm sorry, I can't help you, man."

He rifled through the drawers under the reception counter and in the desk under the stairs. He sat in the wooden chair and pressed the heel of his hand over his hair. Her mouth had tasted of cigarettes. Bits of sand had clung to her knee, her inner thigh. They had fit well, and when he'd stopped he could feel her contracting and expanding around him, squeezing and releasing him. As she dressed, she kept looking at him, not with curiosity or anticipation, but with an analytic bluntness, and he had not been able to tell how he was being processed. But over dinner he'd sensed it clearly enough.

It was past midnight. As part of his duties, he was sure he was required to tour the floors like a night watchman. The second floor was a logical starting point. He hung the five-minute sign and released himself from the cage. His sneakers squeaked over the tile walkway that bordered the lobby carpeting. Fifteen steps up the flight of fake marble stairs he stopped. The reception counter jutted out from under the staircase, obscured by bars. He could see the phone, a couple of pens, a desk blotter calendar. It was odd that there was no tenant roll. Perhaps they were hiding it from him. Perhaps they didn't trust him. Behind his oxygen tank and his opera mementoes, Bob Fields probably was a control freak.

On the second floor were doors to Fields's and the Vietnam Veterans' offices, and a fire door off to the left. He opened the fire door, and stepped into a hallway of dirty pink carpeting and red and yellow floral wallpaper. He eased the door softly shut behind him and listened, a hum of cheap light bulbs and fluorescent tubes, the ticking of old wood floors. He walked the hall, numbered white doors along each wall. Halfway down the corridor was a rest room, with a four-button combination lock. He tried to hear if anyone was inside. Only the faintest drip of water. By the time he reached the end of the hallway he had counted twenty-four doors. Twenty-four women lived on the corridor. She was one of them.

As he made his way back out the hall he heard laughter, gentle at first, but as he stopped and listened from the safety of the foyer, it rose to something raucous, as if the woman were goading him. He let the fire door shut, the sound fading behind it.

Back in the cage he found his job description in his own mail slot. Nowhere did it say that he was to patrol the residential floors. The basement, the lobby, the front door, the door to the cafeteria—these were his areas of responsibility. He was a desk clerk. He was to remain, as much as possible, at the desk.

Around one he considered calling his sister in Michigan. By the time the bill arrived, he'd have the money to pay it, and despite the hour, she would enjoy hearing from him. Before he had been sentenced to prison, he had called her late one night. He had been staying with his mother, and he was trying to prepare himself for his punishment with a sense of optimism, or at least fatalism. "Are you all right?" she had said, her voice husky with sleep. "Have you begun cognitive dissonating yet?" He had nodded into the phone as an answer. "I'll send you something when you're inside," she said. And she had—a tin of chocolate chip cookies and a book called *Adaptation to Life*. A later letter urged him to go on to graduate school in a practical field, and suggested that, as an ex-con, he had a better chance of gaining admission to a good university, due to the nature of what she called his "demographics."

For his first trip to the basement, he took down the flashlight from the shelf under the mail slots, and looked around for a suitable weapon. Wedged between the desk and the wall was an old tire iron, no doubt the instrument of choice. He stood at the elevator, the button pressed, waiting for it to arrive from the sixth floor. To his left was the cafeteria, dark beyond the single window in the locked door. Behind him were the damp stairs. Still, the elevator hadn't come. The wall clock in the cage said it was only one-thirty. The red 6 over the elevator door stared back at him. He supposed this meant that he had to hike the six floors up to see what was the matter. Or he could take the stairs to the basement and pretend that he'd never noticed. When he swallowed, his throat cracked with dryness.

By the time he reached the second floor he was out of breath.

The lukewarm water from the fountain had an unpleasant medicinal taste. He drank heavily, then wet his fingers and patted his brow. He thought of how far he had come to be here. The distance stunned him. He had a sickening feeling that he would never make it back, that he'd never see his mother again. There was some relief in this thought, but there was also homesickness. Philadelphia. The room he had grown up in, the family pictures in the den. He did not have a picture of his father. In prison, in Pennsylvania, this had not bothered him. But free, in California, it appalled him.

Up the next flight of steps, narrow and gunmetal gray, he saw the door to his own little hallway. He could not quite believe that he was going to live behind that door. Had he really committed himself to this?

On the fourth-floor landing he realized that he'd neglected to post a sign on the reception cage. Already he was guilty of abandoning his post. The job was apparently more complicated than he'd been willing to admit. He laughed out loud, his voice startling him. A college degree and ten years of experience dealing with handicapped children, and suddenly he was ill-equipped to handle the demands of adult life at minimum wage. Perhaps prison had fucked him up more than he'd allowed himself to acknowledge. He did not want to acknowledge too much, because he did not want to become bitter. Bitterness he could not afford—it would make him wretched. The word tore at his stomach. Six months of his life and the right to drive a car—a kind of absolute freedom—had been taken from him, all for two ounces of marijuana and a night with a seventeen-year-old girl. In college he had known a rich classmate who'd been caught dealing a pound of coke, and all he had gotten was probation. At the Institute, a Ph.D. confessed to fondling a six-year-old boy with

Down's Syndrome, and he'd only been fired, with a discretion that allowed him immediately to secure another position in another state.

The particular shade of yellow paint on the walls of the fifth-floor landing reminded him of Lucky Andy's. Just twenty-four hours before had been Ana, Lovelock, the hotel room with the honeycomb of light. She had wanted him to stop. He ought to have just masturbated, but he'd never done it, unwilling to submit himself to an exercise in self-intimacy. No one had ever talked to him about it. He had never had the instinct. He supposed he was terribly repressed.

Before he attained the sixth floor, he heard it, a low conspicuous sneering laugh like a half cough. *Heh-heh.* He paused on the steps, and shifted his grip on the tire iron, keeping it to his side, but ready to swing. *Heh-heh.* He rose softly up the stairs. A man sat across the width of the elevator, meticulously smoking a cigarette between his index and middle fingers, his back bracing open the door, a sharp red-handled screwdriver in his other hand. He was dressed entirely in black, black leather jacket, black button-down shirt, black jeans, black leather boots with a silver buckle over each ankle, his legs casually crossed at the knee. He seemed incredibly thin, as if he'd wriggled his way through the ventilation system to get here, as if West could have lifted him up if he wanted, even though it was clear he was over six feet tall.

He looked up at West casually, West climbing the last bit of stairs, trying to keep the tire iron partially hidden. The man's eyebrows were white scars, as if they'd been burned off, and his hair close-cropped in an almost skinhead crew cut. His eyes glared behind thick wire-rimmed glasses. He had big girlish lips. He exhaled smoke in West's direction.

"What do *you* want?"

West stood a bit away, not wanting to tower over him as he lounged on the floor, not wanting to appear threatening.

"I'm just checking on the elevator."

"Nice tire iron." The man touched a long, thin finger to one ear, pressed its lobe, made a glassy stud sparkle.

"You mind getting out of the doorway so that the elevator can run?" West let the tire iron hang from his side loosely, as if it were something he carried all the time just for company.

"Heh-heh." The guy brought his knees up and pushed himself up off the ground. He looked off from his browless eyes over West's head toward the stairs. "It's all yours." He brushed past West carrying both the screwdriver and the cigarette. The elevator door shut and began its descent amidst clanking and grinding. The guy was already halfway down the first flight of stairs.

"Where you going?" West said.

"The kitchen." He was now at midpoint, turning into the short flight of stairs that connected to the fifth floor.

"You live here?" West began following him down. From above, his hair seemed as sharp as needles.

"You think I'd be hanging out in this dump if I didn't."

West tried to keep up without seeming to hurry. "Then you ought to know not to be smoking in the stairs or the hallways."

"Heh-heh." He was taking the stairs down two at a time, using his long legs. A cloud of smoke trailed him. "You trying to follow me?" he called back. "Isn't that harassment?" He let loose a laugh loud enough, West thought, to wake the residents on the fourth floor as he passed through.

"I'm just going back to the desk," West said. He peered down the stairwell and saw through the smoke the black leather jacket

flapping around a bannister. "Would you mind putting that cigarette out?"

"You mind? You mind?" The voice, deep, disembodied,
mocked back, followed by the laugh, originating in the diaphragm like a stage voice. West saw the jacket, the prickly head,
then looked again, and there was nothing. He paused, for an
instant, checking for a sound. Nothing. He sprang over the last
stairs to the third floor. His floor. He crouched, listening. The
elevator clanked past, on its way to the lobby. The door to his
hallway shuddered.

"Hey!" West called out. "Hey, if you're in my hallway, you
mind coming out." He stopped himself, the phrase grating on
him. The asshole. He approached the door. It was still, now. The
son of a bitch was behind the door. West caught the handle,
turned, and yanked the door back as he sidestepped, flattening
himself against a wall.

The hallway was empty. The door to his apartment, at the end
of it, was ajar. He led with the tire iron, poking the door fully
open. It rattled against the inside of his apartment. The light was
on, and he could see almost the entire living room, the built-in
kitchen. He felt along the wall with the tire iron, and stepped
into the apartment. The bedroom behind the open doorway was
dark, and he could not see fully into it. The door to the bathroom, to the left of the bedroom, was shut. He stood in the
middle of the living room, the tire iron raised.

"So you're not a tenant," he told the rooms. "Big deal. Come
on out, and I'll let you back on the street. You know they're not
paying me enough to get involved in something like this."

From the bedroom he swore he heard a choked guffaw. One of
his father's secretaries had been murdered by a boyfriend repeat-

edly stabbing her with a Phillips head. You could hurt someone with a screwdriver.

"I'm not coming in there," he said. "I'm not that stupid." From the bedroom came another garbled laugh and the sound of a match being struck. He glanced behind him at the black phone. It needed him down at the reception desk to make it work. He moved a little closer to the bedroom. He couldn't smell the match. He crept to the wall by the side of the bedroom doorway and turned silently toward the dark opening and breathed in without sound.

The bathroom door tore open behind him and before he could turn, or as he was turning, or thinking of turning, the veneer-coated thick plywood cracked against his ear and crushed into his forehead and jaw. He fell to his knees, tried to right himself, the tire iron pinning his hand to the floor, his head smacking wetly against the wall. Air rushed into his one good ear, and in the other was a high-pitched scream that came from an opening of pain.

She stayed in her room all morning, skipping breakfast, skipping a shower, avoiding Benjamin. Her hands were shaking as she zipped the knapsack shut. Through the thin walls Mildred had kept her up most of the night with bursts of laughter; she was like a broken alarm clock that you had to hit every thirty minutes until you gave up and just lay awake waiting for the next interruption. She had had about three hours of sleep. Now it was eight-fifteen. He ought to be in bed by now.

At the landing she decided on the elevator, for the shortest route through the lobby to the street. She pressed the call button once, twice, three times. A headache glazed the top of her head. Finally she heard the rumble and clank and buzzing sound like an electric razor running in the shaft, and the elevator door opened.

"Hey," Benjamin West said, his eyes hooded under a dark baseball cap. "How you doing."

"All right." She got on and turned her back slightly to him, as she pressed the button for the lobby floor. "I thought you'd be asleep."

He shook his head. "I've got stuff to do. Sell the car. Maybe buy a little refrigerator."

"Sounds exciting." They began a painfully slow descent to the lobby. "What's with the baseball cap?"

He lifted his brim for an instant and showed her a swelling veined and purple like a plum. "I bumped my head in the shower." He pulled the cap down again.

"Oh." She hoped that no one would be in the lobby, but Fields would notice them getting off the elevator together first thing in the morning. He liked to watch everybody's day start and wish all the tenants good morning.

West was tapping her knapsack. "You always take this much to work?"

"Day trip." The elevator door opened and Fields was staring at her, grinning his sickly but unbearably pleasant grin. Everybody loved Fields. "Nice to see you," she said loudly to West. Then she bolted.

On the sidewalk the sun was out. She reached into a compartment of the knapsack for a pair of sunglasses. Pigeons darted from under cars and atop fences, waddled on the sidewalk in germy packs. Already men shrouded by upturned collars and low-riding caps were walking the street, exchanging prolonged cupped handshakes. Within her sunglasses she moved as if under water, passing through the meanness. Girls loomed on the corners, dark and green like trees. She smiled at them, nodded, and they smiled and nodded back. When she turned down Ellis, the sun lost her. She remembered how tired she was. Her shoulders ached. She was still sore. The abstinence had been over twelve weeks, the longest since high school. She was not sure she'd missed it. Cold shade filled her side of the street. She hadn't done anything about organizing the community yet, and Sister Frances would be on her about it, in that gentle way of hers that was not gentle. She held her breath walking by the literacy center, as if passing a cemetery. At the corner she found a pay phone and called. She didn't have to talk to anybody but Rose. Her first sick day in two weeks, working on six dollars an hour. Who could blame her? They would call in Sister Helen to take her classes. No one would suffer. And it was Friday. Suddenly she had a three-day weekend. She crossed to the sun-lit side of the street and headed downtown.

On Powell a cable car creaked past, already stuffed with tourists, the street lined with greasy-windowed stores and fast-food restaurants. Every ten feet someone asked her for change. This wasn't the Tenderloin. She could ignore them without having to notice them. A rumpled man sold watches from a blue blanket. A rambling old hotel sat crated behind scaffolding. To her right was Macy's, and, farther down, Neiman Marcus. The benches in Union Square were populated by young men in oversized football jackets, and gangs of Australian tourists sharing morning beers, their accents twanging.

Farther downtown she passed a window display of an electric train set carrying heaps of gold and diamond Swiss watches through an alpine landscape. Little Hummel figurines appeared to yodel at one another across expanses of lace-capped green velvet hills made rugged by electric waterfalls and jagged quartz ravines. In another window of the same store live kittens played with wax apples and oranges on a low table setting of Italian pottery bowls and Japanese china. Waterford crystal wineglasses dangled upside down from the ceiling. Across the street were a furrier, an Italian shoe store, and the HongKong Shanghai Bank. She had yet to see anything she could afford.

She walked the shortest way to North Beach, and entered a restaurant of tall sliding windows and checked tablecloths; in the anteroom was a wooden bar with overhead racks holding glistening bottles of liquor. Beneath the bottles, two women, in long shorts and button-down short-sleeved shirts, sat shoulder to shoulder on high stools, their elbows planted on the counter, as if they were sharing a milkshake. There was no one at the tables. Amber took a seat at the bar, keeping a few empty stools between herself and the women, and removed her sunglasses and knapsack. The women were younger, perhaps in their early twenties, and they sat silently, one examining the bar in a quiet, thoughtful way, the other, the one closer to Amber, smoking a cigarette and sipping diligently at a drink with a lime in it.

A bald man in a black vest and bow tie came cheerfully out from the kitchen and gave Amber a bar menu. She chose a turkey sandwich with fries, and a Bloody Mary. It came in a tall frosted glass with a celery stalk and a straw that still had the top of its wrapper. She swirled the drink, then took the straw out and laid it on the counter. The pepper, tomato juice, vodka, and Tabasco vaguely resembled a meal. She cancelled her sandwich and fries.

She turned on her stool and looked out at the street. A moustached waiter was hosing off part of the sidewalk, his hair slick with brilliantine and morning sweat. Water sprayed against the window, leaving pearly flecks. Wet steam rose from the pavement. It wasn't yet ten.

The woman two stools over felt Amber looking at her, and raised her fresh glass. Amber nodded with the Bloody Mary.

"Hey," the woman said. "You're not from around here, are you?"

"Not really." Amber paused, and gulped at her drink. "I just moved here two weeks ago."

"Lucky you. My sister and I," the woman nodded next to her, the face of the sister now appearing over her shoulder as if the two women were conjoined, "are making a trip across the country to see relatives, and this is easily the nicest place I've seen."

Amber drained the rest of the Bloody Mary and looked at the two-headed sister. "It *is* nice, isn't it? Where you from?" She gestured to the bartender for another drink.

"The Midwest," the near sister said. She pushed a pack of Marlboro Lights Amber's way. "You want one?"

"I have my own." Amber reached down toward the floor for her knapsack. Her head reeled with a lightness and she felt herself falling. She caught hold of the opposite stool, found the Camel Lights, and brought herself back up to the bar. The woman's sister hid her mouth with a hand; she was laughing.

"Don't mind her," the woman said, offering Amber a light. "She's mildly retarded. She's got no subtlety, but she's nice enough."

"I wish you wouldn't say it that way," the sister said. She got off her stool and came around and offered her hand to Amber. "I'm sorry I laughed at you. I'm Ana."

"Ana." Amber's hands were full with her drink and the cigarette. The sister's face held microscopic freckles and bangs with an incidental part in the middle. On one wrist she wore a narrow white sweatband. Her long shorts were yellow and the blouse was white with blue and yellow birds. Amber set down her cigarette and shook her hand. "I'm Amber."

"Can I buy you a drink?" Ana said.

"Maybe later." Amber felt the back of her neck, damp with sweat. The weather seemed too hot for such a substantial drink. She inhaled on her cigarette, and it loosened the heat inside her. Ana returned to her stool. Her sister was occupying herself with putting the cigarettes and lighter back in their various positions in her purse. She sipped at her drink and looked critically at Amber.

"We were thinking of going to a beach today," she said. "You want to come?"

"I think I'd rather just sit here."

"It's not like you'd be a third wheel, or anything. Some days," the sister nodded back at Ana, "I feel like I'm the only wheel." She took out another cigarette and lit it. It was the wrong end, and the bar filled with a burning charcoal smell. She laughed bitterly. "I guess it's like tennis," she said. "You get as good or as bad as who you play with."

"I didn't know we were going to the beach," Ana said. She held a fruit-colored drink in a curvy glass to her forehead, and let it cool her. She smiled at Amber.

"It's a nice day for the beach," Amber said, trying to be pleasant.

"So you'll come with us?" Ana looked at her brightly.

Amber picked up her empty glass and tipped it at the bartender, who was keeping his distance by the kitchen door. "Vodka and tonic, please." He nodded and moved toward the counter. Her body temperature had cooled and her head felt clear.

She tasted her mouth. When she drank too much, it tasted metallic. Not yet. She lit another cigarette with one of the bar matches.

"We don't have to go to the beach," the sister was saying. "We could go anywhere. The point is, we have a car."

"A Toyota," Ana said.

"What about Sausalito?" the sister asked. "We could all go over to Sausalito for a view. You can probably see this exact place."

"I like this bar." Amber smiled at the bartender serving her drink. She got off her stool, a little unsteadily but still gracefully, and walked over to a jukebox in the corner. The bars Dean had taken her to had sound engineers, people who manned the compact disk player with a silent ruthlessness, never announcing anything but always keeping the music going. She squinted at the jukebox selections, recognized none of the names of the groups or the songs. It made her feel old.

She got back up on her stool. The tonic covered the vodka well, but she could tell it was there, with each swallow, waiting to soothe her. She hadn't thought about Dean in a while, a good sign. She had earned herself a new life. She raised her glass in the air to a toast.

"You look like you're celebrating," a woman said. Amber turned. It was the sister, again. They were both still there, in their shorts and blouses, a couple of harmless tourists from the Midwest. "What are you celebrating?"

"My day off." Amber glanced beyond the sister to Ana. A normal enough looking woman, a little simple and plain in style, but there were a lot of plain and simple people out there. "What does it mean," Amber said quietly. " 'Mildly retarded?' "

"She's got the capacity of a twelve-year-old," the sister said, examining her fingernails. "It's not so bad. She's twenty-five. She does what I tell her."

Amber nodded. "And you're younger."

"Not by much."

She had the easy figure of a seventeen- or eighteen-year-old, before things would change, but it was hard to tell. On her wrist was a bracelet with little gold-colored trinkets. Her dirty blond hair was blown back in swaths and descended in waves past her shoulders. She could be seventeen or she could be twenty-three. Behind her Ana had her back turned, as she looked out the window, where tourists in shorts and broad-brimmed hats were making their way heavily across the street to a psychedelic poster store.

"Look," the sister said. "I'm sorry if I sounded pushy about getting you to go around with us. I just thought it would be fun. Ana likes you."

"I don't even know you guys." Amber sipped lightly at her vodka and tonic, then puffed on her cigarette.

"Whatever." The sister looked at her watch on the other wrist. "We have to go." She took a wallet from her purse and the bartender came over with the check. The sister slid a five over to Amber. "It's from Ana. She wanted to buy you a drink."

"That's all right." Amber pushed the five dollars back.

Ana came over from the window, where she'd gone to stand with her face close to the glass.

"What's going on?" she said.

"Just take it," the sister said to Amber. "Don't hurt her feelings."

"Ana." Amber looked at her mild face, the eyes heavily lidded as if she'd been drinking alcohol. "You don't have to buy me a drink."

"I want to," Ana said.

"Don't be a jerk," her sister said, facing Amber. She patted the five-dollar bill on the counter. "See you."

She took Ana by the hand and they left. The bartender came over and collected the abandoned drink glasses, mopped the counter with a damp rag, and laid out a fresh set of coasters. He stayed behind the bar, his arms folded across the shelf of his belly, while Amber dug into her drink.

"What was that all about?" he said.

"I don't know." She studied the five-dollar bill on the counter next to her. "They wanted me to go out with them. Then they just wanted to buy me a drink. The younger one said the older one was retarded, and she agreed. You got any aspirin?"

The bartender reached under the counter and pulled out a bottle of ibuprofen. "They were probably trying to scam you," he said. "It's a North Beach tradition. Good thing you didn't go with them."

"I bet she was retarded," Amber said. She undid the aspirin bottle and swallowed two pills with her drink.

"They were probably going to kidnap you." The bartender was smiling. "Shake you down. Drive you to an ATM and make you withdraw all your money. Then maybe commit any number of unspeakable acts."

"She was retarded," Amber insisted.

The bartender shrugged. "What do I know? But even retarded people kill." He grinned at her greasily and brought up an open bottle of bar vodka. "Here, let me buy you a drink." Behind her the restaurant felt eerily empty. At least the door to the street was propped open. Ice clinked in her empty glass.

"I've had enough," she said. "How about just giving me my check?"

The bartender looked sadly around the bar and out into the restaurant. "If you leave," he said, "I'll be alone. Then what'll I do?"

She got off the stool carefully and pulled her knapsack from the floor onto her right shoulder. An oily stain shone on his bow tie, circles of sweat ringed the armpits of his white shirt. The checked tablecloths were the shiny, plasticized kind. Most of the bottles behind and above the bar were empty. Flies sailed overhead, en route to the kitchen, where in the window of the door a man was peering out intently at her. She looked back at the bartender. "You'll think of something," she said.

Past noon the street along Bodecker Park hummed with drinking, talking, card-playing, penny-pitching, complaining people, but none of them wanted to buy Benjamin West's car. He took off his cap and mopped the sweat from his forehead with his shirt sleeve. He'd been stationed here for three hours, his car under the sun hot to the touch, a white sign taped to the rear window that said FOR SALE. There wasn't a soul in the park under twenty-five. They sat on benches behind a high fence of pointed iron bars, and sprawled playing cards on an asphalt basketball court. On the four street corners men and women shared beers, lit each other's cigarettes, conversed in low voices, laughed in frantic high notes, the doors to three nearby liquor stores thrown open to the throng and the light. It felt like a cross between a war and a parade. He had had one offer, for ten dollars, from someone in a beret and a goatee with a clear line of mucus running out his nose.

As he drove his sight blurred and the windshield seemed

greasy from the inside out. At a red light he paused to rub his eyes and wipe at the windshield. When he looked up again the light was green and a car was blaring its horn behind him. He stuck his middle finger out the window and drove on. Down a few blocks to the left was a small park with a pair of benches and two diagonal paths that crisscrossed in the middle. He pulled under a flat-topped California cypress with orange poppies blooming in a circle around its trunk. He locked the doors, rolled up the windows to just a crack despite the heat, and curled himself in a horizontal position on the front seat.

When he woke, the low sun was in his eyes and the vinyl seat clammy with his sweat. The collar of his shirt was soaked. He rolled down the front windows and headed for the ocean. He hadn't gone more than two blocks before he saw a phone booth attached to a bus stop. He stopped and got out. He guessed it was about five o'clock. He punched in his mother's phone number, pressing zero first. After a few rings the operator got on and he told her it was collect from Benjamin. The line went blank. The street was a series of boarded-up storefronts and public housing apartments.

"Benjamin?" It was his mother. "Is everything all right? What's the matter?" Her voice was on crisis mode, upset yet authoritative.

"I'm just calling to check in," he said. "I'm sorry it took me so long."

"What? Why are you calling collect? Don't you have any money? Couldn't you sell the car?"

"I just got here." From down the street five black teenagers approached, one carrying a stick the size of a baseball bat. Why should he be afraid?, he told himself. If they were white, it wouldn't frighten him. They were within fifty feet. "Look, I've got to run," he said. "I'm fine. Everything's fine. I love you."

"Benjamin—"

He drove for a while, trying to figure out where he was. He came up a hill and turned left and ascended another sloping road and looked left and there was the whole city, fuming with dusk. He had no idea what had made him come out here in the first place. Was it as far as he could go? Was it the lure of California? The prison library had gotten newspapers from all the major cities, but when he'd shut his eyes and think of San Francisco, all he could see was a golden aura and enough distance between where he was and where he would be. He took a left and headed north, back toward the Tenderloin, the sun sinking. He made sure the windows were tightly shut and the doors locked. He was starving. Breakfast had been scrambled eggs that glistened with undercooked yolk, and white bread faintly toasted accompanied by a little packet of grape jelly. In prison they served the jelly from large plastic tubs, and there was a white margarine that looked like lard.

It was nightfall by the time he found a suitable alley to stash the car. He pulled close against a large old apartment building, up behind a heavy green dumpster. He shut the door quietly. He could hear soft moaning behind a chain link fence at the end of the alley, then giggling.

"Hey." A man stood beside him, touching his sleeve. "You can't park here." He smelled of malt liquor. "You got to move." He nodded at the chain link fence. "This here's a business operation."

"Oh," West said.

"You want a pop? She'll give you a pop for twenty-five."

"I don't think so."

"You sure?" He squinted at West through the dark. "It's a sweet deal. Mattress. Watchman. The great outdoors." West shook his head. "Then I guess you'd better be going."

He drove around, wasting gas. Most of the meters had been decapitated, their coin-filled entrails ripped out. A gang of kids in knee-length Raiders jackets shouted as he passed, offering either to mess with him or help get him messed up. He noticed a car start up from a parking place, and he stopped, reversed, and waited. The head of the driver bobbed, as if he were listening to music while the car warmed up. After a minute the passenger-side door opened and a woman in short shorts and a halter top stumbled out. She staggered a few feet into the middle of the street and spat out a swallow of liquid, then wiped her mouth with the back of her hand. The car pulled from the parking space. Now she stood between West's car and the space. "You next?" she shouted at him. "Or do you just like to watch."

He crossed Market. A few long blocks out, underneath the interstate that connected to the Bay Bridge, he eased into a row of parked cars coated with dust. Beyond the overpass were a few lighted signs for bars and groceries. He locked the car.

It was past nine o'clock by the time he reached the Golden Gate. Cecilia buzzed him in. He was freezing.

"Where you been?" she said.

"Trying to sell the car." He stood at the cage getting warm. He swore he could smell food.

"You didn't sell it?"

"No." He started off toward the stairs, dizzy, his throat swollen.

"Hey," she said. "I got something for you."

He stopped and went back to the cage. She slid a plate wrapped in aluminum foil under the open slot in the grillwork. "I thought you might be hungry."

"God," he said.

"And you got a message, too." She passed him a folded slip of notebook paper from his mail slot. She nodded at his plate. He was just staring at her. "You'd better take that upstairs. Maybe you could heat it up in your kitchen. And, besides, I didn't get you any utensils."

"Thank you." He glanced at the note. It was from Amber. It said for him to come see her when he got back, and it gave her room number. "I mean, really. Thank you."

"Just wait til you eat it." Cecilia was laughing. "Who knows, Benjamin. Maybe I'm just trying to torture you."

As he hurried up the stairs he undid the aluminum wrap. Liver and sautéed onions, a handful of mixed vegetables, and a slice of white bread with a pat of butter. In his room, he ate while he changed. The liver had the texture of a pudding. He washed his hands and face and checked the lump on his head. It looked impressive but it no longer hurt to the touch. He kept the cap on.

Amber's was the first door in on the left, beyond the fire door. He knocked and she opened it almost immediately. She was wearing her leggings and gray sweatshirt and her hair was combed out to her shoulders. The room was as deep and wide as a walk-in closet. In the glare of the overhead light he saw her face had a sunburn.

"Hey," she said. She stood in the doorway, not letting him in. "You just get back?"

"A while ago." He looked out of the corner of his eye to see if anybody was listening. The corridor was empty.

"You want to go for a walk?" She reached behind her and brought out a blue Windbreaker.

"A walk?" But she already had the coat on and the door shut behind her. "Yeah. All right."

"Did you have an okay day?" She was ahead of him, through the fire door, holding it open for him.

"I don't think so. Did you?"

"I'll tell you about it when we get outside."

They passed Cecilia in the lobby, who was occupied with a tenant complaining about lead fumes in her room. "Honey," Cecilia was saying as she waved at them, "we haven't painted that room in two years. Lead doesn't smell that long."

On the street Amber put her arm in his. He waited, wanting her to talk first. She pushed against him as they walked, her shoulder moving into his arm, her face touching his neck. A few steps ahead green lights flashed over an all-night check-cashing operation, and the broad sides of buses groaned past. He brought his arm out from hers and held her closer to him. She forced herself in, touching his skin. He realized he had forgotten to put on a coat. She smelled only of something sweet, like hard candy.

"What's going on?" he said.

"I just want to go someplace." She touched him, felt him, grabbed hold of him through his jeans, on the sidewalk, a few feet from Market Street. "I don't want to be in the Golden Gate."

He thought of the car, five long blocks away, dismissed it, thought of it again. "I don't have any money," he said.

"I don't want to go to a hotel with you." She kissed him, brought her hands around and held him tightly. "I just want to be with you and see if I like it."

"You've had a bad day," he said.

"That's right, Benjamin." She kissed him again. This time he could taste cigarettes below a layer of sweet alcohol. "Now where do you want to go?"

It wasn't until they reached the car that he realized he had forgotten the keys. She stood at the car, expectantly.

"I forgot the keys," he said.

All along under the overpass were cars, coated with varying depths of dust snowlike through the dark. Out on the street a trash can toppled and clattered against the pavement.

"Any car will do," she said.

There were station wagons, pickup trucks, low-riders, in stages of disuse. A Buick with a tinted windshield and bald tires opened on the driver side, but there were no seats, only a floor that felt like thickened, soaked cardboard and smelled of squirrel or rat. He shut the door.

"Who is it?" a woman's voice shouted at them from farther along a row of cars. "What do you want?"

Amber started to laugh. A door opened and the woman climbed out.

"You're not supposed to be here," the woman said. "This is our place. We were here first." She stayed by her car. In the dark all West could tell was that she had short hair and her voice had a young, familiar quality. Amber was moving toward the voice. "Maybe you can come back tomorrow and we'll be gone," the woman offered. "Lisa said tomorrow definitely."

West forced his way between two cars and caught Amber. "We ought to leave her alone," he said.

"I think I know her," Amber said. "Were you in North Beach today?" she called to the woman.

"I don't know," the woman called back. West still had a hold of Amber. "We were a lot of places." The woman stayed behind the open door. "Are you going to leave now?"

"I'm Amber," Amber said. "Does that mean anything to you?"

"I don't care what color you are," the woman said. "I've had a little to drink and Lisa isn't here and I don't think you should come any closer. Tomorrow we're supposed to go, definitely, and it's at least a ten-hour drive, Lisa said, so I'm going to need my sleep if I'm going to help her. She's a lot younger and I'm responsible for her."

"Come on," West said in a low voice. "We're scaring her."

"You're Ana," Amber insisted. "You want to leave a note for Lisa and come back to my place and stay with me?"

"I don't want Lisa coming back to an empty car," Ana said.

"Let's go." West tried to pull Amber back with him. "She wants to be left alone."

"We ought to stay with her."

"What's going on?" Ana's voice was flat and controlled. "You are leaving, aren't you?"

"I *know* her." Amber started off toward her. "Would you mind letting go of me?"

West let her go. Ana's car was at least a dozen cars down, but she was no longer standing by it.

"Where is she?"

"Maybe we scared her off," West offered.

"Fuck you."

Both doors on the driver side of Ana's car were locked. Amber put her face to the window, then walked around to the trunk. "Tennessee," she said. "Lisa said they were from the Midwest. Is Tennessee part of the Midwest?"

"Sure," West said.

She tried both doors on the passenger side. The locked car

echoed hollowly. She turned from it and scanned the two rows of vehicles.

"Ana!" she called. Then she waited, so still that they could hear cars crossing over up on the interstate. West hugged himself, rivulets of sweat against his sides. "Ana!"

He was calm enough now to feel the cold. He made himself be patient. Amber stood on tiptoe, hooding her eyes against the dark with the cup of a hand. Out on the street a man walked a dog, his shoulders hunched against the weather. Beyond the cars there was fog, drifting in clots along an empty avenue. The tires over the interstate made thin musical sounds, like a bow working one string of a violin.

"I guess she's gone," Amber said. She picked her way toward West. "I guess you were right. I guess I scared her."

"*We* scared her," West said.

"I met her in a bar this morning. She laughed when I almost fell off a chair, then she came over and apologized. Her sister said she was mildly retarded. The sister and I had an argument because they wanted me to go with them to someplace, and I wouldn't."

"Weird." West put his arm around her and she drew herself into him.

"Let's get out of here," she said.

As they headed back toward Market he considered telling her. Her face against the wind had an innocent, forgiving quality, the hair blown back. She was smiling to herself.

"What are you thinking about?" she asked him.

"Work," he said.

It was just eleven o'clock when Cecilia let them into the Golden Gate. He walked Amber to the stairs.

"You want to have breakfast tomorrow?" she said.

His face was numb from the cold. "Absolutely."

She kissed him on the cheek. "I'll see you at seven-thirty."

He watched her walk up the staircase, her calves in the black leggings, her soft shoulders. He'd tell her about Ana over breakfast.

"All right, Benjamin." Cecilia smiled. "You're on time."

She showed him the tire iron and the tenant roll and the employee roster—they'd been taped to a pull-out desktop that slid from under the counter. She discussed, at length, the phone system. Everybody calling out had to call through him, and he'd put them on hold, dial for them, then patch them through. His phone would ring as soon as a tenant picked up his or her end. He'd have to be patient. Sometimes the tenants, especially the older ones, would forget how the phone worked, and he'd have to interrupt them talking to themselves or imaginary people to figure out what it was that they wanted.

"But no one used the phone last night, did they?" she asked.

He shook his head.

"We don't give you a master key until your probation is up. You got a problem, you can call Bob."

At eleven-thirty, exactly, she handed him the key to the cage. "Be more careful tonight," she said, pointing at his cap. "Whatever gave you that lump, it wasn't worth it."

She patted him on the shoulder and let herself out. Through the bars, he watched her hurry toward the door to the street, the lobby dark, and his head aching from the cold. She waved as she closed the door after her, her face glistening in the light over the entrance that he was to shut off as soon as she'd left. Then she was gone, quickly, as if late for something, and he knew she was afraid of walking home alone at night.

Amber set her alarm for seven-thirty and got into bed still in her leggings and sweatshirt. She felt slow and light-headed from all the walking she had done and the day of drinking and then the journey through the night to Benjamin's car. The sheets were cool and she drew the blanket up around her shoulders and waited to fall asleep. Through the wall there was no sound of Mildred, but it would be early for Mildred. Mildred did most of her laughing between the hours of three and five. It was past the middle of the month, and Amber had less than two weeks left in her room. She would miss the familiarity of it. Fields had a place reserved for her on the fourth floor—the other women's floor. She had no idea what it looked like up there, but she supposed outside of the wallpaper in the corridor, it would be much the same—a bed, a desk, a chair, a wardrobe, a combination-lock bathroom down the hall. She didn't want to be too close to the bathroom but she wouldn't mind being closer, and she didn't want to be right inside the fire door again.

Her calves ached from the climb up Nob Hill that she had taken at sunset, drunk, to ascend the elevator at the Fairmont for one last drink and a look at the city. Through the rounded windows and the fog coming in, the city appeared to be sinking into a maelstrom of ocean and bay. She'd stayed too long, had anisette, and in the plush ladies' room had impulsively peeled off the pasty skin flapping from a blister. Then her heel had bled and she soaked it up with a peach-colored cotton towel. For dinner, she'd eaten at a McDonald's.

At least Benjamin had done well, the way he'd held back from Ana, the way he didn't accuse her when Ana had run off. She liked how he was always cold and she had to hold him to keep him warm, and how he tried to hide that fact, the way he would bite down on his mouth, and stiffen his shoulders and legs, as if he thought he could will himself not to be cold. She liked that he didn't have twelve different jackets or capes or sets of leather pants, that he dressed functionally. She liked that he hadn't brought up the fact that they'd had sex, that he hadn't teased her or badgered her with it, that they didn't need to mention it. She didn't doubt that they'd get to it again. He was not her rescuer because no one could be her rescuer, but he could evolve—they could evolve.

But now it was past twelve, her chance of sleep draining away from her. She'd be up by three practically by instinct. She turned in bed, forced her head into the pillow, away from the dank, disinfectant-suppressed mildew smell of her room, and tried to will herself to sleep.

Not much later, it seemed, she woke to the throaty odor of smoke and the sensation that her face was covered by a wrap of cold flesh with folds and cracks. It was a kind of dream. She shook her head in it, to loosen herself from it, and it tightened itself to her face and turned against her movement as if it were trying to snap her neck.

"Awake?" said a voice, low and hollow, a laugh waiting behind it, waiting to explode in her ears. "Heh-heh." A fear hit her so hard she hoped she would faint. Her teeth ground against each other. Sweat prickled at the back of her neck. "I knew you'd come around, babe. You always do."

She kicked. He was not there. He crouched at her side, his face not far from hers, his familiar breath of cigarettes and coffee. One hand smothered her mouth and clamped her chin. A knee pointed against her sternum, pushing in so deeply that she thought she could feel herself crack. He was letting her breathe.

"I guess you don't even know who you killed and who you didn't," he said, his face leaning closer. She had refused to open her eyes, but with her lips and the sides of her face she felt the boniness of his hand. Against her eyelids, through the dark, his face descended. His knee pressed harder against her breastbone. "Heh-heh." He ran his tongue over her cheek. "You blew up Andrea, babe. I didn't even know whether I liked her. You blew up some girl I was just trying out. Some kind of East Coast thing. You disappoint me, Ber." He liked to call her Ber. He said it was as cold as she could get. Brrr.

She waited, her eyes clenched shut, tried to feel and not feel with her chest and her face and her hands—where were her hands? She moved her wrists to find them. He held them so tight in his free hand that needles seemed to point against her fingertips.

A light clicked on above her head; that would be the lamp, its color against her eyelids.

"Look at me," he said.

She wouldn't.

His knee dug into her breastbone and he squeezed her face until saliva bubbled at her lips onto his cold palm.

"Look at me."

She looked at him. He'd shaved off all his hair and his eyebrows had been burned to white scars. His eyes dilated and brimmed behind his horn-rimmed glasses.

"Your little explosion," he said, "taught me a new way to part my hair."

He had used to grow his hair long and part it to one side, blow-dry it until it was flaxen, comb it through until each strand had its own luster. Now all there was to his face was a skull with bristle and lips and eyeglasses. She laughed. It came out her nose. His fingers made sockets in the flesh around her mouth.

"So," he said. "What do we do now?"

His hand released her mouth and caught her throat, found her Adam's apple and pressed it until she gagged. He bent his face and kissed her opened lips. She felt his tongue in her mouth, thick and coated with the taste of cigarettes. An orange color swam behind her eyes. She hoped it was unconsciousness.

He let go of her wrists. She was so busy choking, her hands slashed only at air. He had swung himself atop her. She tried to roll him.

"Heh-heh."

He pressed so hard against her throat that her stomach heaved drily and her bowels loosened.

"I never got the chance to tell you." He licked her upper lip. "My warts are back."

Her eyes teared and brimmed and dried out all at once. She tried to kick and scratch him. He was everywhere, but nowhere within reach. She could feel her windpipe begin to flatten. He wrenched down her leggings and tore her underwear. Her breathing came to her through a thin line of pain, as if her passage to air had the diameter of a wire. She tried to relax, to massage the air along as naturally as possible. A high-pitched wail shrieked in her ears. She thought it might be herself, but she was incapable of sound. He had cut her off from sound. She had no sensation anywhere, no sense of whether he was lubricating her, entering her. She tried to make a connection with her nose, to see if there was opportunity. It still required the participation of her throat. Was he talking to her? She couldn't even hear him. Perhaps he wasn't even there, or she wasn't there, she was heading out, leaving parts of herself to him. Her thighs were his, her chest, and whatever was inbetween. All his. She left them to him. Sadness overwhelmed her, to have to leave like this. Soon her whole way of thinking would be left to him. She sensed peripherally her limbs flailing about her, and saw herself a cracked vertebrae twitching with life, her beating heart exposed on a table, her only connections reflexes. Now her back left her, the fact that she had a spine, hips, a little dimple between her shoulder blade and her ribcage, these eluded her, vanished.

Then she felt the pressure on her windpipe easing minutely. The wire of her throat became a cord. She could hear him breathing in shallow breaths. He appeared in her vision, the skull and glasses. His mouth approached, rimmed hers. The length of her sweatshirt arrived at her chin in cotton folds. He pinched her nipples as if he wanted to tear them off.

"I haven't even fucked you yet," he said, her mouth free of him. "I bet you didn't know that. I bet you couldn't even feel it."

For an answer she shrieked and grunted. His face was mottled with bright yellow spots and little twinklings of synaptic stars.

"You took a shit." He laughed and stuck a finger in her mouth. It tasted like nothing she had ever tasted before, muddy and chemical and personal, fecal. "Like old times."

She gagged and trembled and screamed around it. Parts of her twitched helplessly. She was crying, flailing. The pressure resumed on her windpipe. Her hand hit a wall and came back at her, scratching her face.

"Babe," he said. "Babe, go easy on yourself."

Her knees rocketed, her sternum felt as if it were bleeding, if bones could bleed. The matter from his finger clung to her gums and the insides of her mouth. Her right hand struck the windowsill at the head of the bed, ricocheted back to her, was unable to reach his face, to gouge at it, and then cracked back against something of a hard heavy plastic that seemed to break in two and fall to the floor.

"Heh-heh," he said. "The phone. Now there's an idea."

West answered the inside line on the first ring.

"Front desk," he said.

"An idea," a man's voice said, above a clutter of noise that sounded like a television turned on between channels.

"Who is it?" West said. "How can I help you?"

"I could wrap it like this," the man said, deeply, gently.

"You've reached the front desk." West raised his voice for effect. "How can I help you?"

"What the fuck's that?" The voice paused, but West could still hear the white noise. "Babe, could you be still?"

"Look," West said. "I'm going to have to hang up if you don't tell me what you want."

"Ber," the voice said, "I'm going to make you hang up the fucking phone. Heh-heh."

"Hello?" West said. "Hello?" He knew the laugh instantly, felt the lump on his head begin to pain him as if it knew it, too. His ear was sweaty against the receiver. "Hello?"

The white noise died to a rattle, a persistent tiny clicking. Then the line went dead.

So he was in the building, somewhere. He had used the inside line. West selected the tire iron from under the mail slots and headed out of the cage. The floor count above the elevator was lighted at two. At the foot of the staircase he paused, listening, but could hear nothing. He ascended the staircase, leading with the tire iron. At the wide step of the mezzanine, the short door-way, he stopped again. The lobby was sunk in a dark, dank gloom. Above him, from the second floor, came the faint buzzing sound of the elevator, waiting. He waited with it for a moment, peering up the stairs, making sure the landing was empty.

He choked up on the tire iron, trying to find a hold where he would be comfortable and flexible in swinging. He moved softly up the fake marble stairs, his sneakers barely whining as they sought a grip on each step. At the second floor he was greeted by four shut doors—the door of the elevator, the door to Bob's office, the door to the Vietnam Veterans' Program office, and the fire door to the residential corridor. It was quite possible that the screwdriver guy wasn't even here, that someone else had taken the elevator last, that the asshole was a floor or two or three above, terrorizing somebody who West would reach too late. He grasped the handle of the fire door and turned it slowly, making sure it drew the bolt in. Carefully, he pulled open the door, swung it soundlessly back toward him. The corridor was empty. He could hear nothing. He eased the door shut behind him as he stepped into the hallway. Down at the end of the corridor was another door, out onto the fire escape. A stone or brick lay at the foot of the door, and the alarm dangled loosely from the doorway.

West advanced down the hall, looking for doors that were ajar, pausing to see if he could pick up an odd sound. The door to the women's bathroom was firmly shut. At the end of the hall he squinted at the loose alarm system. A trip hinge and joint had been unscrewed. He retraced, slowly, his steps back up the hall. He looked at the carpet under the doorways for signs of light, he looked at the doors themselves to see if they had been forced. He bent down and noted each individual keyhole. Twenty-four doors.

At the last door on his right, Amber's door, he saw it. The keyhole had been widened, the metal bent back and bent in, in tiny jagged petals. He pressed his ear to the door. Nothing. But it had been forced.

He took a soft step back and looked at the door. What did it mean? He couldn't figure it. He turned the handle, pushed the door open quickly, his tire iron raised in his other hand.

A blur of desk lamp caught him as it hit against the side of his face and raked his neck. He stumbled in darkness, rose, turned, swung. He connected solidly with something wooden and large. A wardrobe. He could hear it crack. Wordlessly, he ducked against the shadow of a gesture and the blade of something cold and metal stabbed at his neck. He choked up on the tire iron and swung. He heard a soft groan and felt him fall. His neck burned. The floor gave up a moan. There was no light. An arm appeared to jerk for his legs. He swung, connected in a dull thud. Whipped the iron back against his shoulder and swung harder. A jolt of rebound. Swung a third time, and heard plastic crack and a muted pulpy burst. Once more, he swung. He was out of breath, the room dark. He squinted at the bed. A voice croaked at him.

"Amber?"

The voice tried to clear itself.

He stepped over the shape on the floor and felt near the door for the light switch. He turned it on.

She lay on the bed, holding her throat under a clot of sweat-shirt, her face smeared with a muddy wetness, her free hand emptily reaching for something to cover herself with. On the floor lay the guy, his glasses broken and dented into his face, a moustache of blood coming out his nose, blood faintly drooling from between his lips. His eyes were open, peering through the mangled glasses. A bony index finger lay in a half curl beside the red-handled screwdriver. The tire iron felt warm to West's touch. Amber croaked at him.

As he moved toward her, she kept shaking her head at him, her eyes squinting through tears, her breathing shallow and fast. Between her legs was a brown stain. He covered her up with a blanket, found a washcloth, wet it in her little sink. He washed her face. Then he opened the window above the bed and threw the washcloth out into the airshaft. She was shivering.

He got into bed with her, a narrow bed. He had difficulty positioning himself to hold her. Her neck, at the windpipe, flowered with a redness that was gradually turning purple. He held her and her breathing slowed. She made a sad growling sound.

"It's all right," he said. He thought of telling her the guy was dead. He thought of getting up and calling the police. The phone was in the lobby and he didn't want to leave her. The bed was warm and she seemed cold. He thought maybe they ought to just lie there for a while. He looked again at her neck and realized she needed to drink something hot or cold, he didn't know which.

"We ought to get you dressed," he said. "Can you help me get you dressed?"

She nodded and he got up carefully from the bed. She lay there, shaking her head as if she weren't sure she could get up. Then he remembered how she looked before he covered her. He turned his back. While he stood examining the body on the floor for signs of life, he heard her try to clean herself with the sheet. She was hyperventilating but she sounded on top of it, as if she were managing her crying through her breathing. He felt the pressure on the floor as she got up from the bed. Through the wall a woman started to laugh. He began to shake, then righted himself. The laughter stopped. He reached into her wardrobe and found a pair of underwear, jeans, a T-shirt.

She had taken off the sweatshirt and the leggings. There was a small black mole below her left shoulder, and a brown freckle on the inside of her right thigh. Her knees had little dimples, and her nipples were slightly hard from the cold of the room, from her standing completely nude in it. Her hair was tangled with sweat and sleep, her scalp around her forehead deep red, as if he'd tried to yank her hair out. West gave her the clothes, and looked away as she dressed.

The body still lay on the floor. He had held out a hope that it would get up and leave. He nudged it with the toe of a sneaker. It moved to the touch and then shifted back into its rightful position. The gesture made him feel like a gunslinger, his trigger hand from the fingertips to the heel of the palm still blotchy with color. He supposed he shouldn't even touch the body, that the police wouldn't want it to have been moved.

Amber gingerly pushed past him to the door, dressed in the clothes he had given her. He felt oddly proprietary and intimate. He smiled shyly at her, almost apologetically, as if the whole thing had been his fault.

"I need something to drink," she whispered. She looked at the floor and shook her head. "He really worked over my throat."

He knew to mention the police so soon would upset her, though for his own sake he knew the sooner the better. He patted her shoulder. She slipped out from the room and he followed, shutting the door tight.

In the basement she bought a cup of coffee from the machine, with cream and sugar. She sipped it and stared around the room, avoiding his glance. There was a Formica table with a set of plastic chairs, and she pulled a chair out and sat in it. He remained standing, not knowing what she wanted from him. He wanted something to drink but he didn't have any money, and his thirst struck him as pathetically mundane.

"So," she whispered. She looked at the table. "I suppose I ought to thank you." She wiped her nose with the back of her hand. "God."

He sat in a chair across the table from her, but not directly in her line of view. He was thinking how they really ought to call the police.

"I guess he's dead?" she said.

"Very." He was trying to see the humor in it.

She laughed for him, more like a smoker's cough because of her throat. "I killed his girl friend," she said, her voice a dry rasp.

"What?"

"I killed his girl friend. I was trying to kill both of them, but I only got her. I blew up their apartment. I used to live with him. He was an asshole. But I only managed to kill his girl friend. I guess that's why I said I had to thank you." With her rasp, she sounded like a gangster.

"You're in shock," West said.

"I don't think he would have killed me," she said. "Dean liked to see people twist too much to want to kill them."

"Dean?" West said weakly.

"His name. I lived with him for three years, in L.A.."

"So you knew him?"

"I fucked him for three years," Amber snapped. "I tried to kill him. Of course I knew him."

West rubbed the back of his head. "Maybe you're mistaking him for somebody else."

"What are we going to do with his body?" she rasped.

He laughed. He looked at the veneer wood paneling of the

kitchen and snack room, the fluorescent glow of the tube lights, the exposed tangle of wires that constituted the ceiling, the coffee machine. It was all a rush and swirl that he was both sucked into and pushed out from. He massaged one hand with the other, noting the veins and knuckles, shut his eyes, then opened them.

"You need to clean yourself up," she said. She pointed at his neck, and he felt the open skin, the stickiness of drying blood. She wet a fingertip with her tongue, reached across the table, and dabbed at the cut. It stung. "So we're both killers," she said. "Are you getting the picture?"

He nodded bleakly. There was the fact of his record. He had to wonder whether she had planned it this way—their meeting, their sex, Dean's death, she had initiated all of it. She couldn't have planned it better. Her face under the fluorescent light was pale, her hair in tangled skeins which she was now trying to comb out like an afterthought. Her fingernails were dirty. Through her T-shirt he could see the fragile ridge of her collar-bone and shoulder blades.

"I guess you're thinking it's all my fault," she said. He shrugged. "Well, it is. I shouldn't have wanted to get back at him so badly. But you had to know him to understand what I felt like."

West rubbed the cut on his neck. He was suddenly very tired. "I'll get my car."

"And then what?"

He got up from the table and pushed his chair in, gathered up her empty cup. He'd have to start paying attention to small details now. "We'll think of something."

In the lobby the door to the cage was thrown open and the tire iron was missing. It took him a moment to make sense of it all. He made sure he had the key, then shut the door to the cage. He leaned his head against the bars. He felt her hand on the back of his neck, her fingertips tenderly rubbing the tight muscle. He breathed in, deeply, and steadied himself. He looked up at the clock on the wall above the mail slots. It was only one-thirty.

"We'll have to wait a bit," he managed.

She kept rubbing his neck.

"I'd better go up and have another look."

From the droning sound on the second floor he knew that the elevator hadn't moved. Amber let them into her room and shut the door. In the dark he could feel the body at his feet somewhere. She turned on the light.

Dean lay on his side on the floor, his face still indented by his broken glasses, trails of stale blood etched from his nose and mouth. Dark blood sat in the swirl of his exposed ear. He appeared, almost, to be looking under the bed for something. He wore the black leather boots with the silver buckles, black jeans, a gray T-shirt, and a black leather jacket. West bent over him, put the back of his hand to his nose, then lay his fingers on where the pulse should be on his neck.

"I forgot to tell you," he said, without looking up. "This is the guy who gave me the lump on my head last night."

Amber covered the stripped bed with a blanket. She bundled the dirty sheets in a ball, and stuffed them in a plastic bag. "We should probably hide him under the bed," she said. She reached into the wardrobe and brought out a couple of small plastic bags. She gave West two and kept two for herself. "For your hands."

West tried to remember whether he had touched him yet with anything but the tire iron. Just the sneaker, he had toed him with his sneaker; and he had felt for his carotid. He put on the plastic bags. "What about you?" he said. "Did you touch him?"

"I don't think so."

She picked up Dean by the ankles and West took hold of the wrists. They carried and dragged him a few feet back, then knelt and shoved him under the bed. He wasn't as light as he looked.

The carpet where he had been killed bore only the slightest impression of him, no stain. There was no blood on the tire iron.

"What about that?" Amber said. "Should we get rid of it?"

West shook his head and carefully removed the plastic bags from his hands, to use them again later. "I'd better get down to the desk." He bent to pick up the tire iron and glanced under the bed, saw the back of a body covered with black clothes, Dean's face turned to the wall. "He's still there," he said.

In the lobby he stayed in the cage and she sat on a sofa in the dark. "Still awake," he called softly.

She waved at him through the dark. "Right here."

At two she accompanied him on his inspection of the basement. She bought them both cups of coffee and they sat at the Formica table across from each other. She lit a cigarette.

"Don't," he said.

"Why?"

"I can't explain it. Just don't."

She put it out in the half-filled coffee.

"You didn't have to do it that way," he said.

"I know."

They smiled at each other, shyly.

"I guess I'll go get the car," he said.

"Be careful," she said.

He laughed.

In her room she turned on the light, and moved the desk chair against the door. She got down on her knees by the bed. He was still there. She reached up for two plastic bags on the bed and put them on her hands. She lay flat on the floor and tugged at his heels, then at the shoulders, then at the heels again. Finally she had him close enough. She got on her knees and rolled him out.

He lay face up looking at her, his glasses cracked into the bridge of his nose and jammed against his temples, but she could still see his eyes. His forehead was smudged with dust, and dust coated the tip of his nose. Hairlike strands clung to his lips, which were partly open. The end of his hard, narrow chin wore a goatee of dust. Through the plastic bag her fingers traced his pronounced cheekbones. The glasses crushed into his face looked like they hurt, and she winced for him and pulled them up off the nose just a little. She began to brush the dust from his face. She was crying.

It was one thing to have thought of killing him and to have gone about trying to kill him, but it was another thing entirely to know he was dead, to see him dead, to feel him dead. His nose was still stern and arrogant, but the blood vessels under his eyes had broken and they were beginning to blacken. Still, it was almost beautiful the way there was so little blood, like a dead astronaut. She touched his upper lip. It curled around her fingertip. She withdrew the finger. She tried to remember who Andrea was, not even sure she had met her; she had only seen her clothes, that once, in Dean's apartment. Their apartment. The stirrup pants. She pictured Dean with a whip, riding her. She'd torched the lamb and the bear, their deferential marble eyes. The gyrations she'd used to put them through! Now his head was shaved so close it looked painful. He'd fallen out of the sky from Berlin or London, a European skinhead astronaut. She didn't love him, she'd never loved him; she'd only wanted him, had him, lived with him, and was sucked into him until she felt desperate enough to want to swallow all of him, too, inhale him. Own him. But love him? She shook her head. "I didn't love you," she said. But she was still crying.

Had she loved Josh, or David? Was she one of those women who always had to be with somebody, live with somebody, even if she didn't love? She was now with Benjamin, and she certainly didn't love him. She didn't even know him. And they'd be stuck with each other for a while. She patted Dean's bristly head. He once had such hair, almost like a woman's hair, layered and soft to the touch. Once they'd gone up into the mountains behind Los Angeles, they'd packed a picnic basket and taken a little hike up a trail. They found a stream and sat by it, side by side, the picnic basket behind them so they had to turn into each other whenever they wanted to get something from it. They sat by the stream for a while, the water running clear over a shallow bed of rocks and twigs. She remembered touching his hair by the stream, how it felt like the stream, smooth, soft, running almost down to his shoulders. They had almost identical hair, except his was better, he'd spent more money on it, took better care of it. He was very particular. They had fought over which car to rent for the mountains and which cheeses to buy for the picnic basket. He liked the soft cheeses and she liked the hard ones. They'd bought mostly soft cheese and it ran gooey over their fingers as they tried to slice it onto hunks of French bread. She couldn't touch his hair any more because her hands were covered with cheese. She dipped the hands into the stream. It was much colder than she'd expected, icy. The cheese congealed and broke off into the water and ran down the stream in hardened balls as if they were racing one another. She and Dean had laughed at the cheese. Heh-heh. She'd always hated his laugh, but it was something she got used to by telling herself it came from both his insecurity and his lack of inhibition. He had to laugh like that because he didn't know any other way to laugh. But without hair now his forehead was too big, his face too vast, and it was hard for her to remember any more about him as she knew him. She dried her eyes with the shoulders of her T-shirt. She pushed him back under the bed.

union square

He had made his way out to the lot under the overpass, found the Chevy, put the key into the lock, opened the door, and was halfway into the car when he heard the woman's voice.

"Hey," she said. "Hey. Excuse me. Do you have a minute?"

He heard the click and scrape of pumps over gravel. He pushed himself into the car seat, behind the steering wheel. "I'm in kind of a hurry," he said. He swung the door partially shut so that the window and the dark hid him.

She came up to the car, out of breath. He did not look at her, his cap low over his eyes.

"You've been parked here long?" she said.

"Six or seven hours." He studied the windshield, the interior smears luminous in the dark.

"You haven't by chance seen a girl wandering around, have you? About twenty-five, short hair, bangs."

"No." He kept his grip on the door handle, which was not fully shut.

"Well, she was supposed to wait for me here." She pointed behind him to what he suspected was the Toyota. "She *always* waits for me. I can't understand where she could be."

"Look," he said. "I'm sorry. I'm late for something important." He started to swing the door shut and she grabbed at it. He could have yanked it closed but he would have crushed her fingers.

"Wait a second," she said. "Just wait. The thing is, she's mildly retarded. And the thing is, she's taken the car. And the thing is," she was almost crying, "the girl does not really know how to drive."

"Fuck," West said, still holding onto the door so she couldn't open it.

"What?" Lisa said.

"Nothing." He kept staring out the windshield. "So what do you want me to do?"

"I don't really know," Lisa said. "I haven't thought this through." She paused, pulling gently at the door, trying to see him. "I guess you look all right. Would you mind driving me around a bit, to see if I can find her."

"I don't have the time," West said.

"Just ten minutes. Five minutes. She couldn't have gotten far. It's a standard and I'm surprised she could even make it out of the lot." She drummed her fingers on the car hood. "If you take me a block down each of the streets here, I think we'll find her."

"And if we don't?"

"Five minutes." Lisa pulled harder at the car door. "Will you let me in, or what?"

"The back seat," he said. "You'll have to sit in the back. I spilled a cup of coffee up front."

She let go of the front door and he shut it, then reached around without looking up at her and unlocked the back door. She slid in and the car filled instantly with a smell of perfume and gum and cigarettes.

"Thanks." She leaned forward and put her elbows on his seat back, her face almost touching his head. He could feel her hair. He bent and started the car, pulled from the space without having to look back at her. He wanted to laugh and scream at the same time. "Just try all the streets," she said. "Go slow. It's a four-door Toyota with Tennessee plates." She touched the cotton button at the crown of his cap. "This is some kind of nightmare," she said.

He drove, shoulders hunched over the wheel, eyes set forward. The streets were unpredictably one way, and he had to double back to follow each of them to and from their connection to the parking lot. He could feel her up against his seat back. He'd been gone at least thirty minutes by now, probably closer to forty. The cars parked on the empty streets seemed abandoned, the streetlamps shed diffused misty light through the fog. "I don't know," Lisa kept saying. "I just don't know about this." The streets leading out from the lot under the overpass formed a kind of star. By the fifth street he'd lost his sense of direction.

"What about going to the police," he said.

She pointed to a neon doughnut sign. "Just drop me up there. I'll figure it out."

He pulled up to the shop. In the window a big round clock with orange neon hands said it was a quarter to four.

"Thanks," she said, getting out. He looked away from the light. She shut the door. "See you."

When she turned to head into the shop, he watched her. She brushed her long hair back and pushed open the heavy glass door, sauntered to the counter in her pumps. She did not appear to be in any hurry. Perhaps she knew he was watching and was waiting for him to leave.

He pulled back onto the street, took his first left, then left again. He slowed as he drove under the overpass. The lot appeared to extend for several blocks. Maybe she had just moved the car. Maybe they'd find each other in daylight, unharmed. He took a left into the lot, and followed a rutted, pocked path between the rows of cars. The lot ended in a crush of a half-dozen pickup trucks parked head to head, squeezed into the last bit of space. It had to be four o'clock. He headed farther out.

Through the sheen of fog, the rear end of a car stuck out from the curb like an invitation. It had Tennessee plates. A Toyota. He passed cautiously, all its lights off and the windows dark and clouded. He pulled over ten yards in front and got out quietly. From a safe distance he tried to look through the Toyota's windshield. Too dark. His workboots seemed to thud against the pavement. As he walked past the driver side, he slowed and bent his head at an angle. He thought he could see her, but he wasn't sure. He stopped, angled his shadow to allow the light of a distant streetlamp. She sat strapped in the driver seat, her eyes shut, her hands folded on her lap, holding in place a beach towel draped over herself as a blanket. Her face seemed pursed and slightly contemptuous. She'd made it about two and a half blocks from her parking space in the lot, to a street out in the open, where it must have felt safer. He was glad the window was between them. He could have easily whispered something that would have woken her, that would have embarrassed himself.

He drove farther, until he found a bus stop with a phone

booth. The metal binder that had the Yellow Pages was heavy and full. Under "Doughnuts" he found only one listing for Eighth Street. He dialed the number.

"Doughnuts." It was a young guy with a jaunty voice.

"Look," West said. "I need to talk to one of your customers. A woman from Tennessee. Could you ask if there's a woman from Tennessee?"

"Sure," the guy said, and in the same level voice, "Is there a woman from Tennessee here?" He waited a beat. West was sweating. "You're in luck," he said.

"Yeah?" She sounded as if she were expecting a call. "Who is it?"

"It's me. The guy who drove you around looking for your sister. I found her. She's on Tenth between Harrison and the lot. She's asleep."

"Great," Lisa said, without any emotion. "Are you going to come get me? Or are you going to drive her over and we'll drive you back?"

"I can't. You'll have to take a cab. Tenth, between Harrison and the lot."

"How am I going to get a cab at this hour. Come and get me. I'll pay you. Or we could have breakfast."

"I can't," West said. He hung up and shut his eyes, cracked his neck back against the stiffness in his muscles.

By the time he was finally headed in the right direction, the sky was beginning to lighten, people on the sidewalks, the solstice only six days off. Under the overpass one last time, everything felt coated with a thick, slick texture of oil and a gassy odor permeated the car.

It was a quarter to five when he pulled up in front of the Golden Gate, the sun distinctly threatening to rise, the sky a gray milk. As he got out of the car he saw her standing at the door looking out at him. She opened the door and let him in.

"Well, things are going according to plan, aren't they?" she said.

There were drag marks across the carpet of her room and one of Dean's heels clearly protruded from under the bed.

"You moved him," West said.

"I had to." She shut her eyes and shook her head. "To look at him."

"Do you have anything to cover him with?"

She opened the wardrobe and sifted through her things. "Only the dirty sheets."

"Well." He looked at the floor, began to smooth out the carpet marks with the broad foot of his workboot. "I think he ought to be covered."

They put Baggies on their hands and she brought out the plastic bundle and untangled one of the sheets. They spread it flat on the floor, stained side up, then got down on their knees and rolled Dean out. He landed on his belly and a groan escaped.

"Maybe we should wait until tomorrow," Amber said.

"I don't think so."

They brought one side of the sheet over him and tucked it under, then brought the other side over. West opened the door and checked the hall, went out to make sure the elevator was still there. He came back in and Amber was standing at the head of the bundle, her arms folded across her chest.

"Do you know what you're doing?" she said.

"How could I?" West grabbed onto the foot of the sheet, and she pulled on her end. "I've never done it before."

They bumped him from the room, through the fire door, to the elevator. West hit the button and the door opened and they dragged Dean in, squeezed at a diagonal so that he fit. The elevator droned. They rode to the lobby. When the door opened, faint streams of sunlight were coming through the storefront windows.

They dragged Dean along the linoleum walkway to the door. West went out to open the trunk. Housekeeping wasn't due for another hour and the Popeyes wouldn't open until seven. In the distance something moved toward him with a patient, inexorable slowness. Then it stopped. It had to be at least three blocks away. It didn't move again.

"Come on!" Amber had the door open just a crack, as if she thought the glass hid her.

He jogged inside to the cage, took down the tire iron from the shelf under the mail slots, and set it in the door to the street.

"Don't kick that on your way out."

He opened the door all the way and stuck his back out, then bent and took up his end—the feet—and she took up hers.

"Anyone coming?" she said.

"I sure as hell hope not."

They lifted and dragged the body through the door. It clunked against the tire iron, but the door did not shut. West half squatted as he brought his end of the body around to the trunk, his hands sweaty in the plastic bags. She followed, her knees bent, her face reddening.

They maneuvered Dean parallel to the open trunk, the sheet-covered body bent like a bow between them. He was too long for the car. Amber couldn't get any leverage on her end. In the trunk the spare tire sat taking up space.

"Do something!" she said.

They switched ends, West near Dean's shoulders, Amber taking hold around the knees. They hoisted the body above the trunk. He angled in the head to the deep corner, beyond the tire, and shoved. He tried with Amber to curve the torso around the tire. The legs were still too long. He bent into the trunk and worked the head some more. Still the feet dangled over the trunk.

"You could put the tire in the back seat," she said.

He grunted. It was a good idea, a bit late in coming. Under his jean jacket his shirt was soaked. He reached around the body, snapped out the wrench, and began twisting off the nuts and washers that bolted the tire in place. Whenever a nut came loose it eluded him and clanked around in the rim of the wheel like a roulette ball. The last nut came off and he wiped his face with the sleeve of the jean jacket, then lifted the tire from the trunk. Amber reached in and folded and jammed the feet into the trunk, slammed the hood shut. The bolts and nuts of the spare lay scattered across the pavement. She took the keys from the trunk lock and opened the front door, reached in and unlocked the back door. West brought the tire around and wedged it on the floor between the seats. He crawled in behind it and made sure all the doors were locked.

"The keys?" he said, without looking back.

"I have them."

He pushed his way out and shut the door. "I'd better get inside. At least until my shift's over." He checked the parking meter—it didn't start until eight.

She stared at him. "You're just going to leave the car out front like this?"

"I don't have much choice." He collected the tire iron from the door of the building and headed inside.

"Hey!" she called after him. "Aren't you forgetting something?" He squinted at her. She pointed at a shadow stuck to the rear windshield. "I don't think you want that on the car now."

He moved out to the sidewalk again, careful to replace the tire iron in the door. She gave him the keys. He unlocked the front door of the Chevy, reached in, unlocked the back door, relocked the front door. He opened the back door, stuck his arm in, and peeled off the FOR SALE sign from the inside of the rear windshield. "Thanks," he said. He locked the car again.

In the damp lobby they sat across from each other on mildewed sofas, a hazy heat filtering through the storefront windows. The temperature in the trunk of the dark brown car would rise quickly. It was not quite six o'clock, almost summer, and yet summer seemed already to have arrived in a matter of hours, in the sudden heat of early morning. East Coast, Mid-Atlantic deep summers were like this, the instant or hours of night coolness shifting to the stifling quality of early morning as if a switch had been flicked.

At least he could see the car. At least he would not be walking over to where it was parked to discover it towed, or broken into, or stolen, or surrounded by police. He shut his eyes against the thought and saw himself swinging the tire iron, one-handed, again and again as if his hand was empty and he was just trying to make a point. He'd killed him. He was filled with awe and dread and disgust. It was self-defense, but still killing, sheer killing, and he'd done it. He'd swung more than he'd had to, and he knew that when he was doing it. Was it bloodlust or fear or anger that had spurred him?

"We're going to need some money today," he said. "To drive around, and things."

"We'd better remove his wallet." She leaned forward, then got up from her sofa and came and sat next to him. "You have to know something. His parents have a lot of clout."

"How much?"

"His father is the CEO at Colgate or Crest or something like that."

West groaned. "That'll make the papers."

Someone buzzed at the door and he started, fearing that the trunk had popped or a stench had escaped. The short stumpy frames of two women from housekeeping waited patiently. He let them in.

"Benjamin," one said.

"Hey, Benjamin," said the other.

He didn't know their names. He waved as they bustled past toward the basement. When he returned to the sofa, Amber was gone. He caught up the key in his pocket and went back to the cage. Six o'clock. He hadn't checked the basement a second time, but now the first housekeepers were down there. He could still see the car. He couldn't find the tire iron. He moved out to the sofas quickly, before the next rush of housekeeping came. The tire iron lay on the carpet between the two sofas. He toted it to the cage, and stuck it between the desk and the wall.

The phone rang and he answered it while keeping an eye on the door and the car.

"It's me." Her voice was subdued. "I'll be down at seven-thirty."

"Okay."

"I'm not going to be able to stay in this room anymore. You know that, don't you?"

"We'll work something out." One more housekeeper rang at the door, and he reached under the counter and let her in.

"I'll see you." She hung up.

He smiled as the housekeeper yawned past him toward the basement. Out beyond the door, the unexpected morning sun beat down on the trunk of his car. He felt his pocket for the ring with the two car keys. He put the phone back on the hook. Sunlight crept under the glass door in a long yellow shadow, and cut white bolts through the gray lobby. He stretched inside the cage, and his hand fell on the cut on his neck. It had scabbed, the blood dried into a ridged seal over the wound, where Amber had pressed it with her fingertip.

She brushed her teeth in the little sink in her room, assiduously following the outline of each individual tooth, brushing below the gumline and along the interior of her mouth. She kept taking the toothbrush out and looking at it, the white foam, the yellowed bristles bent out like blown weeds, for signs of shit. She thought she was going to get sick.

When she finished, she threw out the toothbrush in the little straw wastebasket under the sink. On the floor, half under the wardrobe, was the lamp. She picked it up. The dirty white shade was cracked in two places, the hoop frame around the socket bent. The bulb had burst, and in its place was a jagged tangle of filament, the grooved end still embedded in the socket.

She soaped her hands in the sink and scrubbed her face with her fingers. She looked at herself in the square of mildewed mirror above the sink. She couldn't see anything unusual.

She stuffed her knapsack full of fresh plastic hand-sized bags, a T-shirt, another pair of jeans; and she pulled on a black canvas jacket with a half-dozen zippered pockets. She wanted to have a lot of pockets. She rushed through the contents of her wallet. She had $143.75 in cash. She had one credit card. He'd said they needed money. She stuffed the wallet into the zippered pocket at her left breast, looked around one last time, put on her sunglasses, and shouldered the knapsack.

She took the elevator to the basement. As she crossed toward the snack room, she could hear the low, unrushed voices of the housekeeping staff in the tiny bathroom on the stairs. She bought herself a cup of coffee with sugar and cream from the machine, and sat at the white table under the exposed ceiling.

As she started on her coffee, she noticed a brown speck floating in it, a little hardened body, thin hairlike legs. Some kind of ant. She dipped a fingernail into the coffee and pinned the insect against the slick wall of the cup and scraped it out. The napkin holder was empty. With a wooden coffee stirrer she extracted the insect from under her nail. When she lifted the cup to her lips again, two more insects floated to the surface. She made herself repeat the procedure twice, but the insects kept coming. She got up from the chair and threw the wooden sticks with the dead bodies pasted to them into the trash can. She hit the machine once, with the palm of her hand, then bent down to look through the little plastic door into the metal chamber. She couldn't see any ants.

Up the wet stairs to the lobby, she passed the housekeeping staff, the bathroom door thrust open as four of them squeezed in. A woman applied lipstick in a murky mirror, the broad naked back of another woman cut by the gray straps of a bra, as she bent and twisted herself into a dull pink dress. Under the shut toilet stall shone a pair of legs encased in support stockings, descending into a set of worn tennis sneakers.

"Hey, Amber," one of the women said. Amber did not recognize her, but she smiled as she passed.

In the lobby he stood behind the desk, waiting to let in the kitchen staff. She agonized over whether to leave the knapsack.

"I'm going to go out for a while," she said.

He folded his arms across his chest and nodded at her pack. "What's that for?"

"The day," she said. "Our trip."

"Uh-hunh." His face gave a little. "Why don't you just leave it with me."

She took it off her shoulder and handed it to him through the opened cage door. "You can have it," she said. "Now do you feel better?" She unzipped her breast pocket and took out her wallet, removed for her own use a twenty and her state identification card. "You can have this, too."

He set the backpack under the counter, paged slowly through the wallet. "All right." He looked relieved. "I'll see you at the car."

She touched him on the arm. He flinched. She held on for a moment, feeling his warm skin, the light hairs. She gave him a smile and he smiled back. She started for the glass door.

"Hey." He came out from the cage, still holding the door open. "Let me know if you can smell anything," he whispered.

On the sidewalk, she stopped and inhaled deeply. She had no idea what a dead body smelled like. She could smell the heat of the pavement, and the exhaust of traffic. She turned and waved through the door. She couldn't tell whether he waved back.

She hurried toward Market. He'd given her an idea that hadn't occurred to her. She wondered if he had had that problem with other women, of accusing them of thinking of leaving him even when they weren't. She wondered if it were a good idea, if perhaps he had first thought of leaving for himself. When he'd come up to her as she lay in the bed, he'd covered her and wiped her face; he'd climbed into the shit-stained bed and held her. He'd gotten clothes for her, jeans and a soft T-shirt.

She wiped at her eyes and headed downtown. In the middle of the block was a Carl's Jr., washed windows and orange plastic seats, a yellow and brown illuminated menu suspended from the ceiling behind the counter. She ordered two eggs, bacon, an orange juice, a coffee, and toast. She lay a five on the shiny metal counter, and the coins came pinging back to her in loud, expensive-sounding clatter. The meal was served on a brown plastic tray.

Back on the street she could smell marijuana and tobacco and coffee and the beginnings of the day's trash. Sun flashed on the sunken trolley tracks of Market. A discarded morning newspaper lay in damp sections on the sidewalk. A high plaster wall that shielded a construction site was pasted with several dozen posters advertising the same department store. At night, perhaps, they could dump him in a construction site and hope he'd be buried by concrete. They'd just have to find a place no one else was. She wondered if that was possible on a Saturday in California.

She window-shopped back up the other side of the street, looking for ideas. At a Walgreen's, an attendant unlocked the door to a small morning crowd. She had about fifteen dollars. She followed the line in.

The store was already warm from the morning heat. She moved down the aisles, searching for anything that made sense: a carton of heavy-duty sixty-four-gallon trash bags; a can of disinfectant spray; a ten-pair box of disposable surgical gloves, the kind that left a light powdery film on your fingertips after you used them; and a pack of sugar-free mint gum. She put on her sunglasses, and

took her purchases up to the cash register. The order came to
$14.73. She had just under a dollar left, and it made her feel as if
West might not be there when she got back.

She wondered how many gallons were in a body. These were
the bags she used to fill autumn leaves with, bags that held her
clothes to and from the laundromat in college, bags that stored
blankets and sheets during any one of her three westward moves.
They could easily hold a couple of babies or a child, but even
taped together two of them couldn't hold Dean. And she hadn't
bought tape. At least the disinfectant made sense. And the
gloves, too, though she had once heard that they held fingerprints
on the inside.

West was standing in the street by the car, impatiently scanning the road in front of and behind him. An idea hit her with
tremendous force and clarity. Los Angeles. Take him as far as
possible and still make it back for West's shift. Now he turned in
her direction, and his face went soft with relief. He started toward
her, but then looked back at his car. He didn't want to leave the
car. That was good. He was thinking. They were both thinking.
She smiled at him and crossed the street.

"Can you smell it?" he said, as she came up to him. She sniffed
the air and shook her head. "I guess it must be my imagination."

Even through her jeans, the vinyl upholstery was hot. He
fished out her wallet from his back pocket and laid it on the seat.
She let it rest there.

"I was thinking toward L.A.," she said. "Like he never got
here."

His hand slid by her leg as he punched open the glove compartment, stocked with Triple A guidebooks to a dozen states and
a flattened series of road maps.

"My mother," he explained.

He pulled out of the parking space while she groped through the glove compartment.

"So you think it's a good idea?" she said. "Near L.A.?"

He nodded as he drove, concentrating on the road and the impending stoplight. "What about the smell?"

"I bought some Lysol."

He opened the window all the way and headed out toward the bridge. She kept looking at the map. They'd have to pick up 5 somewhere below San Jose. Or they could take the coastal route and dump him near Monterey. She reached up and turned on the radio, took out a pack of cigarettes, and shed her jacket, spreading it on her seat to protect her arms and shoulders from the vinyl. She lit a cigarette and gave it to West, then lit one for herself. The smoke cooled her. She tapped her cigarette out the window. He squinted at the bright road.

"We have to buy you a pair of sunglasses," she said.

"How do you think he got up here?" West said. "Do you think he rented a car or do you think he took a bus or a train? Do you think he used a credit card?"

"Oh." She turned off the radio.

West pulled over into the shade. "We need to figure this out," he said.

Straight ahead was their old parking lot. "Just keep going," she said. "Pull in up there for a minute. Someplace quiet."

"I don't think—"

"—Just do it. You'll see."

The tires jounced over the pocked pavement. They crushed out their cigarettes. She dug into her Walgreen's bag and pulled out the box of surgical gloves and the Lysol.

"Open the trunk for me," she said.

He turned off the engine and got out of the car with her. She

stretched on a pair of gloves and he popped the trunk. She tore off
the sheet. The hips of his jeans were centered against his drawn
legs, his leather jacket still on. She hurried through the pants
pockets first. Nothing. He was like that. He didn't like any
unnecessary bulges.

"I think it smells," West said nervously.

"All right." She picked up the Lysol and flicked off the top.
She sprayed, leaving a damp coat of disinfectant that shone on the
leather and darkened the jeans. Her throat itched and her eyes
teared with the chemical sweetness of it. She coated the floor of
the trunk, pulling and pushing at the body. West reached in to
give her a hand.

"You're not wearing gloves," she said.

He went back to her side of the car, got the Walgreen's bag,
and brought it to the trunk. He squeezed into a pair of surgical
gloves and dug out a couple of the large trash bags. They started
through the pockets of Dean's leather jacket. In a left inside
pocket closed by a metal snap, they found his wallet. The other
pockets were empty. West lay the two trash bags over the body,
and Amber sprayed them. He slammed the trunk shut.

In the car they shed the gloves in another trash bag and rifled
through Dean's wallet. There were seven fifty-dollar bills, a
twenty, three tens, and eight ones. There was a Visa, a Master-
Card, and an American Express Gold Card. A driver's license
with his new address. A St. Mary's College part-time faculty
picture identification card. An ATM card. Amber held it. Her
hand quivered. "There must be five thousand dollars in this account. I'm sure he hasn't changed the PIN."

"Doesn't matter." West took the wallet from her. "Those
things videotape every transaction."

"If we wore something?"

"Forget it."

He picked through the wallet. It was just cards and money. There was no hotel key, no car rental form, no ticket stubs.

"What do you think?" he said.

She took off her gloves and looked out the window at the greasy lot. Her hands were sweaty. "I think he rented a car."

"There were no keys," West insisted.

She sighed, leaned her head back against the seat. "We'd better have another look."

He reached over and touched her with one of his gloved hands, white and rubbery. It made her feel like she was a body in a morgue. She shivered.

"Could they be in the room?" he said. "The keys?"

"No."

"What about the screwdriver? What did you do about his screwdriver?"

"It's in the room somewhere." She opened the door and got out. "It's just a fucking screwdriver, Benjamin. They can't trace it to him."

He got out and looked across the top of the car at her. "All right," he said. "All right. I just want us to be more careful, is all."

"You mean *me*. You just want me to be more careful. You killed him, West. I didn't."

"Not for lack of trying." He marched back and jabbed open the trunk with the key. She stood there, watching. He brushed through the plastic bags and the white sheet. He was wearing gloves and she wasn't. He patted through the pockets again. Nothing.

"Undo his pants," Amber said.

"Christ."

"Hey, you want to be careful, don't you."

Against the hard knees, he undid the pants. There were only a pair of black bikini briefs that looked tight and uncomfortable.

"Check them," she said.

He had been standing back, and now he had to bend in and lift the band of the underwear. His nose was clogged with disinfectant and something that smelled like cooked egg, and he gagged. He made himself look. It was Dean, his penis white and snarled in pubic hair. The summer between high school and college, West had been an orderly, preparing men for surgery. He'd shave their butts and then he'd roll them over, wearing gloves much like these, lather them with Betadine lotion, and shave their balls, all done with a single blade razor. He was famous for never cutting anyone. The men would be embarrassed or aloof or talkative or scared. One guy grew hard in his hand, as he held the penis to get to the growth of hair where the shaft met the testicular sac. He had taken the job because he thought he might become a doctor. He snapped the band of Dean's underwear shut, zipped and buckled the pants. His forehead was beaded with perspiration, and he wiped at it with the bare skin of his arm.

"Now what?" he said.

"The boots."

They were jammed into the near corner, hidden by jeans and various metal protrusions of the trunk. He rolled up a pant leg, the boot a hard black leather with a heavy, shiny silver buckle around the ankle.

"Take one off," she said.

He circled the high shin with one hand, and tugged at the boot with the other. It wouldn't give. He tried undoing the buckle, but it was strictly ornamental. He grunted at it. "It's not coming," he said.

"I can see that." She sighed and went back toward the front of the car, leaving him standing at the open trunk holding Dean's leg. The parking lot swam with the perspiration in his eyes. He wiped angrily at them. His hands sweltered in the close dry fit of the gloves. She returned wearing a fresh pair of gloves. She took the leg from him and jiggled the boot back and forth at the heel. It loosened slowly, giving bit by bit until the ankle of the boot came around the foot. Then he pulled hard. It came off and there was nothing but Dean's foot, without a sock.

"He had a thing about socks," Amber said. "What's in the boot?"

Just inside the top was a narrow little pocket made by a sewn flap of extra leather, that looked like it held a knife or a switchblade. His fingers were too awkward in the gloves to get at it, and he shook the boot out over the lot. Something clattered to the gravel. He picked it up. It was a thick narrow bar of a key chain with HERTZ written on the side, and a pair of keys. He hefted them in a powdery gloved hand, thinking about it.

"Well?" she said.

"These go with us. The boot goes back on his foot." He wiped at his face again with the bare skin of his arm. "I guess we better check the other one." He handed the keys to her and took up Dean's foot. The toes were long, with close-cut nails, and blue veins protruded along the instep. On the sole were dry white patches that flecked when he touched them, and the heel felt like velvet through his glove. He wrestled the boot on, and they started in with removing the second, more difficult to get at because it was attached to the bottom leg. It finally came loose and he quickly sought the inside pocket. There was something but it wouldn't come out. He banged the boot upside down against the bumper of the car. It still wouldn't budge. She took the boot from him and with her narrow fingers worked the contents from the pocket, a tight roll of bills folded into flatness. She undid them: Five one hundreds and six fifties. He whistled at it.

"I was hoping there'd be some money in this," she said, staring at the gravel.

"I guess he was a brat."

She tried to put the money back together, fumbling with it. "It makes me a little sick."

"We don't have to keep it. We could give it away or something."

"Don't patronize me, Benjamin. I know we need it."

He took the boot from her. "You think I like this?" he whispered, starting to angle in with the boot. "You think I like killing somebody and taking his money?" He fought angrily with the foot. "I'm a nice guy." The early morning coffee rose in his throat. He swallowed it back. "I think he's starting to smell again," he said.

She fetched the Lysol and sprayed, carefully holding a gloved hand against West's eyes. He finished with the boot. They covered the body with the sheet and trash bags. He slammed the trunk shut.

They sat in the car, the window down, the traffic on the overpass above them growing heavy. They could hear wind. West could smell himself, ripe with the exertion in the heat. Their used gloves lay in a rubber tangle between them.

"What are we doing?" she said. "We can't just sit here."

West looked at her, tried to make the question flat, neutral. "Should we turn ourselves in?"

She felt around on the seat and found her cigarettes. She lit one and inhaled. She stared at him. She was still wearing sunglasses, and he couldn't see her eyes. "We don't need to be having this conversation," she said. "Just get us out of here, would you?"

He drove from the lot, his ungloved hands slippery on the steering wheel. The door of the glove compartment hung open, but she wasn't looking at anything. She held her knees tight to her chin and smoked her cigarette. He drove toward the city, then picked up the interstate, heading east. To shoot south in the heat, when the Hertz car had to be in the city, wasn't worth the risk.

"Where we going?" she said, not looking at him.

"Across the bridge." He kept his concentration on the road. "And then we might as well head north."

"Whatever." She smoked her cigarette and exhaled out her window. He wanted to ask her for one. The morning was bright and he dropped the visor down. It came unhooked and dangled from the left, letting the sun in his eyes. Slowly she unwound her legs, her feet dropping to the floor mat. She jabbed out her finished cigarette and reached over and hooked the visor into its notch. "I'm all right now," she said tiredly, touching his leg. "Do you want a cigarette?"

"Sure."

They began crossing the bridge, on the lower of two tiers, as if they were driving in a cage. Early sailboats and motorboats slid over the gray water of the bay. Farther out it was blue, to the north. To the south the water seemed brown and polluted and murky with heat.

"You don't think we should have tried looking for his car, do you?" she said. She began going through the maps in the glove compartment.

He squinted at the thought of the two of them scanning hundreds of parked cars over dozens of streets for the right one with the Hertz sticker. It gave him a headache. "Sounds impossible."

She found the California map under the seat and cracked it open over her lap like a newspaper. "I thought so," she said behind the map. "But it's hard to tell with you."

He smoked his cigarette and nodded and smiled. She lowered her map to look at him, then raised it again. "This is very domestic," she said. "You can follow 80 north when you get off the bridge. Maybe it's cooler up there."

As they entered a tunnel he wanted to say that it would be perfect if they found Dean's car, that he was sure they could get away with it then. But they couldn't have gone looking for it with the body, and they wouldn't have found it anyway. Screw the car. But it would have been perfect. They would have driven him down and dumped off the car. He wondered when it was due. He wanted to ask how long she thought he had rented the car for, and when the rental period had begun. Maybe they had less than a week before Dean went missing. Maybe they had only a couple of days, or just a day, or maybe the fucking car was due back at Hertz this afternoon. He came out of the tunnel into the bright heat of the morning.

"What do you think ever happened to that retarded woman?" she said.

"I don't know." He wiped his mouth with his open hand, the smoke of the cigarette stinging his eyes. "I'm sure she's fine."

"You think I fucked up, don't you? I can hear it in your voice."

"I didn't say that."

"You're thinking something, I can hear it. Just tell me, before I scream."

"All right," he said. "All right. I'm thinking about the fucking rental car. You happy?"

"Screw the rental car," she said. "We're going to get away with this. If I didn't think so, I wouldn't have come back this morning."

His head snapped in her direction.

She sucked on her lip. "Fuck."

He stared at her.

"Well," she said. "You thought of leaving too, didn't you?"

"I've got a record." The last of the bridge unraveled into five different exits before him. "I'm not going anywhere."

She pointed at a sign. "Take 80," she said.

He merged into the far left lane, curved slowly into a wide black highway. To the west the bay lapped and dribbled into tall weeds and brown sand, to the east were a series of warehouses and factories and a low range of dusty hills with blackened trees.

"Maybe we can burn him," she said. "I don't think we have the stomach for cutting him up."

"We're just going to bury him." He shifted in the seat, the weather as hot as the Nevada flats. His face cracked with heat, as if sunburned. He took a deep breath. They passed signs for Berkeley. "How much farther until it thins out?"

She studied the map. "I can't tell."

He kept his foot even on the gas, staying just at the speed limit, not letting it drop.

Amber took out the California-Nevada Triple A guidebook from the glove compartment: Attractions Lodgings & Restaurants. In the Points of Interest section was an alphabetical listing of towns with a brief description, population, and altitude. She tried to cross-reference various small-lettered towns on her map with listings in the book. They had to avoid wine country and any place that sounded remotely interesting, but these were all points of interest. When she looked up they were ascending a rise on the interstate and West was pulling over to the shoulder.

"It's been over an hour," he said. "On a grade like this, at least we can see who's coming."

She got out, the interstate filled with station wagons and sports cars. She walked carefully back to the trunk, keeping an eye on the traffic. West waited until she had the cap off the Lysol, then he opened the hood a foot. She reached her arm in and sprayed heavily, quickly, and pulled her arm back out. He slammed the trunk shut. They ran back to their seats and he drove up the shoulder without waiting to see if anyone would let him onto the highway. After a few hundred feet the shoulder crested and they dropped over the other side of the hill. He hit the blinker and they merged.

"That wasn't too bad," he said.

The parking lot of the Napa Valley Mall was a vast field of asphalt baking in the summer, with lampposts glimmering silver and hot from a blur of heat waves and solstitic light. Amber went over the list in her head and hoped they had shopping carts. West pulled up to the Target.

"Hurry," he said.

She dug into her knapsack and found the blue silky scarf, drew it around her head and knotted it at her throat, smiled at him, firmly reset her sunglasses against the bridge of her nose, and pushed her way from the car.

Inside, the air conditioning staggered her and there were no shopping carts. She felt as if she couldn't tell the difference between the shoe department and sporting goods. She followed a wide lane of linoleum that ran the width of the store and found white patio ware and a row of green hosing coiled around giant spools.

In the middle of the aisle a ten-year-old boy hefted a Styrofoam cooler over his head and rubbed it between his palms until it made a squeaking, shrieking sound as if it were a kind of sea mammal. Goose bumps rose along her arms. An older man in baby blue Bermuda shorts and Top-Siders patted the boy on the shoulder. "That's enough, son," he said. Just past them Amber stopped and glanced back. A cooler could be useful, but how? The Colemans had elegant teal wainscoting and rugged white lids. She just wanted to have one in the car with them, to pour a bag of bright clear ice into it and load it with something fresh and cold. A cooler was big and bulky and out of the question.

Near the hoses she found shovels. There were shotguns with arm-length shafts, and large, heavy plows with oversized scoops attached to six-foot wooden poles. She selected two medium-sized ones with relatively light wooden rods and wooden handles at the end coated with cylinders of metal. Together the shovels were heavy and she moved with purpose through the store, corraling the fat neck of a Lysol can and a slick paper box of surgical gloves. At a locked glass case she studied the selection of sunglasses, seeking a pair that were solid and inconspicuous. The circular frames were too John Lennon and everything else ended in sharp pointy corners like the eyes of a Batman mask.

She toted the shovels and the Lysol and the gloves up front to the check-out counters. Long lines ended back in the aisles. People held, set before them, and dragged barbecues; hibachis; softball bats; green and white plaid lawn chairs; inflatable wading pools; bags of coal; sun-brellas; boxed volleyball, tetherball, and badminton sets; an American flag on an aluminum post topped by a golden ball; picnic baskets. She stood between two families, and discreetly invaded the privacy of everyone around her, trying to figure out whether she'd forgotten anything, whether Benjamin needed anything. In the cold blaze of the air conditioning with the heat waiting at the windows everyone seemed sedated, as if they knew what awaited them with the packing and the unpacking and the humidity and the dolefulness and the inevitable dissatisfaction with and deterioration of their acquisitions. By the time she reached the cash register not even the rack of magazines—*Glamour, Mademoiselle, Cosmopolitan, Vogue, People,* all old friends who'd kept her company through menstrual nights and days of influenza—could cheer her. He was waiting out there in the crushing heat of the parking lot, they had each both killed a person, and she had drawn a line between herself and a place—the place of innocence and simplicity, or at least the place of indifferent interaction with humanity—and while it was over-wrought and self-pitying to think of it like this, it was true. She had killed someone. She was complicit in a second death. She was guilty.

In the shade next to the pneumatic complaint of the electric doors, she waited with the shovels and the Lysol and the surgical gloves, while the car circled the parking lot and made its slow, hulking progress to her. She minutely adjusted the sunglasses over her eyes and blinked within their dark green watery walls. She wanted a child, a little girl. The spring of her seventh birthday her mother had thrown her a party in the backyard, with a chocolate cake with white frosting and a big white stuffed bunny and a dozen other little girls from the neighborhood in their pink and white dresses. The old planked picnic table was set with a white cloth and plastic forks and knives, and her mother had combed out Amber's hair into ponytails tied with thin pink ribbons. Over the last ten years since her mother's death some-times this scene would hit her, of the perfect birthday party on an early spring afternoon under a large elm tree, of how hard her mother must have worked to get it just right, and how no one could or would or should ever work that hard for her again, and it would knock the wind out of her. She wanted a little baby girl. She supposed now she didn't deserve her. She'd never have her.

West pulled up, popped on his emergency lights, helped her load the shovels and the Lysol and the surgical gloves into the back seat that already bulged with the spare tire.

"You were in there a while," he said.

"Long lines."

He opened the door to her seat and waited for her to get in, ignoring the waiting traffic. "Is there anything else you think we should get?"

She stared straight ahead through the windshield as she sat on the hot vinyl and shook her head.

He drove them from the crush of the parking lot, all the windows in the car wide open, the lukewarm wind washing through. By the clock tower that rose from the center of the mall it was noon. They passed a McDonald's, the drive-thru jammed with campers and station wagons and sports cars, their windows shut against the heat, the fans of two dozen air conditioners churning in an understated rattle. The odor of the body was there somewhere, under the thin salty aroma of broiled hamburger and fried potatoes, and the tar and gas of heavy cars idling in the noon sun, but she couldn't quite smell it. Soon the smell of egg and sulphur and feet would return, and they'd have to find a place to pull over and spray again.

Up a hill into a neighborhood of new houses glossy with aluminum siding and picture windows, West pulled into the narrow lot of a 7 Eleven. He shut off the engine and looked at her.

"Could you eat something?"

She nodded.

He searched past her for signs of food in the window. "Hot dogs, Slurpees, fruit? What?"

"Anything," she said, her voice garbled and slightly husky, her bare shoulders slumped, and her legs touching at the knees like a girl sitting on a stoop. He plucked up a fifty-dollar bill that was just lying on the seat.

"I'll be right back."

There were Lucite containers full of bagels and breads, the Sunday *New York Times* was already on sale, and in the deli counter were a roast turkey and red potato salad and a thick slab of Boar's Head roast beef and a dozen wheels of imported and domestic cheeses. He ordered a quarter pound of Swiss and a quarter pound of turkey, and while he waited he walked the aisles, gathering a shrink-wrapped box of Pepperidge Farm cookies, the kind his grandmother used to keep in stock, and a crisp bag of unsalted natural potato chips, and a loaf of sliced wheat bread. From the row of glass refrigerators he took two diet Cokes, two regular Cokes, a liter of seltzer, and a six-pack of Amstel Light. He carted it all up to the check-out counter, where an acned clerk stood morosely reading *GQ,* and took a last look around the store. Below the window, set on the floor, were a line of plastic coolers leading to a metal vault filled with bags of ice. He picked up a five-gallon Coleman with crimson trim and a two-gallon bag of ice, and brought them to the register, then went back to the deli to get his order. He was the only customer.

As the clerk rang up each purchase, West loaded it into the cooler, the bag of ice first, the cubes almost blue. When he was finished he sealed the cooler and stacked the chips and the cookies on top. The clerk handed over little plastic squeeze packets of mayonnaise and mustard, and a half-dozen napkins.

"Thirty-two sixty-five," he said.

"Wait a minute." West hurried over to the fruit display against the far wall, and took two navel oranges and a cluster of bananas, worried she would think it all junk food. The clerk sighed and rang up the additional purchases. West squeezed the fruit into the cooler and hefted the entire pile from the counter, heavier than he expected.

Her head was down and she seemed to be looking at something in her lap. He set the cooler on the ground and opened the back door, repositioned the shovels, then wedged the cooler onto the seat. Still, she did not look up. He went around to his side and got in. She turned and glanced at the back. The cooler was already beaded, and the chips and cookies leaned like a trophy on top of it. She started to sob. "Oh God," she said. Tears ran from under her sunglasses and streamed in hairlike lines over her cheeks. She covered her mouth with her hand and looked down at her lap.

"What," he said. "What is it?"

She shook her head, not looking at him, then reached. Her arms folded around his neck and he felt the wingbeats of her heart against his chest. She was soft and damp and he held her as tight as he could, the steering wheel jutting into his hip.

"It's going to be all right," he said. She cried even harder, her sobs hoarsely throbbing. Before he knew it he was trembling with her, holding on, his eyes clenched. He'd killed a person. He was an awful killer. He let out a deep sigh and felt the heat of the day and waited for her, muffled against him. After a moment she pushed away from him and blotted at her eyes under the sunglasses with the shoulders of her T-shirt.

"I'm sorry." She sniffled angrily and looked away, then looked back and smiled embarrassedly at him, her eyes hidden by the dark lenses. "Now what do you want to do?"

He drove them farther up the hill of the neighborhood. Near the top was a baseball diamond, dusty and empty in the heat, out beyond left field on a little slope a stand of cypress trees, their flattened boughs fanned over the white limbs. He parked, brought the cooler out, and set it under the trees. They sat on the grass, dry and hardened by roots. They made sandwiches and ate, and drank the diet Cokes.

After they finished, they loaded the cooler back in the car and sprayed the interior of the trunk. Then West took out the California map and opened it on the hot metal hood. He felt drowsy with food. He nibbled at the cookies. Amber's sunglasses kept slipping down her nose, and she'd push them back up with a fingertip. The baseball field lay empty and sunbaked, and the pitcher's mound smoked with heat.

Down the hill, they filled the car with gas. It was almost two, and over ninety degrees, the station choked with fumes that seemed to find a purchase in the heat. When he paid, the bills came moist from his pocket. She waited in her seat, her hair coming loose from the scarf. As soon as they were back on the road, she unwound the scarf and her hair blew out the window, catching the hot wind.

They followed the weekenders up into Napa. Everyone else had a sun roof and a tapedeck and air conditioning. The radio in the Chevy was either broken or wine country didn't have any music or news. After a while Amber gave up and turned toward the back seat, where she dug from the cooler a handful of slush. They sucked at it and patted the tops of their heads with it, and rivulets of icy water ran down the fronts of their shirts.

Beyond Napa the traffic was stop and go. She opened the bottle of seltzer and they passed it back and forth between them. Cars spilled into and out of massive wineries set off from the road, decked with ivy and sprawling tile roofs and surrounded by terraced gardens. Billboards announced tastings every quarter mile, and West couldn't help thinking that everyone was drunk but them. An old-fashioned train chugged slowly alongside. At its windows people sat at tables with wineglasses and flowers and dinnerware, and smiled out benignly and patronizingly at the stalled traffic. The Chevy appeared to be the only car on the road not from another country, and its moody overweight hulk was like a fat, awkward kid in an elementary-school gym class. Amber shut her eyes against the image, then brought out two bottles of Amstel Light.

"Do we have an opener?" she said.

West shook his head, strands of hair wet against the back of his neck.

A smell gushed forth from the trunk of the car so powerful and suffocating they both caught it at once, as if it had been gathering strength until it was sure it could overwhelm them. They crawled ahead at ten miles per hour in a pool of rotten eggs and old cheese and something like rancid meat. She frantically lit them both cigarettes and they puffed at them, the tobacco a thin veil over the odor.

A road opened off to the right. He bolted down it, as if speed could wash away the smell. Now they were headed the wrong way, but the road was cooler, lined with white-waisted birch trees, the traffic light. He turned the first chance he got onto an even lesser road, then one still more remote, crackling green plant life scraping the sides of the car, the tires pocking over the dirt and stone. He stopped.

Behind and in front of them was a long narrow path with a canopy of greenery and heat. She pushed the door open against a tall wall of weeds and vines. A trail of their own smell led back to the road.

At the trunk he pulled up his shirt and covered his nose and mouth. She looked away, as if keeping watch. He opened the lock, expecting to see the body decomposing.

The layer of untouched green trash bags greeted him. He wasn't wearing gloves.

"I think it just needs a spray," he said, unconvinced.

She looked in, thought about it, stepped back. She slammed the trunk shut, and started down the trail toward the road. "Give me a minute," she said. A few yards away she stepped into the thicket of greenery. He could hear her making water. The air stunk of Dean. West went back to the front seat and found a pair of gloves from the opened box. The Lysol can was a little light. He pulled on the gloves, the sweat of his hands making water marks from the inside, and brought two cans of Lysol back to the trunk.

Her hands on her hips, she looked up and down the path and stood on tiptoe to peer over the weeds and tall grass. They appeared to be on a dividing line between two vineyards. Mounds of dry dirt rested beside last fall's gopher holes. She shook her hair in the heat of the scarf. "You don't suppose we could leave him here?"

For an answer he cracked the trunk, threw back the plastic bags, and began a frenzy of spraying from both cans. When he was finished a mist hung in the air, settling on their bare arms, stinging his sunburn, as he struggled to cover up the body. He shut the trunk. Before she could get in he sprayed the car, exhausting the first can. The mist clung to the metal of the shovels and spattered the open bags of potato chips and cookies. They stood on separate sides of the car, waiting for the air to clear, coughing in it. He squinted his eyes shut and spat a couple times. She could feel sharp pins pricking the lining of her lungs; the air smelled like old garbage doused with perfume. From far off they could hear the thin idle chatter of people tasting wine.

The trail fumed, as West backed them out over the dirt and stone to the asphalt road. She checked the map. They'd agreed on a rift of land near Bolinas, in an undesignated area shaded with green north of Muir Woods. The Lysol made her dizzy. Beside her the muscles of West's arms rippled like small bodies under his skin. He spat out the window and she could feel it coming in the car again. She undid the scarf and breathed into it.

"You all right?"

She nodded.

"I think I know where we're going. You don't need to look at the map."

By nightfall they reached Lagunitas. They could easily get lost in here, the trees in steep gloomy banks, the road dipping and swerving among mountains and hills that hid the Pacific. The sky expressed a bare light, and each road that spilled onto theirs was a dark mouth of asphalt and pine. A group of stork-legged tourists snapped pictures of water past sunset, a cabin with a large sign advertised beer and postcards. He had the distinct sense they were headed in the wrong direction. She'd already made the point several times that if he was searching for the perfect place, he wasn't going to find it.

He wiped his palm against the windshield, stained with specks of cigarette smoke. They were nearing another town, then it'd be a mile and half until the next one. After that were five miles of nothing before suburbia began. The headlights caught the deep trees as the road curved, the ground around the trunks soft and black. He took the curve slowly, thick pines and redwoods as far back as he could see, their branches full with leaves or needles.

"Did you see that?" she said.

"What." He kept driving.

"Back there, on the right. Some kind of road."

"I didn't see anything."

She dislodged her feet from the dashboard and flicked a half-smoked cigarette out the window. "I'm telling you, there was a road. Probably a fire lane. You couldn't even see it."

He sighed. "You sure?"

"Yes."

He pulled over, stopped, waited a moment. The road was dead. He turned around and headed the other way. He couldn't see anything but trees.

"How much farther?"

She shrugged. But it was there, she knew it, out his side of the car, just over his shoulder. She pulled herself next to him. Up ahead, through the trees, the lights of a town shone faintly.

"Slow down," she said.

He dropped to twenty, fifteen, tried not to watch her, not to see the tightness around her shoulders as she looked past him out his window.

"Slower."

He put the car in neutral and kept an eye on the rearview mirror. Through the window he couldn't hear anything but the car, coasting.

"Here," she said.

It was a fire lane as wide as the car, carved out among the trees where they appeared thickest. How the hell had she seen it. He checked the rearview mirror again and the road in front of him. Nothing. He turned onto her road. Branches scraped against the car. Fifteen feet ahead was a bar gate, a red stop sign hooked on it. Beyond it, the lane extended into the woods. He turned off the lights. The car rolled another few feet and then he braked and put it in park.

"Wait here," he whispered.

He got out of the car softly, the interior light blaring for a moment, feeling with the door through his blindness. He traced his way to the front. Through the trees, the sky didn't give much light. At first all he was sure of was the car, and only because he was touching it. Then he could make out the thickest trunks, darker than everything else. The outline of the gate came to him, the circle of the stop sign and the single wing shape of the bar. His feet cracked on dry twigs. He could hear the minute shifting of trees in dry weather, and he could hear her breathing, shallow and consistent, using her mouth as if she weren't getting enough air through her nostrils. The smell. She was avoiding the smell. She caught herself and the sound ceased. Now he saw her; she was leaning slightly out of the window, looking at him. He turned and headed for the gate, stopped. He'd forgotten gloves. He felt for the old pair in his back pocket. He put them on.

At the gate he felt for the latch, the metal cool through the surgical gloves. It jangled and he toyed with its loose jaw, lifted, and the gate moved. He pulled slowly toward the car, the gate wider than the road. The gate cleared the car and he pulled it all the way over to the other side. He got back into the car quickly, shutting his eyes temporarily so that the interior light wouldn't blind him. He eased the car from park to neutral. The tires sagged into the mulch of the lane. He shifted into drive and crossed slowly through the open gate. Beside him Amber groped on the seat, found the box of surgical gloves, and put on a pair. He let the car go forty or fifty feet past the gate. They were in a tunnel of trees, thinner out Amber's side. He took the key from the ignition, holding onto the one that worked the trunk, felt back with his free hand, and found the two shovels lodged against the cooler and the spare tire. He got out of the car quickly and shut the door, opened the back, which didn't activate the interior light, and pulled out the shovels. When he closed the door, he got down on his knees and felt around on the ground to make sure nothing had dropped from the car. Then he took the shovels with him to the trunk.

She was waiting for him. Her gloves glowed against the lid of the trunk, her thumb on the keyhole. He gave her the shovels and opened the trunk. Under the trash bags was a swamp of smell that they could barely breathe through. He pulled at the sheet, unraveling it, limbs thudding softly against the floor of the trunk as he untangled them. Quickly he felt over the body, removing the cracked glasses. He fought the odor, breathing through his teeth. He felt loud.

"You go on in," he whispered. "I can take him myself."

He forced his hands around the body, took hold above the waist, below the ribcage. The head banged against the metal side of the trunk. The feet were stuck. She let go of the shovels and pulled at the neck as he lifted at the waist. Dean hung over the bumper. West worked at the feet, the boots. They appeared to be caught against an interior frame. Finally he got them free. Dean did a slow somersault onto the ground.

"Fuck," West said.

The smell spread like a pool of something spilled, and he pulled at the body, dragging it into the woods. Amber dusted Dean's path with the blade of a shovel. Branches cracked around them. Then she was ahead of West, swinging at the woods with the shovels, her face stung by little cuts and scratches.

The body, dragged over tree roots and grass and moss and weeds and twigs, made a heavy whooshing sound as it gathered bits and pieces into the crevices of its clothing. She held the shovels against her face to block the branches. Occasionally she would stumble, and West would bump into her, and the body would jam into West. It was slow going. When she thought they'd covered about fifty yards, she stopped, and he let the body drop.

Tree roots were dense within the ground, and they had to feel around for a soft patch. Little insects came to life and gnawed at them. As they dug, she swore she could hear things feeding on Dean like termites in wood. She dug faster. Sometimes their shovels met with a loud clang, and they shushed each other. The earth came easily. Before long West was in a pit, while she worked along the top of the walls. When it reached the height of West's waist and appeared as long as Dean, West pushed himself from the grave. The body lay in a low mound a few feet away. He pulled it over to the edge of the pit. Before he could roll it in, she touched him quickly. She got down on her knees beside Dean. West thought she was going to help. She just stared at the body.

"I don't think we need to say anything," West whispered, "if that's what's bugging you."

"No," she said softly. Through the surgical gloves she felt Dean's face, the thick lips, the ridged chin, the groove between his nose and his mouth. She breathed deeply. He was under there somewhere, under the decay, the smell of too many cigarettes and a particular kind of cooking salt and white wine and the curry he liked to work with, maybe a pinch of saffron. His smell. He always thought the saffron was too expensive, but he bought it, and he used it sparingly, showing her just how much. Then there was the faint scent of the bear and the lamb, a furry toy smell, and the smell of their pillows, side by side on the bed, a whiff of his shampoo and conditioner, mint and honey. Leather. French roast coffee. Books. His students' papers. Ink. The curled lime-sweat of his body. "Dean," she said. She pushed him and he rolled once and trembled on the lip of the grave and fell heavily into it, a complaint of metal buckles, the scrape and thud of his bones meeting and settling on the bottom of the grave. She reached around her for the nearest pile of dirt and swept it in on top of him. Then she got up and got her shovel and began heaping the dirt over him.

When they finished they used the backs of their shovels to pound the dirt flat over the grave, to smooth it out across the width of the patch. A few twigs and rocks over the grave worked well. Maybe it was too perfect, maybe they should have tried a less ideal spot. West tamped the shovel once more over the mound. On their way out to the car, they tried to resurrect obstacles of branches and saplings.

When he put the car in reverse, little white lights glowed from the rear bumper, and he could see his way along the fire lane through the gate. He stopped, got out and shut the gate, backed the car carefully from the lane.

They drove along the road for almost a mile, almost to the next town, before they realized they hadn't turned on the headlights. He switched them on, then almost veered off the road.

"What about the shovels? We forgot the shovels."

She nodded to the backseat. "We've got them."

It was just past ten o'clock. If he hurried, if he concentrated, if he got lucky, he'd make it back to the Golden Gate in time for his shift.

"It's done," he said.

"I know."

In his room, while he worked at the lobby desk, she examined the furniture and the wardrobe and the two feet of kitchen for signs of herself. She stood in the doorway of his half bedroom. They would sleep facing each other or turned away, the bed too narrow for them to lie side by side. Or they would spoon. She'd work during the day and he'd be down in the lobby at night, and in the fifteen days left in the month they'd share the bed four times. She sat on the bed. Four times. Would he want to hold her? Would they have dinner first, a few drinks, go to a movie on Dean's money or go out dancing? In L.A., at the places they went, you didn't dance. You listened and stared and glared until you'd drunk enough that it seemed worth the bother to shout above the music. On those four nights would West get up in the morning with her, go down to breakfast with her? Would they have breakfast alone in the apartment, breathing into steaming cups of coffee, eating cereal? He didn't even have a refrigerator. Would he say things like: *I like what you're wearing today;* or *What did you dream last night?;* or *Do you want to meet for lunch?*

They'd sit at the card table on folding chairs and sip instant coffee and not have anything to say except: *Have you seen the paper yet?; Do you think they found him?; What are we going to do about the car?*

She rose from the bed and went into the other room. The phone sat on the little table. She unfolded a chair and picked up the receiver and waited.

"Yes?" West said. "This is the front desk."

"It's me." She shifted herself in the chair and swung her legs up on the table. "What are you doing?"

"What do you think?" West said.

"You're mad at me." She paused for a second, giving him a chance to deny it. She could not even hear his breathing. "Hello?"

"We shouldn't be tying up the line."

"I want you to talk to me," she said.

"When do you think the car was rented," he said.

"I don't know," she snapped. "Why don't you just try to find the damn thing?" She hung up the phone.

It rang almost immediately.

"You're coming around," West said.

She leaned her head back over the chair, the plaster and paint of his ceiling cracked in almost indiscernible lines that ran the length of the room. She felt along the phone cord. "Hold on a minute," she said. She set the phone on the floor and went into the bedroom, where she gathered up the army blanket and the pillow. She came back and lay next to the phone, positioned the pillow under her head and pulled the blanket over her, the room damp and cool, the carpet laced with an industrial cleaner surrendering to mildew. The army blanket was softer than it looked, as if he'd taken it to summer camp with him as a child. In the corner was a sewed name tag. Benjamin West. She wondered if he were ever called Ben. Benny. Benji. She laughed, holding the phone to her.

"What's going on?" West said.

"Your blanket," she said. He was drifting away. She wanted to hear him. "Do you have any brothers or sisters?"

"A sister," he said noncommittally.

"I have a brother." She shut her eyes and saw him, frantic in his law office in New York, the twisted crease of his tie through the too-tight shirt collar. "You're going to make us hunt for that car tomorrow, aren't you?"

"Oh, yes."

"Christ," she said tiredly.

"So what about your brother," he said.

"My brother." She placed him again against the ceiling, a face she'd grown up with, pale, babyish, an imperious nose. He had the back room, above the garage, and his own television set—a big circular picture tube stuck on a wood and plastic pedestal. He liked to tinker with it. He broke his leg once while skiing, he was thirteen and she eleven, and she remembered the bitter adolescent smell of him because he couldn't bathe himself properly for six weeks, the cast extending from his toe to his hip. He'd gone to Harvard. She visited him once. They sat on his floor with several of his friends and ate Oreo cookies and drank milk. They played squash in the basement of one of the dorms. It was December and rainy, dead wet leaves brownishly translucent on the asphalt paths, the tall dark windows of a quad library beaded with moisture. He'd gone to law school there, too, then clerked for a judge, wound up on Wall Street. She hadn't seen him in five years, their father's funeral. He was a full-blown lawyer then and he wanted to settle the estate. They fought. She was just finishing up Santa Fe at the time, sending off résumés to L.A. art galleries and law firms. She let him handle it. Her father was in debt. All she now had from the house were a few things in storage at her brother's brownstone. She supposed she might never see them again. Every time she moved she dropped her brother a card. They used to call one another on birthdays, before their father died, but not anymore.

"I guess that makes sense," West said.

"What?" She couldn't recall exactly what she had been telling him.

"That you and your brother don't talk. I'm not sure my sister and I would if my mother weren't around."

"Oh." She was thinking about a little rocking chair that was at her brother's. They both grew up with it, but the chair was hers, a child's chair, knee-high, made of finished wood, the seat smoothed and hollowed, the back a curve of polished wooden poles descending from an arch. The rockers were worn through the varnish. She'd always imagined her own child in that chair. There was a toy chest, too, which she'd set aside, almost as big as the wardrobe in her room downstairs at the Golden Gate, but horizontal instead of vertical. There was a green furry teddy bear that she kept wearing out and her mother kept restuffing and patching, until it was half its girth, had buttons for eyes, and was a blue corduroy material. She called it Dickie.

"Dickie?" West said.

"I'm going to hang up now." She was three-quarters asleep, and she felt her hand reaching with the phone. The clatter woke her slightly, and she turned into the blanket, so she wouldn't have to think of any of herself exposed. Through her shut eyes the overhead light pulsed. She would have liked to reach over and pick up the phone and ask him to come up and switch it off for her. She smiled and ducked her eyes under the blanket. She hadn't been to L.A. in what seemed like a very long time. There were a couple of stores she wouldn't mind going to, with Dean's money, so that she wouldn't have to feel so underdressed on Union Square. She could get two blouses and a skirt for under two hundred dollars. She wondered how she'd look in stirrup pants. She was evil. She didn't like being evil, but it gave her an edge. "The quills," her mother called it. Her father had them, her brother had them, and she had them; but her mother didn't have them, lecturing her in the kitchen, wagging the wooden spoon coated with spaghetti sauce. "I certainly hope you're not part of that ostracization, young lady." She got up clutching the army blanket, found the light switch, and flicked it off. It was too dark; there were no windows. She turned the light back on and went over to the bathroom and turned that light on, then crossed back and shut off the living-room light. Now it was bearable, although the carpet looked cold. She could not imagine sleeping on it.

Half asleep, she gathered the blanket around her and went out to the elevator. It opened immediately. She stepped on, the door shutting quickly behind her, nearly pinching the cape of her blanket. The elevator descended slowly, each few feet accompanied by a pause and a slow roll under the floor. He'd been in here on the floor between them, wrapped in the soiled white sheet, the material so worn she could see the pinkish paleness of his face through it. She checked the floor. His DNA had to be somewhere, a strand of hair or a fingernail sliver.

The elevator opened onto the lobby and she stepped out into the large darkness around the small glow of the cage. West was staring at her.

"What's up?" he said. "You seemed to be nodding off pretty

good on the phone." He came out from the cage and they sat across from each other in the dark lobby, cold air pressing through the storefront windows. She drew her knees up into the blanket.

"We're not going to get away with it," she said softly.

"Come on," he said. "We're doing the best we can. You've just got to quit talking about it."

"Don't be an asshole," she said. "The point is, we need to close this thing. We do all we absolutely can in the next day or two, and then that's it. We don't do anymore. Because I'm so sick of this thinking. I haven't slept right in thirteen weeks. And I've lost something that I can't ever get back. Do you know what that's like?"

He smoked his cigarette. He did know. It was beyond angst, beyond guilt. It was fucking Ana. It was sitting in prison for six months. It was killing Dean when he didn't have to kill Dean. It was the person on the floor, unconscious, recoverable, that he struck and struck until it was only a body. It was that thing inside you, the thing you grew up with, the idea of yourself, your sense of your own sanity, decency, humanity, that shattered and evaporated, making you less than you had been before.

"Yes," he said, looking at her. "I know what it's like."

She sighed and studied him through her half-open eyes. He smiled. She knew he knew what she was talking about. She smiled back and shut her eyes and listened to her breathing begin to slow. He knew, all right. It was why she liked him.

On their way to the parking lot West made himself examine the bumper of every parked car. There was one Dollar and three Budgets, but no Hertzes. The upholstery of the

Chevy smelled of food left in the cooler, dirt, a patina of Lysol. And Dean. They opened all the windows. West emptied the cooler and sprayed it with Lysol.

The interior of the trunk was a pool of odor that he had to reach through to reset the spare, most of the bolts and washers misplaced. He loaded the shovels in as a wedge, while up front Amber went over a map of San Francisco. He slammed the trunk shut and got in, saw the map.

"Where to first?"

She yawned and pushed her sunglasses up the bridge of her nose. "I need a cup of coffee."

"We'll do a couple blocks. Then we'll get some coffee. All right?"

Parked cars lined the length of the street, the newer models with high rounded trunks and bumpers, a curved sloping style of their tops and sides that made them all look like rental cars. He kept trying to lean over her to get a better look. She didn't see a single rental car.

"I saw four on the way out. Are you sure?"

"Hey." She smiled fakely at him. "I'm not even looking. I'm just tanning the right side of my face."

"They don't all have decals," he said. "Have you been looking at the license plate frame? Or the left rear quarter glass—there's usually a sticker there."

"Shit."

He took the newer cars one at a time, so that she'd have plenty of opportunity to examine their rears. She checked the bumper, the license plate, the quarter glass. In the middle of the block, at a shiny blue trunk, the frame of the license plate had printed on it HERTZ RENTALS AND SALES.

"Here's one," she said. He stopped the car and she opened her door.

"Wear a glove," he said. "Don't touch anything without a glove."

She reached back, pulled on a pair of surgical gloves, and got out from the car slowly, conscious of her hands. It was only eight o'clock and no one was on the sidewalk.

"Don't get in," he said. "Just see if the key works."

The Hertz was a four-door with tinted windows. She could barely see inside. It would be just like him to have tinted windows. She felt in her pocket for a key, positioned it in her hand, and pulled it out and into the keyhole and turned. Nothing. She removed it from the keyhole and tried it the other way up. Nothing. She fumbled with the second key. A stoplight turned down the block and she could feel traffic coming. She gave the second key two quick tries. Nothing twice. She slipped back into the Chevy. "Let's get out of here," she said.

"But the other cars," he said.

"Later. We're being too damn obvious."

In the rearview mirror were two cars, too tired or lazy to bother blowing their horns or changing lanes. "Fuck," he said. He stepped on the gas and lost rubber as the car squealed down the street.

"Easy," she said.

He was three quarters into his first turn when he realized it was one way the wrong way. He veered onto the street again, and at the next intersection found a turn he could make. Halfway up the block he pulled over at a fire hydrant.

"We need a better system," Amber said. "If we knew the make—"

"—They're all the same damn make." He got out, slamming the door after him, went over to her side, and leaned against her door, sweat popping out on his scalp. He felt as if the top of his head were frying.

"Maybe we shouldn't bother," he said.

She looked up at him through her sunglasses and shook her head. "That's not what I'm saying."

"I thought you thought it was a bad idea."

"I just want to get it over with," she said. "That's all."

"You sure?"

"I'm sure."

On Market as they pulled around again, she saw a store with leather garters and a cat-o'-nine-tails and skinhead masks in the window. She got out, went in, and bought herself a pair of black stretch gloves. For the next seven-and-a-half hours she and West worked the streets of the Tenderloin and south of Market. They found eighty-three Hertzes, some with wads of parking tickets flapping from under their windshield wipers, others with pillows or blankets stuffed under the rear windshield as if the car were an abode. Sixty-seven blocks, one hundred and thirty-four lanes of parked cars, eighty-three Hertzes. She kept count on a notepad. She was going to quit at a hundred and fifty.

She eyed the smeared windshield, sighed, and tried to bring herself to say the thing she'd been dreading saying for the last few hours, the thing that seemed inevitable. She sighed again. "I suppose we ought to try some parking garages." Her voice was barely audible.

"I know." West drummed the steering wheel halfheartedly and grimaced at the dashboard coated with cigarette dust.

"We'll just look at a few of the bigger ones, where he'd feel safest spending the night."

"There wasn't," West said slowly, "by chance, a parking ticket stub in his wallet."

She looked at him, her face reddening. But they'd both gone through his wallet. There was no stub. He'd be too afraid of losing it and getting overcharged. "No," she said.

At a large hotel perched atop an underground parking lot, he pulled the car in and took a ticket from the automatic machine at the gate. It was a narrow lot with cars parked three to an aisle, fifteen facing aisles to a floor. Some of the cars were parked head to head, and with their boxy palindromic shapes it was hard to tell whether she was looking at the rear or the front windshields. Several aisles down and one car in on her right she saw a flash of yellow decal quite clearly. "There's one," she said. On the third and last floor she spotted another. But they were both blocking other cars, and she had Dean's key.

"Forget it," she said.

West took the ramps down to the exit. The attendant examined his ticket. "Couldn't find a space?" he said. "I know there's plenty of spaces."

"We changed our minds," West said.

"I still have to charge you a minimum." He slid the ticket through the slot in the register. "Two-fifty."

The next garage had only a single floor, but the fine print on the ticket said to be out by 10 P.M. or leave the car overnight. She saw one Hertz. The attendant was watching them. A good parking lot, but he'd have been shut in at night, or shut out, depending on his plans, and nothing in his wallet or boots or jacket indicated he'd bothered with a hotel. West pulled the car around to the exit. The attendant bent down on Amber's side, his face a few inches from hers. "What's the matter?"

"It just didn't feel right," she said, his face greenish through her sunglasses.

"Uh-hunh." He looked through the car at West. "All right." He waved them out of the lot.

Across from Macy's was a multistory modern garage with a ground-floor deli. She spotted seventeen Hertzes. She wished they had a duplicate of the keys. West parked on the roof. On Amber's lap was a damp piece of paper on which she'd sketched a map of where the cars were. He started to open his door, his shoulders and neck tight.

"I'll go," she said. "It'll be less conspicuous." She kissed him on the cheek.

In her white sneakers and jeans and T-shirt and scarf, she looked pretty conspicuous to him, but she was a woman and at least she didn't look poor. He opened both the back doors and got in and lay down. He yawned. The sky was beginning to pinken. Soon the fog would come in, the air growing cool. She'd left her jacket slung over the front seat, and he pulled it onto himself. When he shut his eyes, he could feel the sky above the car.

He opened them again at the urging of his foot. Amber was shaking it. The sky was gray and thick. He rubbed the dust from his eyes.

"Let's get out of here," she said.

He got himself into the front seat and started the car. She went around shutting the open doors. His vision was fuzzy and he felt cold. "Where to?"

"Union Square."

There was no line at the exit, and the fee was only seventy-five cents. He turned into the street. "Maybe we should give up. I could live with it."

"I don't think so," she said.

The corners were full of panhandlers and street musicians, a few of the shops already closed. At Union Square she made him turn right. In the middle of the block, on the left, was an entrance to a parking garage under the square.

"Yes," she said.

Only two floors, all single-vehicle parking. No elevators, no fresh paint. No camera surveillance. He took a swing around the upper floor. She found seven Hertzes. On the lower floor were two more. He pulled into a space and she got out.

"You want me to go?" he said.

She'd tried every single one of the Hertzes so far, and she wasn't going to let him start now. "It won't take me that long."

She headed for the ramp to the upper floor, passing a row of big-backed cars hunched against a far wall. One of the Hertzes was among them, but she was saving it for the walk back. It caught her eye again; it had something jammed against the inside of the rear windshield, one of those stuffed animals. She stopped. It was a ball of dirty coiled white fur with black ears and hooves. A tiny marble eye stared out at her. A lamb. She went up to the windshield and stared at it, the little black hooves, the distinctive tight curl of the fur, the shy eyes. With her gloved hand, she touched where the lamb pressed against the windshield.

She took a deep breath, glanced around quickly to see if anyone was watching. Only West was, squinting at her as if she'd lost her mind. She reached for the driver side door and tried a key, both ways. She nearly broke it off in the lock. She tried the second key. The lock moved with it, the door clicked. She pulled the handle. The door swung open. She looked back at West. He was getting out of the car. She shook her head. He stopped. She looked into Dean's car. There was a map of San Francisco across the shotgun seat and in the back were a travel blanket and a Thermos and a pair of black sneakers and a gray T-shirt and a hardback novel and a balled-up sleeping bag and the backside of the lamb sticking out from the rear dashboard. The car smelled of cold cigarettes, and underneath the radio the ashtray hung out full with ash. She reached over to the glove compartment, opened it, pulled out the rental contract, and shut it. She shut the door and locked it. She went around to the trunk and tried the other key. The trunk whined open. Books swayed in a stack within an open duffel bag that held underwear and socks. There were a combination-lock leather suitcase and a toolbox and a spare tire. She shut the trunk. The lamb glared at her from behind the rear windshield.

She headed back toward the Chevy, her legs numb, as if they might fold under her. West was beaming at her, and she could feel herself grinning back, her teeth gritty with caffeine and ash, her stomach tight. She straightened her sunglasses self-consciously. She had to look ridiculous. She didn't care. She'd found the car. They'd found the car.

She got into the Chevy with him. They sat there, their doors shut, staring at the wall of the garage. She took off her gloves and reached across the seat for his hand.

"I can't believe it," he said.

L.A.

e could not imagine L.A. He'd been near it only once, when he was six years old, sponge boulders at Universal Studios and getting lost in Disneyland with his sister. They'd sat under a sign at a hospitality office which said LOST PARENTS PLEASE CLAIM YOUR CHILDREN HERE, and he had cried and hated his sister for losing their parents until they finally came, looking full on Disneyland snacks and slightly embarrassed. They had stayed at a campground south of the city, with pit toilets and no showers, near the beach, and he tried to bodysurf, and the first wave knocked him so hard into the ocean floor that he surfaced with eyes full of sand, and had not dared the Pacific since. He knew L.A. only from television shows and the L.A. newspapers that he'd read in prison. He envisioned twenty-lane freeways and treeless streets and carjackings every block and air the color and taste of lead. The Triple A guidebook devoted forty pages to its hotels and sixteen pages to its attractions. L.A. was endless. They wouldn't be able to manage it. Or the Chevy would break down en route and they'd be stuck, having tried so hard to cover their tracks that all they did was make them deeper. But what if he went and dug up the body and drove it down there with them and stuck it somewhere in the city?

Amber had said to forget about the body, to think only about the car and Dean's apartment. You had to narrow it down to close it. If you kept opening it up, you'd never close it. She was right. He could just see trying to dig out the body at the end of his shift, in broad daylight, so he could ferry it down to L.A. It was a matter of timing. He had only one day off from work before the car was due, and he wasn't going to send her out there. So forget the body. An image struck him of returning from the grueling trip to L.A. only to discover a row of police cars patiently awaiting his arrival. Amber had already bought him a pair of driving gloves and plotted the entire course of their trip. She had thought this through. He was impressed and unnerved.

At two he took the tire iron and descended the stairway to the basement, his pockets full of change. He had a chocolate bar and a soda, while taking a halfhearted look around. He could hear the television going behind the locked door of the children's room, and the low voices of people talking. He didn't have the key. If he knocked, would they actually open up to allow him to kick them out? He bought another soda and headed upstairs.

He was asleep at the little desk under the stairs when the phone rang.

"It's your break," Amber said. "Are you coming up or not?"

He headed upstairs. On the second-floor landing she was waiting for him. She opened the fire door to the corridor and there was an old woman with neat white hair, standing in the hall in a bathrobe lined by a fake fur collar, smoking a cigarette and tapping the ash out onto the dirty pink carpeting.

"Mildred?" Amber said. It was the woman who lived next door, who laughed through the walls at nothing in particular.

"Hello, dear," Mildred said mildly. "Who's your friend?"

"The desk clerk. I broke the lamp in my room and I wanted him to have a look."

"Nice to meet you," West said.

"Don't let him report you," Mildred said to Amber. "They'll charge you for it."

"He won't tell anybody," Amber said. She gave West a shy look. "Will you?"

West shook his head.

"You two an item?" Mildred smiled. "That's nice." She flicked off more ash from her cigarette. "Well, I'll leave you to get on with it."

They stood in the hallway for a moment, listening to her moving around inside.

"You think she heard anything?" West hoarsely whispered to Amber.

Amber shrugged and unlocked her door. "Don't worry about it."

Her own room felt cold and stale, like a car that hadn't been started in days. The lamp stuck out from under the wardrobe. He set to work reshaping the metal hoop around the socket. Amber thumbed through her clothes, took several pairs of jeans and shirts and underwear, then her shampoo and toothbrush and deodorant. She handed the clothes to West. He was still examining the room.

"What is it?" she said.

"The screwdriver."

She got down on her knees and checked under the bed. It lay against the far wall. Her arm was too short to reach it and the carpet was full of dust bunnies and hair balls. She got up.

"It's under the bed," she said. "It can wait."

West set the clothes on the bed, got down on his stomach, and crawled partway under the bed. He rose and jammed the screwdriver in his back pocket.

"Ready?" She didn't bother to hide the irritation in her voice.

"Ready."

She opened the door to the hallway for him, and he went out carrying her stack of clothes. Mildred was in the hall again, smoking her cigarette.

"I can't stand the smoke in my room," she said. "You know how it is. The smoke ends up in your hair and you spend all day trying to wash it out."

He kept on toward the landing.

"You're not moving in with him, are you, honey?" Mildred asked when West had passed through the fire door.

Amber shook her head.

"I won't tell anybody," Mildred said.

On her way up to the third floor, trailing West, her face felt hot. She was getting sloppy, she'd been distracted by the trip to L.A. He had only been fussy and nervous. But he was right. Maybe they should try to get the body. Could she go herself? Should she offer to cover for him while he went? The sun would rise around five-thirty. He'd finish by then, if he left now. She should tell him to go. She wanted him to go. He was right.

He was standing in the outer room of his apartment, looking

at her pallet on the floor. "You going to sleep out here?" he said.

"Listen," she said. "If you want to go after the body, you can. I'll cover for you. Maybe you're right. But you have to go now. What do you think?"

He looked at her, unsure of whether she was parodying him. She wasn't. "We'd have to drive it all the way to L.A.."

"So?"

"I don't even know whether I could find the place again." But he could. He could see it quite clearly, off an overgrown fire lane, a niche forty-eight steps into the forest so perfectly bounded by a circle of redwood and pines that it was practically an announcement for a burial spot. The tamped soft earth that he could dig through in a minute.

"Just go," she said to him. "Go now!" She twisted her hair and glared at him. If he'd only just go. "Go!" she said.

He gathered his jacket and the set of driving gloves she'd bought him, and found his car keys and his baseball cap. "Here's the key to the front desk. I'll be back by six, before housekeeping or maintenance. Christ. Why didn't we think of this earlier?"

"Don't answer the phone," he said to her as they hurried down the stairs. "No matter what. It's better that people think I'm busy with something else than that you've taken my place."

"You know where you're going?"

"Yeah," he said grimly. "I know."

Then he was through the door and she was watching him go, the street dark. He waved once, then began to run.

She retreated to a sofa and sat down. He was gone. She tapped out a single cigarette and placed it in her mouth, her lips dry around it, her throat sore, her face still hot. He really needed her.

He needed her to distinguish the fire lane from the trees and to stay in the car while he opened the gate and to lead the way through the brush and branches and to help lever the body back into the trunk. It would be hard in the dark. And then he'd have to back out of the lane, shut the gate, and what about refilling the grave? Would he remember to refill the grave? Did it matter? She looked at the cigarette. He wouldn't want her to smoke in the lobby. She shouldn't smoke. He needed her. Why did she always stay behind while he went out into the dark? She should have just gone. That heavy body, bone, dead weight. He had to go.

Benjamin. It was too nice a name for a killer. Amber had some trash to it. Ambers could wind up where she was, but Benjamins shouldn't. She got up and walked to the door with her unlit cigarette, the lighter jammed into her pocket. He'd bring the car with the body right up to the door again, wouldn't he? Benjamin. She contemplated lighting her cigarette and opening the door every minute or so to exhale. Not subtle. Something had happened to her brain and subtlety had tiptoed away. Why was she the one who had to wait? Was it better to wait or to go? The dark lobby or the dead body in a dark forest? Behind her the phone rang in the reception cage. She glared at it. It kept ringing. She would note the time and when he returned tell him, if anyone asked, to say that he had been on break. The phone continued ringing. She turned to look at the street and saw a face staring in at her from the sidewalk. She screamed. The face ran off the door. The ringing stopped. She ran to the cage and let herself in and switched on all the lobby and exterior lights. Mildew bubbled high on the walls. She lay her hands on the reception counter, the cigarette rolling loose, her hands raw and chapped from having been in gloves all day. She steadied one hand and picked up the cigarette. With her other hand she dug out her lighter and struck it. She lit the cigarette.

Over the Golden Gate Bridge the night was starry and the moon out. To either side the ocean met the bay and an overgrowth of trees dangled from the bluffs, and he thought—out here ought to be good enough. But it wasn't. They'd agreed it wasn't. He came off the bridge and the road curved up the hill and his rearview mirror caught the city, like shiny needles sticking up from a bed of light.

The car clucked uphill, the casing of the transmission had to be slick with oil. They would buy a couple quarts for the trip. Implanted reflectors winked at his headlights and whined against his tires when he changed lanes. The bay rimmed by the lights of Sausalito and Tiburon came into view, reflecting a black, empty sky. For a while, car dealerships mounted the road on either side, as if he were in New Jersey. At 4:12 he reached his exit, took the overpass across and down into a town with yellow flashing stoplights and an AM-PM minimarket and undoubtedly a speed trap hidden behind a grove of trees or a closed gas station. He settled in behind the wheel on the lifeless road, and made himself stay at thirty-five.

The road was not as he remembered it, everything turned around, the lighted signs all pointed the wrong way and on the wrong side and in the reverse order. But it was definitely the right road, at one point serpentine and hilly, now widening and flattening through yet another town, past a darkened high school, the comfortable generic darkness of a road at night in a familiar car. His hands seemed foreign on the steering wheel and he wanted to take the gloves off, but better to leave them on, to get used to them, so as not to forget to wear them when he needed them. He felt behind him for the shovels, groped only air and the vinyl of the back seat, was about to pull over when he realized they were in the trunk. Everything was in the trunk. He didn't have a flashlight, but inside the trunk, hung on a plastic-coated wire, was a tiny pointed light like a refugee from a Christmas tree. He hated Christmas, couldn't bring himself to say the name of Jesus without wincing, in elementary school he had skipped over the word when having to sing songs. It was a Jewish thing, even though he was not particulary religious. He loved the sound of the mourner's Kaddish, the stoic repetitive lyric of it, *Yisgadal, veyis kaddish veyis haseh, veyis halal, veyis haleh.* His father, ashes under a brass nameplate in the cement ground of the cemetery. He'd given West the Chevy a decade ago, bought from a cousin for five hundred dollars. It sank in the short driveway, with its charcoal vinyl top and dull brown body. West had never had a car. Its ride was smooth and his father had covered him on insurance that first year. Then out of college he had landed the plum job at the Institute en route to a Ph.D. *Yisgadal, veyis kaddish veyis haseh* for his Ph.D.

He had never applied to graduate school. He took the tests, mailed away for the crisp forms. He could just not bring himself to fill out and send in the application. It seemed false to him, graduate school, an escape. He did not like the graduate students who served as pre-docs at the Institute, competitive and petty. He could not imagine five or seven years with people like them, and he did not like himself for aspiring to be one of them. He kept his tiny office at the Institute, thinking that eventually he might overcome his hostility to graduate school, half hoping that he could rise above the Ph.D.s without having one himself. After a few years, people stopped asking him about whatever happened to his ambition. When he turned thirty he suffered the cliché of a crisis, and made his girl friend comfort him. No doubt that helped drive her off. He felt he hadn't accomplished anything, that he had been one of those people who was supposed to, that in college, Phi Beta Kappa, high honors, he had earned the right to this supposition. What had happened? Inertia, depression, self-doubt, cynicism? Three weeks short of his father's death, he sat with him one late afternoon in his hospital room overlooking west Philadelphia, the old red brick buildings graying and cracking, shingles sliding off of roofs. His father's voice was hoarse from a second tracheotomy, recently closed as the hospital staff moved to seal him up piece by piece, shutting his case. His father asked him to massage his feet for him—they stuck out from the bottom of the bed sheet like two bricks. West squeezed Keri lotion onto his hands and began rubbing. "That's good," his father rasped. "That's nice." No matter how much lotion West massaged into his father's soles and insteps, they did not seem able to retain it, his toenails yellowed and calcified like teeth encased in plaque. "What are you thinking?" his father said. West shook his head, concentrating on his father's feet. The sun shot through the window and lay across his father's bed. "The sun's nice," his father said. The skin of his feet, under the superficial lotion, was as dry and tough as when West had begun. "Have we bonded?" his father said. "What?" West said. "Have we bonded? You know, the father-son thing. You're the psychology major, and I want to know whether we've bonded." "Sure," West lied. His father looked away and stared at the sun. "How's the car?" he said.

"It's a piece of shit," West said aloud to himself in the car, his voice bouncing back from the windshield. "But it runs."

He was a few miles out now. If he was lucky, he'd make it back by six, the sky already beginning to lighten, a grayness creeping in behind him from the east. Loose gravel pinged as it shot up under the car. The road narrowed, and from either side the head-lights caught what seemed to be sets of eyes. He slowed. They were deer, their ears alert, their snouts tilted at a haughty angle. He wanted to pull over and get out for a minute or two. He could see white chests, tan hides. Some of them had antlers. He didn't know anything about deer. There were forty or fifty of them in his rearview mirror and alongside the car and up the road a few hundred feet. Their eyes took the headlights and then their jaws glanced back as if to avoid being struck. Through his wide open windows he thought he could smell cold fresh fur, glistening nostrils, droppings. Animal. He could kill one of them and stick it in the trunk with Dean to cover the odor. The deer trailed off in his rearview mirror.

He dropped to fifteen miles an hour and picked up the fire lane, the steady lightening of the sky a help. He pulled in, stopped far enough from the gate, and shut off the headlights. He could discern individual branches of trees as if through a gray fog, and he clicked at his headlights again. It was practically dawn. He'd miscalculated the time and arrived at dawn. It was too light. He was fucked. He glanced through the rear windshield and could see the road and across the road and the shallow of trees rising up the hill just as plain as day. The whole goddamned day had crept up on him and was now all around him. He was fucked. Chances were a dairy trucker would spot him from the road as he was lugging Dean to the car and by the time he had him situated in the trunk there'd be a police helicopter clacking in the sky and half a dozen squad cars bearing down on him through the gate. But where was his daring, his ambition? Did he have absolutely no ambition? If there was anything in his life to get ambitious about, it was this.

He swung the gate open, pulled the car through, and stopped. How much farther in had they gone? Trees leaned over the windshield. He eased the car down the fire lane, impossible to see fifty yards in, and it all looked the same. He'd just have to work his way around, look around. They hadn't packed the dirt so hard.

He plowed through the brush, concentrating on counting his fifty steps. Tracks wouldn't matter, once the body was gone, and he *was* taking the body. At fifty he paused and looked around, the trees too tall and summer thick, the redwood wet with morning, the bark of the eucalyptus white like driftwood. Everywhere he looked seemed to be good for a grave. He tried to keep within a certain distance of the fire lane, as he ranged farther from and closer to the road, where sometimes he thought he could hear traffic whirring past, the soft whooshing displacement of air.

About a hundred feet farther in from the road than he'd calculated was a bed of relatively soft dirt situated within a copse of trees. He tested it with his foot, toed into it. He began digging. Daylight lit the woods, sweat ran on his back and under his arms. The dirt came easily, at times filling itself in just as he unloaded yet another shovelful, his hands hot in the gloves. He was digging deeper than he thought he should have to. What if it wasn't even a grave, or what if it was a grave but not the right body? He gave a little scream at the thought.

He was digging systematically, left to right, left to right, when his shovel caught on something. A flap of black leather appeared and was instantly covered with loose grains of dirt. Dean! West dropped to his knees and reached through the dirt to the leather, his gloves filling with dry brown granules. The son of a bitch was heavy. He caught up the shovel, and went to where he thought Dean's head was. H aimed near the neck and struck the shovel through the dirt, then swung hard forward on the handle. Dean's head rose through the dirt, his caked face youthful without glasses, dirt funneling from his nose and mouth. West wedged the shovel against the graveside. He hurdled Dean and positioned himself at his head, reached through the dirt for purchase under Dean's arms, and pulled. Dean hammered him against the head of the grave. He caught his breath, dug his boot toes into either side of the grave, and pushed himself higher with his knees as he pulled at Dean. Something shone hotly on his head and he looked up and was caught by a ray of sun. He gave as hard and as vicious a pull as he could as his toes extended and sprung him from the grave and he fell over the side onto the floor of the forest and Dean fell on top of him.

He caught his breath, Dean's bristly shaved head orange with clay against his face, the smell of him at first indistinct but then growing to the powerful odor that he easily remembered. He rolled out from under Dean and brushed himself off. Piles of red-orange dirt lay all around him, and he kicked at them, trying to guide them into the grave. Sunlight showered everything he wore—his boots, his pants, his shirt, his socks, his jacket—all stained the rust red of deep soil. He began sweeping as much of the dirt as he could into the grave. Dean lay face up on the ground, his scalp orange, his shut eyelids the color of orange juice. West bent and took hold of his legs near the shins and gave a pull, testing the weight. He could not help wishing he'd brought an axe to divide him into more manageable pieces.

He set off with Dean toward the car, Dean heavier than before, loaded up with dirt that bled from his pants and his shirt and his jacket and his leather boots and taking on the twigs and loose brush of the forest floor. West kept moving, backstepping his way toward the fire lane, turning to see if he could spot the car, hunching his shoulders against any possible witness. He came out on the fire lane before he really saw it, the car a glint of brown metal a hundred or two hundred feet away. He practically ran backward with the body along the lane, sunlight slanting through in musty yellow bars, traffic on the road beyond, the soft roll of rubber over pavement. He left Dean behind the car and hauled the tire out, set it by the side of the car. Dean lay curled as if cold, his face dented by shadow. He got down on his knees and forced his arms around Dean's waist and pulled and lifted and heaved, aiming for the trunk. Dean jounced in, his head banging on the hard metal side as he landed on his knees and then settled, one arm loosely thrown out toward West like the gesture of a question. West reached in and unlocked the remaining angle of the knees, folded the head in, the neck tight over the handle of a shovel, the feet jammed below the loose hanging interior light. He went up front, got the Lysol, gave him a spray, covered him with bagging, and slammed the trunk shut.

Back up the fire lane a blue truck with red lettering flapped past. He ran toward the open grave, his hands and arms ahead of him, batting back branches and leaves and needles. He arrived dizzy, the lower left quadrant of his back beginning to spasm. He took up the shovel, kicked at the last loose fallen piles of dirt, and headed for the car.

Now he was done, now he was really finished. He launched the shovel and tire into the back seat. Five minutes past six. He backed the car from the fire lane, stopped, got out, swung shut the gate, felt and heard in the distance oncoming traffic, and spun the car onto the road. As he drove he watched the rearview mirror and saw a tan pickup bearing down on him. He gunned the car. Birds reeled overhead in a haphazard pattern of flight, as if they could smell him.

The door rang again and Amber looked up, hopeful. It was just Tildon, who worked in the kitchen. He sauntered toward her, light on his feet. Ethel would follow in exactly two minutes. It was a thing they did, switching who arrived first but always arriving at exactly the same interval, both their hair wet, as if they thought no one knew they were sleeping together.

"New job, hunh?" Tildon said. "You're one of the team now." He reached through the bars and shook her hand. Ethel entered soon after, carrying a folded pink sweater tight to her chest. She smiled at Amber and kept going. She was terminally shy, a little shorter than Amber, a little chunkier. It was two minutes to seven. Amber unlocked the cage and waited. The front door rang and without looking she let the person in and slid from the cage, leaving it slightly ajar.

"Where is he?" the day desk clerk said. Amber shrugged. "You were at the desk. I saw you."

"Somebody had to let you in," she said, not quite looking at him.

"How long have you been covering for him?" He bustled into the cage and immediately picked up the phone, punched in numbers. She leaned her back against the wall by the elevator and wished she could have a cigarette. "Bob," he said breathlessly. "It's Mike. Your boy's gone AWOL." She knocked her head lightly against the wall. He'd missed change of shift. She wondered how long she should wait for him. God. He was fired. Six dollars an hour and he was fired. He'd slipped off the bottom rung, and he didn't even know it.

"Good morning," Mike was calling out to people coming down for breakfast. "How you doing? Good morning."

The door buzzed, and West pushed his way in, his jacket powdered with dirt. He didn't even see her, as he made his way directly to the cage.

"Benjamin," she said.

"What's been keeping you," Mike said.

"Is Bob here yet?"

"He's on his way."

On the counter in the cage the log book was already open, his name clearly written at the top of an incident report.

"You weren't here for change of shift," Mike said. "That's a gross violation. And Amber was behind the desk—that's another one."

"Mike," Amber said, "I wasn't behind the desk. I just reached in."

"Then he left it unlocked." He turned to West. "Whatever."

"Let's just see what Bob says," West said evenly.

Mike laughed and shook his head. "You prison guys, you think you can get away with anything, that it's some kind of affirmative action deal."

West stood at the counter while Mike wrote, his face reddening all the way to the neck, where it was cut off by a collar and tie. He'd abandoned his post. He was going to lose his job, his shitty job, his shitty apartment. Maybe it was the best thing that could happen to him. Maybe he had aimed too low.

The door rang and he let in Bob, a floppy hat protecting his head, a hand holding a cane he wasn't even using.

"Good morning," he said to a few Vietnam vets who lounged

on a sofa. "How's everybody doing?" They nodded at him and concentrated on a game of gin that they had going.

Bob strode to the cage. "Good morning. Benjamin, could I see you in my office as soon as you get a chance." He held out a hand to Mike, and Mike ripped the incident report neatly from its perforation and handed it through the bars. Bob gave a wave to some more residents on their way to breakfast, and got in the elevator.

West checked to see if he'd left anything of his in the cage. He didn't want to have to return with someone watching over his shoulder to make sure he didn't steal. Amber waited by the cafeteria door, gesturing a cup of coffee at him. He took his time climbing the stairs to the second floor. He'd been to meetings like this before. He was in no particular hurry.

The door to Bob's outer office was thrown open, smoke already beginning to fill it. West passed by the opera souvenirs, trying not to look at Bob until he had to. Then he was in Bob's office and Bob was smiling at him and telling him to sit down and he sat and Bob offered him a cigarette and he took it and Bob smiled at him again as he lit his cigarette for him and he inhaled, the menthol unfamiliarly cool.

"Would you mind shutting the door," Bob said.

West reached back from his chair and caught the door and pushed it shut, feeling a sadness as it swung to; he would have liked to have remained on the other side of it.

"So you've been with us five nights," Bob said, glancing down at the incident report. "And you were missing from your post from at least six until seven-fifteen today?" West nodded. "Mike says here that maybe you got locked out. Let me ask you this." Bob leaned forward and cocked an elbow on his desk. "How long were you not at your post?"

"Since four," West said.

"You were on break between three and four and then you weren't at your post since four? You want to tell me what happened."

"I had to go and get something on my break. I got locked out and didn't come back until I knew someone would be awake."

"I see." Bob inhaled on the cigarette. "What did you go out to get?"

"It's personal," West said.

"You left the cage open."

West nodded.

"Is there anything else you did, in terms of neglecting your work?" West shook his head. Bob studied his cigarette. "Tonight's your night off. Tomorrow, as they say, is another day. Let me ask you an unfortunate question. Would you prefer to be fired by someone you didn't know or would you prefer to be fired by me?"

West took a long inhalation off the cold cigarette. "By you."

"Well, then I'll probably fire you tomorrow. I can't see how I can't, Benjamin. You leave your post for three and a quarter hours, with the cage unlocked. If I don't fire you, someone else will. You know how it works. And I can't exactly cover it up, not only because of the fact that it's already been recorded, but because the possibility clearly exists that worse events could happen with you at the desk. You know what I mean? You've undermined the credibility and authority of the front desk. That can only be reestablished by letting you go." He shook his head. "I like you, Benjamin. I don't know you, but I like you. I could tell you how it was when I got released from prison, but what does one guy's story have to do with another?"

"Nothing," West said. He got up to go.

Bob held up his hand. "I'm not done, Benjamin. I'll tell you what I can do. I won't fire you officially until your next night on the job. That way, you get a couple more nights here, and you can also resign. If you decide to resign," he smiled up at West, "I can let you stay in the apartment a week. If I fire you, you only get one night free."

"I'll think about it." West found the handle to the door, his hand surprisingly shaky. For a moment he couldn't open it, and when he finally did he hurried to get out.

"You can leave it open," Bob called after him mildly.

He was through the outer office and halfway down the stairs when he heard someone saying his name softly, persistently.

"You all right?" Amber said.

He nodded, not quite able to speak. She followed him back up to his apartment. He began gathering his clothes together and throwing them into the trunk. Then he stopped and went to the sink in the two-foot kitchen and scrubbed his hands with dishwasher soap.

"I'm fired," he said. "Fired or resigned."

"I'm sorry." She touched him on his shoulder and he shook out his hands in the sink and reached back and drew her close, pressed his face in and took a series of steadying breaths. She held him. She heard something ticking and looked past his hair at her watch. Almost eight o'clock. She felt guilty but there it was. She eased him from her shoulder. He grabbed for his cap.

"I'm ready," he said.

In Dean's rental car she swung up the on-ramp to the highway with a sense of elation. They were really going.

She was going to L.A. She hadn't expected this, this trip, this sense of adventure. Behind her came West, looking all bottled up within the layers of windshields. She stretched her fingers inside her gloves and stared at the road, as they breezed out of town, past the airport and down the peninsula. On the radio were nothing but newscasts and music shows in foreign languages.

Just a few miles beyond San Jose she felt as if she were in the country, the hills gold and green, livestock mingling in grassy swells. The highway narrowed to just two lanes, and West came alongside her for a moment and waved, then dropped back. The sun was flat on the car hood and even with her sunglasses she squinted and she wished she had bought him a pair. They coasted down the center of a valley between two low mountain ranges, and she imagined the road might have been a river once.

An hour out of San Jose was a sign that said CORRECTIONAL FACILITY, the side of the highway lined by a chain link fence topped by coils of barbed wire and interspersed with low watch-towers. A group of squat buildings huddled in a dust-blown circle. Beyond them was a tall cinder-block structure with barred tiny windows like portholes. West was looking, too. She wondered if they had co-ed correctional facilities, and if there was a difference between correctional facility and prison and penitentiary, if there really existed a distinction between enforcing penitence and providing correction. If she was caught, where would they send her?

Below Salinas the valley floor widened, rows and rows of lettuce and pickers bending in the fields under the noon sun and long trucks pulled up like huge animals to absorb the full crates. Pickups and old cars tilted on the shoulder of the highway, and on a narrow trail through the lettuce a tin-roofed refreshment van waited. Her throat ached and she felt desperately thirsty. She told herself it was an emotional reaction. In her rearview mirror West put on his blinker.

She rose along the off-ramp and took the overpass to a gas station, pulled through to the last pump, and got out. The Chevy came up behind her and West shut off the engine and opened the door. Part of his arm was sunburned and his face flushed with heat. A warm wind blew, carrying fumes of gas and potato chips and beer. She began to feel dizzy in the sudden heat. She started filling the car. Ten feet away West was doing the same, pretending to ignore her. When he finished, he got down on his knees. The transmission was too hot to feel, but oil dripped slowly onto the pavement. When he rose she was looking at him and he shook his head at her. She went into the minimarket. He inhaled deeply and was surprised that he could not smell Dean. He waited a minute, hoping she'd finish inside. The black vinyl hood of the car was so ingrained with dirt it was practically a dark shade of brown. It had been a miserable ride down so far, the hugeness of the scenery making him feel so small, so minute, that his only wish was not to exist. As the car sat in its puddle, the engine emitted pinging and crinkling sounds as if eroding before his eyes.

In the minimarket Amber was examining a long line of glass refrigerators against the far wall. A lame air conditioner rattled behind the cashier's, and the rest room was locked. West bought four quarts of motor oil, a cigarette lighter, and a liter of soda. He wasn't hungry. Amber had a bag of Pepperidge Farm cookies and a shrink-wrapped sandwich and an aluminum foil pouch of potato chips, along with a bottle of Calistoga and two oranges. He wanted to scream at her.

He moved the Chevy from the gas pump to the paltry shade of a baby eucalyptus. When he poured in the oil a little curl of smoke rose and the inside of the car gurgled. If it died on him they could always move Dean and double up to L.A. But maybe he wouldn't go back. Why should he? He could go all the way to Mexico. If she gave him a few hundred dollars he might be able to last until he could get himself a job in Mexico. It sounded so promising, so outrageous, so much like what a convict would think. Maybe he'd do it anyway. He finished with the oil and shut the hood. Amber waited in her car, sipping at her Calistoga, looking at him shyly. What would she think about Mexico? L.A. wasn't two hundred miles from the border, and then he'd be in Baja. He'd have to look at a map. Mexico. He didn't know anything about it. He headed back into the minimarket. He got his own shrink-wrapped ham and cheese and bag of chips and brought them to the cashier, a guy of about his age with mutton chops and a goatee.

"I saw you pouring oil out there," he drawled while he rang up West's purchases.

"Yeah." West nodded.

"How far you going?"

"Pismo Beach."

"Well." He slid West his sandwich and chips. "I've got a tip for you. The lady in the rental car." West started to look. "Don't look," he said. "She's got a thing for you. She was watching you pour that oil as if you were pouring it onto her." He laughed.

"Thanks." West collected his purchases and started for the door.

"Hey," the guy called after him. West turned, his back holding open the door. "What's with the gloves?"

West shrugged. "For doing the oil."

He grinned at him. He seemed to have one tooth that was all silver. "She wears gloves, too."

On the highway he pulled behind Amber and began to unwrap his sandwich in his gloves, staring at them. Why the hell was *he* wearing gloves? It was his car. He yanked the gloves off as he drove down 101 in the glaring noon heat. His hands seemed swollen and flushed. He ate his sandwich greedily and concentrated on the fields of green lettuce, the matching mountain ranges, the other cars, Amber's car. His eyes hurt from the bright sun and his T-shirt was drenched with sweat. He took a swig of his soda. A car shot by on his left, a rich fucker in a sporty foreign convertible with black windows, a chrome tailpipe, translucent exhaust. He was doing eighty, maybe eighty-five. He'd bet the asshole never got a ticket. It was easy to think about how much money his classmates from college were making, and which percentile he was in. He should have just gone to graduate school. But now what? What was there for him? Mexico? He'd get a job at a bar in a beach town and die in abeyance.

Uphill trucks were lumbering and panting, and he stayed behind Amber in the middle lane, eucalyptus and cypress filling a bright green mountainside. After the pass they descended toward the ocean, flat and grayish blue, palms with old fronds up around their coconuts like beards and palms with thin anorectic trunks. The town against the water was mostly a series of gas stations and hotels, but there were bungalows with shingled roofs and larger houses with Spanish tiles and treelined streets that ran down to the shore. He loved the ocean, its limitlessness and depth. Pismo Beach went on for six exits, then the route headed inland. On the flat parched road between Arroyo Grande and Santa Maria, he began to smell Dean again. He flashed his lights at Amber. They got off at Nipomo, drove along a road swirling with dust, and came out on a deserted soccer field with a withered cypress shading a corner of one goal line. In the distance, along a horizon of sagebrush, were a line of trailer homes and a sign for a grocery store. He parked behind Amber and got out, wearing his gloves and carrying the Lysol.

"You want me to do it?" she said.

He shook his head and unlocked the trunk, pulled back the trash bags. She was looking over his shoulder. Dean was face down. The soil had changed the color of his leather jacket to purple. West sprayed thoroughly, then shut the trunk.

"We could switch cars, if you want."

"We're only a couple hours out," he said. "It's no big deal."

They walked around the parked cars, stretching, the sun still fairly high, the heat paralytic. She ran her gloved hands along her arms as if to brush it away.

"You ready?" he said. He was already getting into his car, not even looking at her. The perspiration had partially dried on his shirt, made a crust against his skin. She'd said and he'd known that it was almost five hundred miles, but it seemed longer to be in the middle of it.

There was no on-ramp where they had exited, and they had to follow a parallel road, squeezed between an arid ranch and 101. The road curved suddenly away from the highway. She looked in her rearview mirror at him and raised a hand in question. He pointed to keep going. They rounded the border of the ranch and came upon small houses and large fields and a red barn with a huge hole in its roof, as if a meteor had dropped. The road seemed to be curving back to the northeast. She kept looking at West and he kept nodding his head. At another stop sign there was no hint of 101. She wondered if he were enjoying this obvious failure on her part. It seemed to her that she should head back the way they came, and figure it out from there, but she knew that wasn't right. She took a left. The road dipped and headed through woodland as if it didn't care where it was going and she was thoroughly confused and in the rearview mirror West appeared almost horrified. When the brittle trees and brush had shadows, they seemed to intersect and not lie in any meaningful direction. Her odometer said they'd gone only three miles, weeds tall against the sides of the road and the sun's rays tipping her visor and diffusing across the surface of her sunglasses. Then the sun came around the car and hit her high on the shoulder from the side window. Her front right tire caught a pothole. The road ascended above the brush and she could see across the valley. Directly below her and not a mile away was the highway. She waved at West behind her and he gave a smile back. The road dipped again and in a half mile a sign appeared that said they were a thousand feet from the highway entrance. She adjusted the air conditioning to its coldest level and upped the volume on the radio, even though the music was country.

At Ventura they found a drive-thru fast-food restaurant with three lanes, all five cars deep, a greasy goo of burgers and fries, the sweetness of Coca-Cola syrup. Above West's shoulder was the hum of the highway. He was glad she had stopped. The last bit to L.A. looked desolate and carnivorous to him, the way in the Triple A guidebook it wound through mountains and broadened to a half-dozen lanes. It'd be better at dusk.

After he got his food, he followed Amber out a wide avenue, through a neighborhood of too-green lawns and stunted palm trees, across a set of railroad tracks that bit at his tires, to a gravel lot that hugged the beach. The sand was gray and the water green, and the sun appeared to be sinking quickly. There were no cars for a long way in either direction, and he got out smiling at their isolation.

They picnicked on the beach, halfway between the lot and the water, the sand still sunbaked warm but the air beginning to cool. No one was in the ocean, the nearest people tan specks against the dusty curvature of hills to the north. He ate without words, looking at Amber, wondering what it would be like between them if they didn't have Dean. He kept an eye on the car and tried to imagine it without the body. When he finished he lay back and stared at the enormity of the sky over the water. Sometimes Amber talked and he only half listened, and sometimes he talked and he didn't even bother to follow what he was saying. All he felt was dirty. He sat up and took off his shirt.

"I'm going for a swim," he said. "You want to come?"

"Benjamin." She sighed. "What about the car?"

"I don't care about the fucking car." He sat on his butt, taking off his clothes as if he were a kid.

"Okay." She sat on the sand with him. "All right." She pulled her T-shirt over her head. When she looked up again he was already running toward the water, his butt even paler than the rest of him. She had thought he would wait. She rushed out of the rest of her clothes.

Though the water appeared mild and flat as she hurried toward it, she could not see him. She kicked through it until she was up to her waist, gritting her teeth, the temperature much colder than she'd expected. Then she dove and swam out a few feet, soft swells lapping against her forehead. When she came up for air, he was there, almost hiding behind a swell, alternating between treading water and floating on his back. Sometimes he made little dives, and came up with his hair slicked back and his shoulders squared away from her, as if he'd forgotten about her. She swam over to him. Her lips felt blue and she moved her arms to try to keep herself warm. He saw her and smiled.

"It's freezing," she said.

He dove and came up again, closer to her but not too close. "I know." His teeth were chattering. "I just needed to get clean." His shoulders were twitching with the cold. The northern hills looked glazed with a kind of frost. "Come over here," he said.

"I don't think so."

He made a reach for her and she treaded water backward away from him.

"Come on," he said. "I'm not going to do anything."

"No."

He made what he thought was a playful lunge for her and she reared back against the water, pulling herself with her arms and pushing herself with her feet, and kicked him in the stomach. A sharp pain reached him through the icy numbness of his skin, and he doubled up in the water, his head under, swallowing brine. She'd knocked the wind out of him. He emerged coughing and spitting and shaking his head hard, water flying off his scalp in small pellets. She was already a good distance away, toward the shore, swimming with her head down and her arms taut. He waited, his face hot against the cool air and the cold water. She reached shallow water and jogged to the sand, where she broke into a run toward her clothes. He watched as she pulled on her underwear and jeans and bra and T-shirt. When she was tying her sneakers he made his way in slowly, feeling the water against his shoulders as he swam, feeling her tracking him. He climbed from the water and she was standing at their place on the beach glaring at him. He walked up, embarrassed more by his own nudity than anything else. He got into his underwear and jeans before he would look at her. He had water up his nose and in his ears and his gut still hurt.

"I'm sorry," he said.

"Right."

"You didn't have to kick me so hard."

"How was I supposed to know."

He stretched into his T-shirt. He had a bit of sunburn on his face and he could not help but feel good, crisp, fresh.

"You ready?" he said.

"Just fuck you," she said, and he backed off. "You're a son of a bitch."

He nodded and bowed his head, his ears hot. She was breathing hard.

"You scared me out there," she said quietly. "Do you understand?" She headed off toward the car. When she looked back as she opened the door he was sitting in the sand, picking the crystals from his wet feet. She took a deep breath and let her hands shake, let her whole body shudder itself out. She could really pick them. She massaged her forehead and looked at West pulling on his socks. Lying there in her bed with her mouth full of feces she had heard the absolute stillness of Dean as West continued clubbing him with the tire iron. She covered her mouth and shut her eyes. He was just West. He wasn't anybody terrible. She heard him and looked up. He was wearing gloves again and spraying grimly into the open trunk of the Malibu, and an image of him in the trunk with Dean sailed slowly across her mind. Careful, she told herself. When he glanced over to see if she was watching, she feigned looking at the open map on the seat beside her. He got into his car and gave a quick toot on his horn and she started the Caprice, turned on the headlights, and made a slow half circle in the lot.

Soon they were ascending the long roll of land that separated L.A. from the rest of the world. It was still dusk, endless before the solstice, the highway far wider than it needed to be at this time of day, the traffic bare as it struggled over hills and dipped and climbed again. There were a few bedroom communities planted on the slopes, their lights quaint against the russet and azure spreading of early night. She came to a dark stretch of highway muffled by rhododendrons, and a roadside sign said she'd reached Los Angeles. She had twenty miles until her exit. For the first time in a while she looked in her rearview mirror and there he was, the eerie outline of his baseball cap backlit by the old wide set of his single headlights. The road, under the halogen lamps and the last burst of sunset, was turning steadily orange and she had a vision she was driving on fire. L.A. was her place, and that would make everything easier to handle. She hit a cusp in the highway where downtown came into view, a line of grim ocher glass. She tried to tell in her rearview mirror how he was taking it, but it was too dark.

They lost even more traffic as they neared the city. She took Highland Drive through a break in the rhododendrons and suddenly she was shooting by signs to the Hollywood Bowl and she was in town, the lights glaring at her. She pulled into the first gas station, West trailing behind, keeping his distance, and got out and prepaid and began to fill Dean's car. Already the air stung her eyes, and her throat constricted and felt coated with tiny particles. She finished with the pump, sealed on the cap, and led West from the gas station down Highland, teasing him as she slowly crossed the wide barrage of noise of Santa Monica Boulevard,

making him see the riot of the several thousand façades that lined
it, as if more people lived there than in all of San Francisco.

On a dark street she parked and opened the trunk. West stayed
in his car, as if sensitive to setting his feet on L.A. pavement,
until she gestured impatiently for him. They methodically emptied Dean's things into the back seat of the Malibu. He'd brought
a lot of stuff. It looked like he'd planned on ten days, he'd found
her on the third day. She could just imagine what he had hoped
to accomplish the rest of the week.

She got back into Dean's car with just the map and the full
ashtray for company, a rental car again, a sterile, infallible box.
The air conditioner blasted coldly at her face and neck and under
her arms, and the radio was crowded with a hundred different
stations. There was too much music in her head and she had the
volume way up, not that Noc-Noc Club noise that Dean made
her listen to. She rolled along in her big yellow box on wheels.
She could see Dean's expression when he saw the color waiting for
him in the Hertz garage, the forms all signed, too much of a
hassle to change it. She turned onto Melrose. There was a Cuban
restaurant they'd had a fight in, where they let you bring your
dog and the ceilings were twenty feet high and the floor was a
smooth polished concrete like the inside of a nice garage. They'd
ordered too much food because the waitress had lied about the
size of the tapas, and Dean had wanted to argue about the check
because of the waste and Amber asked him not to and he called
her a coward. There was a used bookstore where Dean liked to
shoplift. Once he got caught at a gourmet supermarket on Beverly taking a frozen eel, and he'd argued with the clerk that it was
part of his culinary education. The clerk had confiscated the eel
but let Dean go. There were a hundred other places they'd been
to and fought in, she always keeping her voice to a whisper and

he mocking her as his voice rose, loud and as hollow as his laugh, and he'd be enjoying the people feigning not to watch but obviously watching them as he railed at her and railed at them watching him.

She passed stores lined with lights as if it were Christmas, and shops that put candles in their windows and used tubes where neon moved like a liquid inside the glass. Farther out were apartment buildings and fuchsia trees planted in squares of red soil, provincial L.A.. She crossed La Cienega and rode up a hill past a cineplex. She pointed out a parking space to West, and waited with her blinkers on. When he came out to her car he was wearing gloves and his cap. He walked over to her side and she got out, the keys still in the ignition and the car buzzing and beeping.

"It's back around the corner," she said. "You can't miss it."

He got in, barely looking at her. He'd seen the yellow and black sign. He shut the door and she tapped the roof of the car and he drove off down the block while she went to wait by the Chevy. There seemed to be trees everywhere, trees and pavement, downtown far away and all around him, as if it existed in one sense and was the orange towering place he'd seen, and did not exist at all in another sense and L.A. was just a massive county-city of a million short buildings and a lot of nice trees.

Taped to the inside of the check-in booth at the Hertz garage was a long explanation for night-drops, which he read twice. He withdrew the contract from the glove compartment and proceeded up the ramp to the second floor. Hertz cars filled all the parking slots and in a corner by the elevators a man in a white cap and white overalls was vacuuming out a blue Taurus. He saw the Caprice and examined it warily, as if concerned for his own safety. He nodded for West to proceed to the far wall, where the line of night-drops sat, freshly discarded, and a metal strongbox glowed on a nearby pillar. West parked the car in the line and got out, clipped the key chain to the inside fold of the contract and dropped it into the box. He walked around the car once, checking for signs of himself or Amber. She'd done her usual thorough job.

On La Cienega, the blocks were incredibly long and the street much wider than any city he'd been in, but beyond the first block there weren't that many people out, and he practically ran. The uphill grade of the road began to increase, and he was short of breath, and at the top of the hill a number of hotels began slowly to come into focus. L.A. at ten o'clock at night appeared to be an all right town, and he felt exhilarated, a number of stores along the avenue still open, their light falling on the sidewalk, their windows full of books, records, baguettes, bottles of wine, beach clothes, Persian rugs. At a liquor store he bought six-packs of beer and soda, and a bottle opener.

On the dark street under the bright night sky the bag was heavier than it ought to be, a warm wind full of fumes blowing in his face. Maybe they should skip Dean's apartment, but he wanted to see it. He laughed softly. He could feel himself wanting to be mean, wanting to be hard, cruel, impervious, in control and out of control. He hadn't even had a drink. How many people wandering around out here were killers? Why didn't he feel released? In Amber's room that night a door had opened and he'd walked through and that was his release. But that was a logic he did not believe.

She was sitting with her legs dangling from the car, smoking another cigarette.

"Everything go all right?"

"Sure." He dumped the bag of cans and bottles between them, and got in, his face sweaty and his hair plastered with perspiration. It had been forty-five minutes between his departure and his return. She lit a cigarette for herself and one for him. Her hand outside the window clutched the groove between the top of the door and the car roof.

She had them park around the block from where she thought Dean's house was. The sounds of television poured from dark open windows. They locked the car and walked without talking, watching the houses. Occasionally the thrum of an air conditioner broke through the grass rustle and creak of insects, and from Melrose came a screech or yelp or howl from someone who was having a good time, and the steady subdued din of a club that had its doors open. Dean's place was the front first floor unit of a two-story fourplex with a white brick base and white wood siding. They walked by it slowly, his entrance to the side, the upstairs neighbors awake with the lights off and the variable bright shadows of television illuminating their walls, both back units dark.

At the car they gathered together everything that wasn't theirs. She paged through each book, awkward wearing the gloves, then felt around in his shirts and socks and finally his underwear, where she found two loose keys. They repacked the duffel, squeezing in everything Dean had kept in the back of the car, working through an odor not like before, but like very old garbage that if let to rot might eventually cease to emit anything noxious. She took the combination-lock suitcase, which was lighter than the duffel, and set it on the sidewalk.

"Give me five minutes," she said. "Then bring the rest of the stuff."

She lit a cigarette, took a few quick hits, and surrendered it to West. She started off around the block.

He got back into the car and smoked the cigarette to add

another layer to the odor. Adjusting the rearview mirror, he followed her as she reached the corner, where a tree got in the way and all he could see were the street and the dark houses. Then he saw her under a full paloverde, touching her hand to the scarf around her hair.

She crossed the street at the fourplex, clearly a better place than they had lived, better neighborhood, larger windows with venetian blinds made out of rice paper. She climbed the four steps to the side entrance, opened the storm door, set down the suitcase, and turned the keys in the separate locks. When the door was open she brought the suitcase in and shut both doors quietly behind her.

A spacious room with high ceilings, the air stale and smelling of ancient cigarette butts. There was a big desk along the far wall, made from a door laid on trestles, and a large, wide bookcase against the near wall. She was standing on a pile of mail, shoved through a slot in the door. She gathered it and stood, listening. Through the high ceiling she could just make out the sound of the upstairs neighbor's television set. She breathed through her mouth loudly, once, as an experiment, the echo of it running through the rooms of the apartment. She carried the suitcase across the floor and set it against the one empty wall, between the two windows. She walked carefully back to the front door and got down on her knees and felt around for any missing pieces of mail, the air hot. She wanted to take off her scarf and sunglasses. When she heard the faint scrape of the storm door opening, she hurried to the door, opened it, put a finger to her lips, and let him in. She shut the door noiselessly behind him and guided him by the elbow into the safe middle of the room, where he set the duffel on the floor. He wanted to tell her that she could probably take off her sunglasses. She gestured to him to wait, and made her way along a narrow hall to a second room with a dining table and chairs. Beyond it to the left was a doorway to a smaller room and to the right the hall continued on. The smaller room, she discovered, was the kitchen, with a double sink and dish-drying rack and a refrigerator and an oven with a four-burner stovetop and glass-fronted cabinets. The air smelled of ground ash. Back through the living room and down the hallway she found a rectangular bathroom and a large, plain square bedroom with a king-sized bed. The bathroom had the smallest window of any room, and on a towel rack she felt a series of thick towels.

She went to the little window, swung it open, draped it heavily with one of the towels, and shut it tightly. She shut the bathroom door behind her, the room darker than it had been before. It took an excruciatingly long time to find the light switch. When she switched it on, she was, despite her sunglasses, blinded. She had to reach out for a wall to keep from falling. She tried to breathe deeply, to steady herself, the air powdery and close. Her lips were dry and she licked at them and they stung. The floor of the bathroom was an art deco mosaic of tiny black and white hexagonal tiles, the walls ivory, the towels on the rack an oceanic blue. In a chest-high armoire were miniature bottles of shampoo and conditioner from a local hotel where he must have stayed between the hospital and moving in, along with additional blue towels and washcloths and a four-pack of toilet paper and a tin of Tiger Balm. Behind the mirror above the stark white sink were two matching jars of Vaseline, a pump bottle of toothpaste, and a set of nail clippers and nail scissors and several boxed bars of expensive facial soap. A blue bathmat was folded crisply over the side of the bathtub, and the tile above the bath was a deep, dark blue. Although there was a shower head there was no curtain. He liked his baths. He liked to smoke cigarettes and sometimes she would come in and soap his back and perhaps even his chest with a large loofa, and he would smoke his cigarette and when she was finished she would get in the tub with him, the water warm through her clothes, and he would have to peel them off her. On the blue tile shelf at the foot of the bath sat a similar sponge and a razor, a dish of orange facial soap, a dish of white soap, a plastic bottle of shampoo, a plastic tube of conditioner, and a pump jar of bath and shower cream that was made in Italy. As a child he had had sensitive skin and had required oatmeal baths, his mother perched on the side of the tub as she soaped him with a cloth.

On the floor beside Amber as she knelt at the tub was the stack of mail she had gathered, and she saw quite clearly the Crane's envelope and the elegant, arrogant embossed return address. She tore it open despite her gloves and read the short note about wanting to help him out this once, as if they didn't share this exchange every month, and the check it partially hid, written in green ink from an unpredictable fountain pen so that she had to squint at it to reassure herself of the quantity. Ten thousand dollars. She lay the check face up on the floor beside her, and patted it still. Below the sink, the plumbing cast an argentiferous glow. Ten thousand dollars. It was too much money for him to leave lying around, and she would have to deposit it. She wondered if it were like all the other checks he had received, that it required no response and would never be acknowledged, not even when his mother had called and he had talked to her in a low sullen voice. She wondered how much was in his savings account. He was an only child, but he suspected that his father would eventually cut him off completely, even through his mother, and he was saving in the face of it. When Amber had lived with Dean he'd been receiving only two thousand a month, to subsidize his seventeen-thousand-a-year teaching salary, and she knew he had about thirty thousand in his savings account and he'd been thinking of opening a more sophisticated account with a broker and investing a portion of the money, but he didn't like to talk about it and they weren't married and she stayed out of it. On principle he had never paid for her for anything; they either split the bills or alternated. She did not resent it—that was the way it had been with Josh and David, too. But they had worked for their money.

She used the scissors to open the rest of the envelopes cleanly. He had a large MasterCard bill, for all the new toiletries around her and for a dining-room set and a computer and printer, several dinners out and a number of new books. The bill wasn't due for another two weeks. The rental car had been charged on his family's American Express Gold Card; his mother would be paying it directly. It was easy to remember the rhythm of the months with him, the Visa bill arriving early and the MasterCard in the middle and the P.G.&E. and PacBell near the end. His rent wasn't due for another two weeks. Her arms felt tired from dealing with the slips of paper, and her legs stuck out asleep in front of her. There was an invitation to a gallery opening on Caribbean art and an announcement of a poetry reading and a letter from someone he knew in Santa Barbara, where he had grown up and gone to college, the writing so cramped she couldn't even tell the sex of it. The faculty newsletter from St. Mary's College had an item on him. His own book of poems was being published by a local press of national stature, and the introduction was being written by one of the foremost language poets. A letter from the publisher came in another envelope, with a check for five hundred dollars against royalties and a note saying he hoped Dean was fully recovered. There was a postcard from a student vacationing on

Bali, saying that Dean had changed her life and she was terribly grateful. A booklet of coupons offered deals at Jack in the Box and Kentucky Fried Chicken and Payless Drugs. A flimsy envelope contained just an old photograph of a little girl in a plaid dress with a note on the back: "Here she is at three. I wanted you to have it," with no signature. Amber turned the photo around again: the little girl, her reddish brown hair parted to one side, had a chubby round face with a smile lacking teeth, and she was holding a big leaf up to the camera, a leaf—because of the angle of the picture—that seemed almost larger than her head, and she wore a white blouse under the red and green plaid dress and her knees had faint patches of color as if she had recently crawled, chasing down that leaf. For some reason there were no trees around her—she was standing alone in an alley lined by brown brick buildings that ended in white daylight behind her. Amber put the picture back into the envelope and lay it delicately on the floor beside the check. Andrea at three.

The door to the hallway opened and West came in, his eyes clenching against the light, and shut the door quickly behind him. He took a seat next to the sink, at a diagonal from her, and held his gloved hands to his eyes. A few envelopes lay unexamined. Should she bother? She felt exhausted, the small of her back in a dull pain against the side of the tub, her legs numb. She pointed her toes and stretched her legs until her knees locked, then bent them and stretched them again. She picked up a fresh envelope. West finally took his hands away.

"It's getting late," he whispered.

She scissored off the end of a number ten envelope and dug out a typed letter from a New York friend of Dean's whom she'd met briefly. The guy was offering a rambling mixture of praise and criticism for Dean's "manuscript." She dropped the letter on the floor.

"Anything good?"

"A ten thousand dollar check," she said softly, as she cut off the end of another envelope. "A MasterCard bill. A picture of the woman I killed when she was three."

He reached out and tapped the watch on her wrist. He was right. It was late. She didn't care. The latest envelope held a form letter from someone offering to be Dean's broker for any of his larger acquisitions—"From cars to condos. From televisions to vacation packages." She shook West's hand from her wrist, and reached for the last envelope. It was clearly another credit card offer, but she opened it anyway. Guaranteed preapproval. West turned off the lights. Again it felt hot and close in the bathroom. He opened the door and the less-stale air of the apartment drifted in. She wrenched open the bathroom window and removed the towel, then shut it tightly.

In the kitchen she dumped the junk mail into the garbage, then navigated her way to the living room. His duffel and suitcase looked like rocks jutting up from the hardwood floor. Under the desk of the door on trestles she could see a two-drawer metal filing cabinet.

"What do you want me to do with his bags?" West whispered.

She shook her head for him to shut up.

She slid the top file drawer open, its plastic wheels making a low rolling sound in their metal tracks. Inside were a few hanging files. The thought of taking them back to the bathroom made her legs numb. It was past one o'clock. She'd have to call in sick a third straight day. That would probably be it for her. She emptied the top file drawer, then the bottom file drawer. Behind her

West began to follow, and she turned and stopped. He was a shadow against all the other shadows in the apartment.

"Just wait here," she said, the mild tone of her voice surprising her.

He sat on the floor by the suitcase and the duffel bag and listened as she worked on setting up the bathroom. After a while the door shut. He got up, slung the duffel over one shoulder, and took up the suitcase. He bumped softly along the hallway to the bedroom. He lay the duffel and the suitcase side by side on the bed, then backtracked toward the kitchen, where he found a can opener in one of the drawers. In the bedroom he cracked open the combination-lock suitcase, and unzipped the duffel. The dresser against the near wall smelled of wood and varnish. The underwear, as he removed them from the duffel, shone in a variety of colors through the dark. He put them in their drawer in the dresser, stacked the books by the side of the bed, and started in on the suitcase. In a closet he hung and set the clothes where he assumed they ought to go. Still, something did not feel right. He sat on the end of the crisp bedspread, folded up the duffel, and closed the suitcase which now would not shut. He hauled the suitcase and the duffel over to the closet, and set them on the floor so that the duffel draped the suitcase. He knew what was bothering him. Almost everything was brand new. That made sense.

He left the bedroom and paused by the crack of light at the bathroom door.

"You finished?" he whispered.

"Go on out," she said through the door. "I'll meet you at the car."

He hesitated. He felt an urge to take a memento, a book

perhaps. She wouldn't like that. At the door he paused again, thinking she might come out from the bathroom. He slipped out onto the landing.

She listened for a moment, then took a deep breath. She could still smell the fire from his files, and in her hand was the curled newsprint of the tiny article Dean had carefully extracted from the *Times* about the explosion. He had let it slide as a tenant error. He'd wanted to settle it between them and now she imagined that they had. She'd read parts of his manuscript. He was moving away from the I in his last poems, but he still saw himself as a kind of Christ. Some of the new poems were about colonialism in Africa, and although they were probably derivative, she could not help but like them. There was a thin file on her, too—VISTA application guidelines, VISTA sites in northern California, the phone numbers and addresses of her brother in New York and her former boss at the L.A. law firm—and these she now confiscated. A file on St. Mary's College had a letter of reappointment for the fall term with a small raise, and a letter of condolence from the Department Chair with a copy of a direct-deposited check, a donation from all the faculty to him. A memorial scholarship was being set up in Andrea's name, and the department faculty had already made a similar donation to it. There was a file on his health insurance and medical claims information, a file on the receipts for all the new furniture and equipment he had bought, and a file on his finances. He had thirty-two thousand dollars in a brokered account at an investment bank, and twenty-seven thousand in a savings account at his regular bank. He had five thousand dollars in checking. One file indicated that discussions on cover art for his book would occur in the near future. She could see the cover bearing just his face, that haunted skeletal quality, heavy on shadow. Several pictures of him had hung framed on the walls of his old apartment, Dean looking into the far distance and not liking what he was seeing, Dean bare-chested with belted jeans clinging to his scrawny waist, Dean with his head in his hands, when he had his hair, the thinker agonist. She had the checks and bills she needed and the deposit slip, had already made them all out and forged his signature and addressed the envelopes. She stretched her legs and went out to review the bedroom.

She smoothed the made bed, and ran her gloved hand across the top of the dresser. She opened the closet and saw the duffel. Under the duffel was the jimmied-open suitcase. She reached in and brought it out and set it on the bed. She opened and closed all the drawers in the dresser. Here, he'd done well. She tried to jam the suitcase together. He might as well have slit the sides open with a serrated knife. She got up from the bed and lifted the suitcase, then smoothed out the spread. A damn suitcase. She toted it from the bedroom, along the hall, past the dark bathroom, the dining room with the new table and chairs, to the living room. Eventually he would have bought a sofa and a coffee table, a glass one with a greenish copper frame, and he would have set fat candleholders on it with candles in luminous colors, and he would have bought a stereo system and had a few vases. He liked flowers with large heads and huge petals, gerbera daisies and sunflowers and Easter lilies with their white trumpets. He would have added an overstuffed chair and an ottoman, and moved the desk into the bedroom. Or maybe he would have kept the apartment barren, to mirror his new skinhead look. The desk was his claim as a starving artist. She opened the door out and pushed at the screen door gently as it scraped over the cement landing. She reached through and set the suitcase on the landing, then took the keys with her damp gloves and turned them in the

locks. She gathered the suitcase and hurried down the stairs to
the driveway, the night so much brighter than his apartment. She
crossed quickly to the opposite sidewalk, glancing at the upstairs
window above Dean's, dark enough for her to conclude that the
television was no longer on.

The Chevy seemed shut and empty for the night. She got in
the passenger side, shoving the suitcase in ahead of her. He
looked up from a sip of his beer.

"It's been almost a half hour," he said.

She positioned the suitcase between them. "You should have
told me that you broke it."

He sighed and leaned his head over the seat back, rubbed one
gloved hand over his face. He placed the beer between his legs,
and started the car without looking at her. With an effort he
remembered to turn on the headlights. The beer was warm and
he sipped at it in the dark spaces between streetlamps, his shoulders tired. They passed Dean's house. She still had on her sunglasses and scarf. When he dropped her at a supermarket on La
Cienega, he said, "You look like a terrorist."

She hurried into the store. Soon it would be three, then four,
and they'd have a daylight burial on their hands. After a few
minutes she came out with a thin plastic bag. In the car beside
him she licked the stamps and pressed them onto their separate
envelopes, and he drove toward the hills until she saw a mailbox.
She got out, dumped the envelopes into the slot, and set the
suitcase by the box. When she returned she was smiling.

At three-fifteen they passed near the Hollywood Bowl and
drove under 101. Out the other side were low hills with a hairline
of condominium blocks and apartment houses. A grove of trees
perched on the rim of a reservoir, the white dome of an observa-
tory shone in the distance, a large cemetery sprawled below. The

amalgamation of Universal City bled orange to the west. Up beyond the Hollywood sign grew wild brush on softer dirt. Everyone went up there. Along all the freeways were areas of overgrown weeds and tall burned stalks. "Pull over for a minute," she told West. He stopped in front of a McDonald's.

"I'm a little lost as to where to put him," she said.

"Take your time." He opened another beer, handed it to her, then opened one for himself. Through the large glass window of the McDonald's a skinny white guy running an electric brush mop was looking out at them. West made a careful legal U-turn. At 101 he got on the northbound ramp. After he merged he took a long swallow of beer.

"I remember coming in," he said. "There were places."

She nodded and sipped at her beer, too warm but she made herself. She lit a cigarette and handed it to him, lit another and inhaled deeply. Let him handle it.

They drove out 101, the lights of near and far places receding in the wake of the car. Dean was back there, where the wake began, in the trunk. She'd see him again. She didn't want to; she'd buried him once and stood in his apartment and gone through his files and examined the childhood photograph of his new girl friend. They were leaving L.A. For what? She was going to slip off the last rung, too, the six-dollar-an-hour shit-work rung. She imagined calling her brother and asking if she could come stay with him. He'd say yes. The plane ride east, being met or not met at the airport, crossing the hearth of his brownstone, the cold mechanical welcome inside, a hint of warmth but essentially distant and strange, as if they hadn't even grown up together. She didn't want to go back. She didn't want to live in the Golden Gate either.

"Fuck!" he said suddenly.

"What?" The beer had spilled in her lap. "What is it?"

He nodded at the rearview mirror. She leaned into him and looked. She could see the wide square headlights set in a shadowy oversized grill, the black shining hood and the encased blank siren of a police cruiser, tailing them at twenty yards.

West took the first possible exit, the asphalt under the tires broken in jagged pieces. Midway down the ramp he met a pot-hole that seemed to shake the engine loose. Quickly he took a right. Under yellow streetlamps were old hushed row houses, the fence of one yard topped with a paste of glittering broken bottles, another home left gaping at the bulldozed wreckage of its missing twin. He needed another turn. As he took it, heading still farther from the highway, the cruiser almost disinterestedly turned onto the block he had just departed. West coached himself from accelerating.

"Floor it," Amber said. "He can't see you."

"He's got radar, for Christ's sake. He can see whatever he wants."

They were on another street of a grid of streets that spanned a pocked neighborhood, long blocks of infrequent houses and dark vacant lots. By the time he found an intersection, the cruiser had already picked him up again, and there were no buildings as he turned. He felt vulnerable and obvious driving along the bare street. When Amber looked out nonchalantly, the cruiser was coming down the street perpendicular and the turn indicator was already winking at her, the steady combined movement of the car and its lights official and yet bored. Abandoned tires and other car parts lay on the gray sidewalks. An emaciated dog circled itself in the opposite lane, its bared yellow teeth nipping at the empty night. They were going twenty-five and the cop, now having followed again onto their street, was also going twenty-five and was, she estimated, only a half block or so away, the distance minimized by the flat, open landscape so that he might as well have been tailgating.

Up ahead the street rose and dipped, and West accelerated slightly. When the street leveled there was nothing but the rumpled flatness of buckled pavement and unpaved lots stretching out to a dark horizon.

"You all right?" West said. She nodded. Her head was extraordinarily hot in the scarf and all she wanted was to take it off. She took it off. She took her sunglasses off, too. Her eyes stung from fatigue and she sniffled as if she had been crying. She hadn't. West eased off the gas and readied himself for the right turn in about a quarter of a block that he could already see and that would head them back toward the highway. In the rearview mirror the cruiser effortlessly began to close. "Do we have a story?" West said.

"Maybe he won't smell it," Amber said. "Maybe his mind will freeze up and he won't notice anything obvious."

West shook his head slowly. The cruiser picked up speed and was coming on hard, wasn't even thirty feet back. It flashed its headlights at West as it kept coming, and he began to brake and pull over. The cop tooted his horn and brushed by him, taillights on, still accelerating, the rear of the cruiser wagging as it picked up speed. West was stopped by the side of the street.

"Weird," he said aloud.

"I guess he was just fucking with us," Amber said.

Exhaust kicked up around the cruiser, and by the time it had vanished behind a line of houses the smoke hung like fog along the street. West turned and started back the way they had come. Wearily Amber put on her scarf and sunglasses.

As they reentered the freeway the sky was steadily suffusing with light, the halogen road lamps growing dim. Grayish-orange flashes of other cars passed. From the trunk a fetidness spread.

"Any ideas," West said.

It was her fault. They shouldn't have had to bury him twice. She hadn't thought it through. She'd been spontaneous. She shut her eyes and felt the darkness and the vague yellow beams of oncoming cars.

"We could stay another night," he said.

"After what just happened." She paused for words. "We'd still be down here with him."

West watched the sky, again checked the rearview mirror, the various sets of headlights behind him, the fading purplish glow of Los Angeles. All around him was the rhododendron life that hugged the freeway and beyond that the lighted streets and parks of L.A. He took the next exit, and came down onto a six-lane road.

"It's Van Nuys," Amber said mechanically. "I used to live here."

"And?" West said. "Come on! It's four fucking thirty."

She waved her hand. "There are dumpsters."

He U-turned and crossed back under the freeway. "And here," he said.

"I don't know." She rolled down her window. They were suddenly in the hills, the air fresh. "I didn't have a car." Ahead were the bald backs of the Santa Monica Mountains, the road wide but sparsely lighted. Frazzled strands of wild brush approached and waved at the car. "This could work," she said.

Farther into the hills he took a right off the boulevard and then a left, to darker shadows of lean trees and the prickly shapes of pruned bushes. A deer loped in what appeared to be a meadow tall with overgrown grass. He stopped the car, shut off the lights, and they got out, the road perfectly paved and the shapes of massive houses partially hidden by old trees and stone walls distinct against the lighter shade of the hills. A goddamned suburb. They crossed the street, waded through the tall grass, and came out onto a little playground with a woodframe jungle gym and a split-oak seesaw and a large sandbox with a lacquered wood retaining wall. Paths of cedar chips ran between the various amusements. They saw the deer over by the swings and the deer saw them and faded cautiously from sight. Out the other side of the playground were discreet houses, the kind of neighborhood where no one left any lights on because they employed more sophisticated means of security.

At the car he gave her the shovels and she set them on the grass border of the sidewalk. He swept away the plastic bagging and got Dean by the shoulders and she took the knees and they pulled him out as quietly as possible and hurried him across to the playground, where they rested him by the sandbox. West went back for the shovels while she stayed with Dean. One day a child would dig too deeply past the sand. She would have liked to have felt something for the body at her feet. She bent down to touch his face through her glove. It felt crookedly set in his skull and she stood quickly and noticed that her tongue was impatiently clicking against her teeth.

West brought the shovels. The sandbox was a bit larger than her room at the Golden Gate. He started backhanding powdery mounds. As she dug, she worried that the bottom of the box would be closed instead of opening into the earth. He brought out the first shovelful of dirt and heaved it past the wall, careful to release just beyond the wood partition. When he dug in again, he headed the plot toward the wall. She worked quickly to clear the remaining sand. He dug now with soft half-swallowed grunts, his breathing loud through his nose. The dirt began to feel very heavy, damp, and it fell in clots from their shovels beyond the wall and he wondered if they were going to hit a waterline or a sprinkler system. By the time they were in it up to their hips he could feel his sneakers soaking with water. It was maybe two and a half feet deep, maybe three. The sky was the color of ash. He climbed from the grave and helped her out.

It was so light they could see the partially hidden gables and roofs and antennae of the obscured houses around the park. They hoisted Dean between them, his face the color of the sky and his clothes crusty with old dirt. They stepped over the sandbox wall and set him by the head of the grave. They each took hold of a wrist and dragged the body headfirst into the opening and along it until it lay fully on the floor of the plot and they were both on their knees. West released a wrist first. Amber held on, Dean's arm stretched along the wall of the plot. She let go and the hand fell against his thigh and was still. His head had fallen back so that his throat was exposed. West lay the first shovelful of dirt over him, trying to work quietly, and then a second and a third so that the air between Dean and the floor began to fill, and then West gave up trying to be quiet, the light of the day accelerating. Soon the plot was filled to Dean's temple and his ears were covered and he looked as if he were floating. She got up from her knees and got her shovel. In another few minutes he was covered except for his boot toes. The white sand within the box had swirls of dark dirt through it, and there was dirt all over the green lawn. They filled the rest of the grave, stood on it, and used the backs of their shovels to pack it. They added a little more dirt, trying to make it level, then retreated to their respective piles of sand and released them over the plot. A large section of sand was coffee-colored, and they had to resift it. West scraped the blade of the shovel over the grass and respread the cedar along the trail.

They came out from the tall grass onto the street. The trunk of the car was open and from an invisible house they could hear classical music playing. He stored the shovels under the sharp light bulb and pressed the hood shut. In the car they shucked their gloves and he made a three-point turn and drove back down the hill. It was just before six when the car merged onto the smooth wide surface of the freeway, the sky white. Wearily Amber pulled on her gloves again, reached into the supermarket bag for the scissors, and began to cut up the credit cards and bank cards. By the next exit she was finished. She opened her window as they drove out 101 and released fistful after fistful of plastic confetti into the roaring air.

"You drive," he said.

embarcadero

By Santa Barbara he was asleep. She took the exit marked TOWN CENTER, the ocean disappearing behind her. The street came up lined with supple palm trees and park benches and frontier-style lampposts, brick sidewalks. She climbed from the car into a sea-breeze-cool morning, loaded the meter, and went around to West's side, where his elbow poked out of the window and his head lay back against the top of the seat and his other arm rested lazily in his lap. She didn't want to wake him but maybe leaving him asleep like this was like leaving an animal in the car. She nudged West's elbow. His eyelids fluttered and he curled away from her touch. She squeezed his upper arm and he gave out a whimper.

"Honey," she said. "Honey, come on. Wake up."

He stared at the dashboard as its features sharpened—the dusty radio with its wide orange needle, the blackened teeth of the broken air-conditioning vent, the shut glove compartment with its puckered release button. At his window her arms were folded and her chest leaned in. He rubbed his eyes.

"Where are we?"

"Santa Barbara." She paused to see how he was taking it. He wasn't yet fully awake. "We need to stop for about an hour. I was hoping you'd come with me."

"What?" he said.

"I need some things." She opened the door and pulled at his arm. "Let's go."

He swung his legs out. The edges of his vision seemed fuzzy, as if parts of his eyes were still asleep. He pushed himself from the car. A line of tall, dark-windowed storefronts met him. "You've got to be kidding," he said.

She was already on the sidewalk and heading to a place whose last name was Salon.

"Amber!"

She gave him a little wave and the door shut after her in a hydraulic hush. In the store window his image shimmered, heat beginning to melt the breeze along the sidewalk. He pulled open the salon door to an air conditioning so subtle it felt as if he were still outside but had somehow moved closer to the ocean. She was standing with her back to him, across several arrangements of pale clothes, paging through a rack of skirts.

"I'm just going to get a skirt," she said without looking at him. "And a summer sweater. There's a shoe store down the street and I might have to look there, too."

He smelled himself in the air conditioning and was embarrassed. A saleswoman kept an eye on them from a brass tree hung with linen suits.

"Are you going to help me," Amber said to him. She was

holding up a black skirt in one hand and a khaki skirt in the other.

He shook his head at her. "Black."

"With a white top," she said, "or celery green?" She started behind him to a glossy oak credenza piled with folded cotton sweaters.

"White."

She rehung the khaki skirt and took up both sweaters. The saleswoman appeared at her side. "Would you like to try these on?"

"Please."

Amber followed her through the store to the dressing rooms, cabanas around a pool of carpeting.

"Should I get your friend?" the saleswoman said. She wore a twin set the color of weak tea, and trousers with a dulled plaid pattern. Amber locked herself into the dressing room. For the first time she looked at the price tags, the sweaters each ninety and the skirt two-twenty. She took off the sunglasses, then the scarf. Her hair seemed flat and brittle. The green ribbed summer sweater worked better with the skirt, a long swirl of thin jersey with a fitted waist, but the neck was lower than she'd expected. It was still nicer than anything she owned. She got back into her old clothes and put on the scarf and the sunglasses. When she opened the dressing-room door, the saleswoman was waiting for her.

"I'll take these," she said, handing over the skirt and the green sweater.

The saleswoman tried to swallow her look of surprise, but Amber saw the way her eyes had started back in her head and her frozen smile cracked. It made her sad.

At the register she paid in cash. The saleswoman ran the four $100 bills under a hairlike laser of light next to the register.

"Well, thank you," she finally said, giving up a large paper bag with a wooden handle.

"Thank you," Amber said. She looked quickly around the store for West, but he wasn't there. On the sidewalk it was already unpleasantly warm. He was not in the car, either. At least she had the keys. Over forty minutes remained on the meter. She leaned against the front of the car, the sunbaked hood hot through her jeans, the town feeling like a suburb to someplace else, snobbish yet parasitic. Atop the high hills perched little fortresses, and pine and eucalyptus trees covered the slopes down to the coast. A helicopter spun over the ocean, its bubble opalescing in the sun. A brilliant purple fuschia tree browned before her eyes, the petals curling. She was thirsty. In a café, large transparent juice dispensers lined a long counter, and bread and croissants lay tilted in tiers of display. West sat at a corner table, sipping a beer. She bought herself a pineapple orange juice and led her awkward bag of clothing over to him.

"What'd you get?" he said.

She sipped at her juice. He'd managed to buffer himself with several unoccupied tables, but she could still hear people chatting across their latte and cappuccino. They looked as if they worked in offices, but she'd seen only stores. Maybe they all caught the ten o'clock helicopter to L.A.

"You ready?" she said.

On the sidewalk under the withering heat she heard him ask her as gently as he could just what the fuck they were doing in Santa Barbara. She looked down at the pavement and realized she'd forgotten her bag in the café.

"Would you?" she said.

In the shoe store, she sat on a thick black leather cushion and rested her freed bare feet on the cool tile floor, while she tried on a half-dozen pairs of shoes. She finally selected a black open-toed sandal, with leather straps woven over the foot. The saleswoman said she liked Amber's taste.

It was extraordinarily hot when she emerged, and she guessed she was late. She hoped that Benjamin was taking care of the meter. At a pharmacy with too-cold air conditioning and a locked glass case of gold Rolexes she bought him a ninety-three dollar pair of Ray·Bans. Her shoes had cost one hundred and fifty. It had been a good morning. A few blocks up, in a red-tile roofed minimall, she found him an oversized blue cotton short-sleeved shirt wash-faded to a shade of denim.

He was waiting at the car. His shirt smelled of beer and his eyes were hooded by heavy lids. She gave him the sunglasses before he could say anything. He muttered to himself, put them on, took them off, put them on again. He bent and looked at himself in the sideview mirror. He gave her a sweaty hug.

"Could you drive for a while," she said.

He grinned at her, hidden behind his sunglasses, impenetrable. "I'm drunk."

"I don't care. I just want to try the whole outfit on."

Outside of Santa Barbara, at a stretch of railroad and wild grass, he adjusted his rearview mirror to look at her. She had her top off.

"Benjamin," she said.

He set the mirror back and hummed as he drove. Almost noon. He lowered his sunglasses and saw how blue the ocean was, the wild grass bright yellow. Road signs warned of brush fires. A silver train emerged along the tracks and passed him, its ceiling observation windows glaring with sun. She leaned up against the seat. The momentary touch of her elbow at the back of his neck made him start.

"Pull over," she said.

He pulled over onto a narrow shoulder with weeds crackling under his tires. She threw a shirt into the front seat.

"Try it on."

He took off his cap, his hair oily and stuck together in thickened strands. Behind him, she got out of the car. He took off his T-shirt, wiped his face and towel-dried his hair with it, then dabbed his underarms. He got into the shirt. It fit very loosely, as if too big, but that was the way it was supposed to fit. She had crossed the highway to the other side, and was looking at the ocean. He tried to comb his hair with his hand, then got out of the car and crossed the road. She smiled at him. She wore the long black skirt and the light green sweater, which showed her neckline to her breasts. Her legs were bare.

"What do you think?" she said.

"You look great."

"I mean the shirt. Do you like the shirt?"

He nodded, slightly hungover. She reached and took his hand. They descended through tall scratchy grass to the railroad tracks, crossed them, and maneuvered down a steeper slope to a jagged line of large rocks set against the ocean. She sat on one rock and he sat on another. She tucked her legs under her and faced the sea. The sun grew hot on his shoulders.

"So we did it," she said.

He tried to think if there was anything left of Dean's in the car. "What about his keys?"

"On the freeway somewhere."

"We probably ought to get back."

"In a minute." She stretched out on her rock. The ocean

sounded at her head and the sun pinned her to the flat, smooth surface. She took a few deep breaths. She wasn't wearing any underwear. She wondered if he knew. She reached her arms behind her and felt the air at the end of the rock and another rock beyond it. She shifted her shoulders until she was comfortable. The sun concentrated on her skirt.

"Hey," he said.

For some reason he was standing on her rock. She'd fallen asleep, the rock hard against the back of her head, her arms thrown over her eyes. She opened her arms. Even with his sunglasses on she could tell he was perplexed. She fluttered her fingers lightly. He got down carefully on his knees and allowed her arms around him. She kissed him. He was lying on top of her, rich with old sweat, bitter, a tang. She found his hand and guided it under her skirt. He took a sudden breath. She was already wet and his fingers moved thickly. She felt for his zipper. He helped her.

"Take off your shirt," she said to his lips.

He hurried out of his shirt, glancing at the slope to the railroad tracks and the bank upward beyond that to the highway. She drew him back in again, took him as a shade against the sun. His zipper was open and she pushed down his pants. They stuck against his hips. With her feet she reached the heels of his sneakers and pushed them off, one at a time, onto the rocks below. He wasn't wearing socks. He wasn't wearing underwear. She pushed harder at his pants. He was trying gingerly to enter her, the rock hard against his knees. She moved his pants with her thighs as she held him, then pulled them down his legs with her hands and pushed them off with her feet. They landed on another rock. He seemed torn between wanting to go on and wanting to recover his clothes. A horn blasted up on the highway. Some trucker. He was frantic for his clothes but he could not bring himself to pull out from her. She had no clothes to give him. He was nude under the sun, and she moved with him, conscious of the rock against his knees. Her back hurt. She concentrated on the movement inside her and the feel of his back and thighs and hip and butt, vulnerable to anything tall that would come along the tracks and the highway. She held him close, making him move with only his pelvis, and reached under his leg and cupped his balls in one hand, squeezed and palmed and stroked them, while with the other hand she opened his buttocks and slid her finger inside. He shuddered and shuddered and she could feel the wet warmth of it within her. His sunglasses had slipped to her chest and he kept looking away from her, up toward the highway and out to the ocean, while she felt him where she wanted to and he continued to come. When he was done she held him in and moved against him, carefully, searchingly, until she found the motion and the meeting between him and her that she wanted and she repeated it and repeated it while his mouth hung open and his eyes drew shut until she managed to release herself.

After a while he drew himself out and got up, his shoulders burning and his ass cold and his knees red with indentations from the rock, and crawled among the rocks for his clothes. He dipped the tail of the shirt into the water and wiped himself thoroughly. He pulled on his jeans and his crotch still felt sticky and his penis seemed immediately to be chafing against the rough lining and the meanness of the zipper. He looked up at the sound of another trucker's horn. Amber was already making her way over the railroad tracks toward the highway. He wanted to call to her, to make her wave at him, to shout her name. He felt his way over the rocks and found his sneakers wedged between the haunches of two boulders. He sat and pulled them on and retied them. He put his sunglasses on and started over the rocks to the slope. As he moved, half climbing, half walking, the jeans rubbed him uncomfortably.

She was lying on her side in the back seat, in her new clothes and the old scarf and sunglasses, facing a wall of vinyl. He slipped in behind the wheel and put on his damp cap.

"You don't mind driving," she said drowsily.

"Not at all."

He pulled carefully from the narrow shoulder back onto the highway, the sun directly above the car, a deep blue sky. The sunglasses made everything less sharp, softened it so he felt he was driving in a pillow and he could put his head against it. His eyes kept shutting on him. He took the sunglasses off and the glare was too great. He pinched his thigh and stuck his mouth out the window, shifted in the seat, toyed with the range of his speed. With the sunglasses on everything was green and with them off everything was white. He kept them off. Fragments of cars passed over his shoulder. When he looked at his odometer, he was oppressed to discover that they'd gone only ten miles. There was not even a gas station. He was thirsty. In the back seat, she slept. The highway veered from the ocean into a range of white hills shot through with eucalyptus and cypress. The sun beat hard on the dark vinyl roof and the dark brown metal of the car, and he inhaled deeply for the telltale odor. There was only the pink briny scent of her and him.

At last she woke and leaned sleepily over the seatback by his shoulder.

"You want me to drive?"

At the pull-over, a side of her face held the lined pattern of the car seat in varying shades of red. He touched the marks softly and she held her hand there against his. She wasn't going to hate him all over again. She let him kiss her on the lips, and then he crawled into the back, pulled the door shut after him, and let sleep flood him.

When he woke they were in a parking lot, the sunstruck ocean in the distance white and the road white and cracked in front of him. She was standing by a soda machine, sipping a diet Coke and smoking a cigarette, talking to a guy whose shoulders were squared against the approach of any competition, his head tilted to catch her words. She nodded slightly at West when she saw him, and continued talking. West was awfully thirsty but he didn't want to appear territorial. He got out the other side of the car, and stood gazing at the ocean and a tin and tile town set below a ridge of burned golden high grass. He reached in the front seat and claimed his sunglasses. He stood, counting time, then sauntered over to the soda machine. The square-shouldered guy was telling Amber a story about ten raccoons laid out at five-foot intervals along the middle of 101, as if they'd lined up like dominoes to die. Amber was nodding and sipping her soda and taking quick hits off her cigarette and blowing the smoke to one side. West bought a drink and went in search of the rest room.

Several road campers had pulled into the lot, and people sat in aluminum lawn chairs looking at the gas station and the ocean, as if they planned to stay through the midafternoon heat. West urinated in a damp, syrupy closet that made him stand on tiptoe, then tried to wash his hands in a sink, but it gave no water. In the rust-spotted mirror his hair had dried to a stiffened part. Beneath a two-day stubble little red pimples showed along his jaw. The paper towel dispenser was empty. In the lot the people in lawn chairs were drinking beer from thick foam holders. West wondered if maybe they lived there. A man in an old-fashioned tank top with fleshy upper arms caught West looking at him, glared, and West headed to the car. Amber was ten feet from the roadkill guy, calling her last good-byes. She stepped carefully into the passenger side of the car, laughing and giving a wave, and West got in and started the Chevy and pulled from the station. For a moment he kept an eye on the rearview mirror.

"We're making shitty time," he said.

She pointed at a gauge. "I filled the tank. You slept right through it." She sniffed her sweater. "This is going to the cleaner's tomorrow."

The highway passed under a series of overpasses and started uphill along the coast. He wanted to ask her whether she had approached the guy or he had approached her, why she even had exchanged a word with him. The stretch of Pismo Beach blew past him, and the highway headed into the mountains again along an uphill grade. He felt as if he knew the map by heart now, as if he knew the whole damn constellation from here to Philadelphia. The sunglasses seemed to make his face hotter and he took them off. She was fiddling with the radio, barely able to pick up static. They were still going uphill, the highway widened to three lanes, cars passing on either side because he was moving too slowly. He squirmed and shifted in his seat, pressed the accelerator to the floor. The car seemed to be rolling backward. He let go of the wheel and stretched his fingers, took some weight off the gas. In his rearview mirror the ocean turned momentarily gray under a thin movement of clouds. Amber finally gave up on the radio. The car crested the mountain and began picking up speed as it rolled downhill. Across the tops of the dull green trees he could see a series of hills in the near distance that they'd have to ascend. All the other cars appeared to have wide bodies with tail fins and brake lights that slanted like eyebrows. The front of his forehead screamed with hunger.

The room at the Tenderloin King was about eighty square feet, including a closet built out from the wall, significantly smaller than any unit in the Golden Gate. The clerk beckoned for West to enter. A narrow metal-frame bed took up most of the space, with a little night table and a chair folded against a yellow wall. There was one electrical outlet, the carpet a purple that hid the dirt, no windows. Above the bed, a crack ran along the top of the wall. West got down on his knees and examined the baseboards. No holes. The tan bedclothes smelled sharply of mildew. The overhead light was a single bulb. On the night table was a lamp with a torn shade, plugged into the electrical outlet. He tried it. It didn't work.

"Three seventy-five?" he said.

"Three fifty, if you commit to a minimum of three months."

"I'll have to think about it."

"Uh-hunh." The clerk stepped aside to let West from the room.

"Can I see the bathroom?"

The clerk locked up the room and led him down the hall to the bathroom. He dialed the combination, unhooked the padlock, opened the door. The foremost curve of the toilet bowl practically reached the hallway. He pulled at a chain light and pointed to a loop and latch on the doorframe. "See," he said. "You can lock yourself inside when you use it."

"Where's the shower?" West said.

"Another stall. Same kind of setup. You want to see it?"

West shook his head.

Walking down the stairs the clerk said, "You ever been to France?" West didn't say anything. "It's kind of like a French setup. One of the one-star hotels. Not much amenities, but enough. One star." The clerk nodded his head to himself. "Better than none."

On the sidewalk people were drinking quart beer, smoking cigarettes, exchanging half-hidden packed handshakes. West self-consciously stepped over a syringe laying in a crack in the pavement. There were gangs of kids in their early teens, who were shorter than he and wore knee-length Raiders coats, who looked like they could beat the crap out of him. He walked close to the curb, eye-checking, not focusing. If he lived in the King, Amber would never come over. Everything about him would begin to smell of rot, and he'd have to go to the agencies, and a social worker would take his case, and eventually he'd get on a program for ex-cons and develop a skill and wear a tie and sweater and be head of interoffice mail delivery at a corporation and polish his act and apply to and be accepted by graduate schools because of his interesting demographics and progress toward his Ph.D. and when he was forty or forty-five be released into the clinical or academic world, meet someone, get married, buy a home, have a car, work, retire, die. In prison, he had sat in a circle with eleven other soon-to-be released inmates and their rehab leader, as they went around, one by one, and responded to her first attempt at a confessional question: Who would you most want to be? He heard the names of athletes, scientists, authors, rock stars, fathers, teachers, followed by exactly why that person was the person to be. When his turn came he said that he didn't want to be anybody else, because he couldn't. "But if you could?" the rehab leader said. "I can't," West said. "For the sake of the exercise," the leader said. West shook his head. "No," he said. "I'm not going to be anybody else so I'm not going to think about being anybody else." "Come on," said an inmate to his left, who had just confessed that he was bulimic and had tied it to wanting to be Betty Ford. "No," West said again. "I see his point," another inmate said. He had worked with West in the infirmary. "But he should still answer the question." "Will you answer the question?" the rehab leader said. "There's only one person left after you, and everybody else has answered it." "This is ridiculous," West said. "He shouldn't *have* to answer the question," an inmate with a Long Island accent said. "It should be optional."

At a gaudy wreck where the rooms were five hundred dollars a month and came with hotplates, a clerk told West quietly that if he could get on public assistance, he'd qualify for a better situation. "Just take a place for a month," she said. "By that time you ought to be able to work something out. What's a month?" One of the Vietnam vets hanging out on the corner of Leavenworth and Geary chewing forcefully on a half-dozen Chiclets suggested he try the East Bay. "They've got some stuff over there," he told West. "And the weather's a little warmer." West accepted a Chiclet from the vet and kept on. Two men were kneeling on the sidewalk inspecting a plastic bag, a knife loose beside them. They glanced at him as he came down toward them, then went back to their work.

Under the overpass, the Chevy sat shoulder to shoulder with rusted-out carcasses of automobiles. He got in and opened the window. The windshield was yellowed and streaked from cigarette smoke, the dashboard coated with a fine gray dust. He found a loose cigarette, and smoked. He ought just to take what was left of his share of Dean's cash and shove off for someplace he'd never been before and see what would happen. He inhaled deeply. He was thirty-one, soon to be thirty-two. He was standing at a window again. She was standing on the other side, she was what was beyond the window. He wished he could vanish into his own self. He wished he wasn't so damn conventional. He wished he didn't love her. He lit another cigarette. He had to push away, separate himself. He knew the damn window, he didn't want to stand at it anymore, he had stood at it through high school and college and the first three or four years at the Institute, and then he'd willed it to disappear. But it had come back around his thirtieth birthday and since then he couldn't shake it. He wanted the damn window. He wanted what was beyond it, and he was ashamed of wanting it. He was ambitious. He wanted her. It made him sick.

As he came up Ellis, Amber was already standing outside the entrance of the literacy center. She opened the car door but stayed on the sidewalk.

"They're letting me keep my job," she said. She was wearing her sunglasses and he couldn't tell her expression. "I can't make it right now. I've got a meeting. I really do."

"I never said you didn't," West said.

"Are you all right? You look a little upset."

"I found a place at the King. I'm already moved in."

"Already?" she said. "That's good, isn't it?"

"I think so."

"Tell me where it is and I'll be over afterward."

He saw himself waiting in his room for her. "Did you check the L.A. paper today?"

"Nothing about it." She started to shut the door. "Look, I've really got to go. It's called King? I'll meet you there at eight."

She shut the door and hurried back into the building, wearing a skirt and a blouse he hadn't seen before. He turned off the motor and lit a cigarette. Her hair had seemed different, too, as if she'd had it cut.

He bought a poor boy at a Korean deli and a bottle of Five O'Clock bourbon at the liquor store next door, drove a few blocks up, and parked. In the rearview mirror he could see a couple of prostitutes staffing the streetcorners. Across the street in front of a Laundromat a woman with long stringy blond hair sat on the curb, her head between her knees. She held a Styrofoam cup in two hands. Every now and then she looked up at nothing in particular. He could ask her to join him. She had holes in her jeans, and a thick dog-eared paperback. A bus blew past. He looked along the street for a likely place to urinate. It was six o'clock and still daylight, and he'd drunk a quarter of the bottle. The woman across the street gave him a cursory look and resumed examining the pavement. He trudged down Ellis, aware of people in doorways measuring him, making them know he was aware of them. He passed the literacy center, hard to tell with the angle of the sun if there was anyone inside. The next street was his street. Leavenworth. He let out a loud laugh at the name. No one seemed to notice. Girls were out at the corners, and men dressed as girls. A hopscotch chart was chalked in white on the pavement. Empty King Cobra cans rattled against a chain link fence, the air smoky and cool as fog crossed Leavenworth like exhaust from an invisible vehicle.

The lobby of the King was dark, the reception window a sea green with the purplish face of the evening clerk. He buzzed West through the door to the stairs, the stairwell hot and dank. West opened the second-floor door to see if it was any different. Two kids sat crosslegged in the hall, playing jacks on the hard carpet. "This is the woman's floor," one said to him. He shut the door and continued up the stairs, his bladder so full he had sharp pains as he climbed. The hallway of the third floor was empty, but the door to the toilet was locked from the inside. He stood in the hall, waiting. After a few minutes he retreated to his room. Instantly he noticed that the trunk had been moved. From along the corridor came the faint, sickly flushing of the toilet. He shut the door locked and hurried down the hall. A man in his eighties or nineties doddered from the bathroom, his shoulder scraping the wall. The floor of the stall was marbled with green veins of mildew. West locked himself in and urinated, his back against the door and a twenty-watt light bulb in his face.

In his room he lay on the bed and realized he'd left the bourbon in the car. He tried to make himself want to retrieve it while at the same time he tried to believe it was better not to have it. A dull pain gathered behind his temple. The ibuprofen was in the trunk. He had no water. He sat up on the bed and looked at the door quizzically. It wasn't more than two feet away. He'd thought he'd heard a knock.

"Yeah?" he said.

"It's me."

She was early. He looked around to see if there was any way to improve the place. He straightened the collar of his shirt. At least he was wearing her shirt. He extended his arm to the door and opened it while sitting on the bed.

"They let me up." She took in the room quickly and decided to pretend it was not there. "You want to go get some dinner?"

His tongue still felt thick from the bourbon. He nodded and nabbed his jeans jacket from the trunk.

"No," she said gently. "The sweater."

He dropped the jacket and picked up a crimson sweater with a crew neck and pulled it on. It was a sweater his ex-girl friend had bought him and he both liked it and hated it. Amber waited in the hallway. He drew the door shut and she held his hand as they walked out the corridor and down the stairs.

He blinked at the daylight, the dull pain in his head now fist-sized and hot. He squinted at her.

"Where's the car?" she said.

For a moment he thought he'd left it out by the Golden Gate, or in front of the King. He was starved. He began walking up Leavenworth toward Ellis, remembering. She was still holding his hand.

"I forgot to tell you," he said thickly. "I have a job interview, too. Fields set it up. Selling vitamins by phone."

"You don't want it," she said.

"That's correct."

Three black teenagers approached from up the street, and he and Amber didn't say anything to each other as the guys passed, the long football jackets swishing widely. West felt an elbow in his side, hard, short. He stumbled against Amber but kept his balance. He did not stop walking.

"What happened?" she said.

The pain in his side was like a piece of ice, and he wished he could apply it to his head.

"You all right?"

He kept walking, thinking maybe some more bourbon would help, maybe it wouldn't. The fog came at them. As they passed the literacy center, he picked up the pace. The blonde in front of the Laundromat was gone. The side window of the Chevy lay shattered on the street and inside the car, in tiny blue chips and cubes. "Fuck," he said. Maps and guidebooks sprawled across the front seat and on the floor where the bourbon used to be. The

radio bore cut marks, but it hadn't been budged. He opened the
trunk, got a shovel, and tried to remove the fragments of glass
from the car. She picked up shreds of pieces and put them into
the cup of her hand. The tip of her index finger began to bleed,
and she sucked at it. She could see the slightest sliver of glass
embedding itself within the grooves of her skin. When she held
her fingertip a certain way, it reflected back at her. She began to
laugh, she couldn't help it. The blood ran down her finger in a
hairline. She sat in the car, glass fragments scrabbling into the
folds of the vinyl. West was trying to punish the shovel as he
threw it back into the trunk. He came around and got in, his eyes
clenched against the pain in his head. He slammed the door,
started the engine, looked over at her, and noticed the blood. He
tried to examine it closely. "It's a sliver," he made himself say.

At a Safeway he wanted to leave her in the car while he ran in,
but she refused to sit at the open window. There was a napkin
from the Korean deli on the front seat, and he wrapped her finger
in it. The blood bled through the white folds in dark Rorschach-
like patterns. The security guard at the door of the Safeway
noticed, but said nothing.

They found in the pharmacy aisle a pair of tweezers, antiseptic
cream, and Band-Aids. On the way to the cashier he picked up a
carton of white bagging and a roll of masking tape.

"Did you want to get something to eat here?" West asked.

At the last aisle of the store, the produce took up most of the
wall and was arranged in greenery under miniature sprinklers.
There were radioactive-looking tomatoes and seven different
fungi and baby artichokes and giant artichokes, three varieties of
avocadoes and packed cartons of bean sprouts, four selections of
carrots and a dozen different types of lettuce, orange and red and
yellow green peppers, and squash and zucchini and arugula and

gingerroot and snow peas. She chose two seedless oranges from Israel and an apple from Wisconsin.

She sat in the car with the door open while West began taping a sheet of white bagging where the window used to be. She sterilized the tweezers in the flame of her lighter and poked at the groove of her skin until she could clearly see the sliver, entered in her fingertip so fully that it was difficult to tell which end it should come out. She put pressure on one point and the sliver seemed to dig deeper. She dug against it at the other end and a hole opened, and she pushed harder and it opened wider and the crusted point of the sliver poked out. She applied pressure with her thumb to the closed end and tried to snatch the point with the tweezers. Blood was gushing out as if she'd popped a tiny artery and she shut her eyes and opened them and tried to focus. The glass point teased her. The tweezers caught it in its narrow clamps and she pulled and the sliver came out and she looked at it for a moment, it was about a half centimeter long, and let it drop to the pavement of the parking lot. Blood welled and bubbled from the cut. The finger hurt more than when the glass was in it. Benjamin was still patiently taping the window. She sucked her finger, then applied a dab of antiseptic and a Band-Aid.

"How is it?" West said.

"I think I'll clean it better in a restaurant." The finger throbbed within the Band-Aid and she leaned back against the seat. When he shut her door she felt a line of pain go all the way up her arm to her shoulder. White plastic was stretched taut over the window, secured by thick strips of tape that ran along the frame and looped over the door. She felt as if she were looking out from her own body bag.

"Where do you want to go?" he said.

"I think I just want to go home, if you don't mind."

"I'm sorry about your finger."

"My mother." She started to cry, and took a steadying breath. "My mother used to say that there were two ways of dealing with splinters. You either went in there after them, or you let them work themselves out." She could taste the salt in her mouth, and she looked out the window, saw only the white plastic. "Benjamin," she said. "I'm really, really sorry."

"It's all right."

She wiped her eyes with the hand that didn't hurt. "You have to know that we're going to get away with it. You do know that, don't you?"

He nodded.

"So?" she said.

"So, that's good," he said.

They drove alongside new palm trees standing in a line down the middle of Market, their high arched fronds tinged purple in the slow dusk.

"Nice palms," he said.

As she looked past him out his window, all she could see were the trunks, wide with stitched triangulations of bark. Then the stand of palms ended and there was a used car lot on the other side of the street. At their evening meeting, Sister Frances had mentioned that the literacy center had a car to lend her, that it was part of her duties to go around and look at the operations in Richmond and Oakland and San Jose and Marin City. There was a conference in September that she was supposed to attend in Seattle, and she could either fly or drive. She wanted to drive.

West took the car around to the Golden Gate. The fog was moving fast and low and he could not see beyond the third story. He stopped in front.

"Well, I guess I'll see you," she said.

He touched her arm. "Take care."

She nodded and got out of the car and shut the door and walked over to the front of the building. Cecilia buzzed her in quickly. She crossed toward the stairs in a hurry, her finger screaming at her and her eyes blurring.

"You going to be okay, honey?" Cecilia called after her.

"Yes," Amber said. She reached the stairs and began climbing. As she neared the mezzanine she stopped to see if he were still there, waiting. He was.

He began to move, as if he knew she had finally looked. He passed a large flatbed truck groaning and shrieking behind orange traffic cones, its tires flattened as it inched along. On the bed of the truck was a tall concrete base, tiered and inlaid with bronze plaques, atop which sat a bronze cowboy on a horse. There was a hole in either streetcorner, one where the statue had come from, the other where it was going to. He was so busy looking he missed his turn. On Van Ness he took a right, and nearly hit a young couple in evening dress. He pulled to the curb and reached across and tore a hole in the taped white plastic sheeting on the passenger side. Now he could see. A face peered in at him. It was the young man with the neat pucker of his black bow tie.

"Buy a fucking window, pal," he said.

West blared his horn at him and headed out Van Ness. Cold air rushed through the eye in the white bagging. Where the bay ought to be was only a bed of fog. He turned left, passing rows of two-story hotels, the Sandpiper, Ocean View, Sea Crest. He'd come this way to retrieve Dean. Blue chips of window glass glinted at him from the crevice of the seat. He parked near a grocer's, and bought a quart of beer and the afternoon newspaper. It was still light. He left the car where it was and walked a half-dozen long blocks to the bayside, where deserted benches lined an asphalt path and through the breaks in the fog he could see the lights across the water turning on almost one by one. He sat on a bench, drank his beer, and read the paper, every now and then checking over the top of it to keep track of the lights and whether it was late enough to head back.

In the Tenderloin, in the dark, he looked for a parking space. He found a metered one that was free until eight in the morning. He taped sections of the newspaper to the window frame to cover the hole in the plastic. From the trunk he took out the cooler. He pictured himself filling it during the nights with ice and beer and some fruit for breakfast, until he made enough money from vitamins to move.

Although it was almost midnight, it felt too early to him. Across the street he could see sets of smallish young men with brilliantined hair leaning against cars, smoking cigarettes, wearing shorts and thin jackets or only T-shirts despite the cold.

"What's up?" one softly called to him. "You can come over here, if you want."

There were women in doorways and out on the sidewalk as he walked. He held the empty cooler under his arm like a football, and walked close to the curb. From a small barred park he heard shouts and whispers, as if people weren't sure how to talk. A line of shopping carts hooked around a corner, protecting a curved row of full sleeping bags. On his old street he turned left. The light over the doorway of the Golden Gate was out. He passed slowly. A security guard sat at a desk pulled up close to the door, a small lamp shining on the surface of his open log book. The reception cage was dark. In the shadows of the furniture West wondered if he could see her. She was leaning back in a sofa, staring out the storefront, directly at him. He kept looking. At his desk the security guard twitched. He yawned and pushed his chair back, got up, and disappeared outside of the light. West approached the window. The overhead bulbs of the lobby clicked on, and the spotlight over the door burst into a whiteness shining in his face. He stepped back into the darkness of the street. After a moment, he was able to see into the Golden Gate. The entire lobby was empty, save for the security guard, who paced patiently back and forth in front of the reception cage, waiting to turn off the lights.

On the sidewalk as West headed toward the King, a woman was beating a little girl with a moccasin, while a man stood nearby smoking a cigarette. "Apologize!" she screamed at the girl. "Now you apologize!" The girl laughed and ducked under the moccasin.

"You keep missing her," the man said.

"Don't I know it," the woman said. "And I've been practicing all night."

Fred G. Leebron's stories have appeared in numerous publications, including *Grand Street, TriQuarterly, North American Review,* and *Ploughshares,* and in anthologies including *The New Generation, Flash Fiction,* and *Voices of the Xiled.* He has received Fulbright, Michener, and Slegner Fellowships for his writing. He teaches Creative Writing at the University of North Carolina in Charlotte, where he lives with his wife, the writer Kathryn Rhett, and their child.